RIGHT WHERE SHE BELONGED

"You were the best thing that ever happened to me," Parker said, with such force that Alexandra held her breath and stared at him like she was nineteen again.

In slow motion, Parker bent his head to kiss her; Alexandra watched his handsome features until they blurred, and her eyelids naturally drifted closed. When she again felt Parker's lips, they were slightly parted and settled purposefully on her own. His hand squeezed her tightly around the waist; the other hand lay along her jaw, the thumb touching her bottom lip and urging her to answer his kiss.

Alexandra felt her senses spin. She knew only the need to press her slender, trembling body closer to him, to let his kiss reclaim her . . . She was experiencing a pure joy, outside of reason, which made her feel she was right where she belonged.

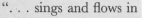

D0802847

SANDRA KITT
SERENADE

PINNACLE BOOKS
WINDSOR PUBLISHING CORP.

To Alice *and* Alice,
who made last year possible

PINNACLE BOOKS are published by

Windsor Publishing Corp.
850 Third Avenue
New York, NY 10022

The P logo Reg U.S. Pat & TM off. Pinnacle is a trademark of Windsor Publishing Corp.

First Printing: July, 1994

Printed in the United States of America

Chapter One

One of Grandma Ginny's old wives' tales was that if it rained on the day you got married, the union was doomed to failure. It was a pessimistic, rather sobering notion, but one that kept reverberating with humorous irony in Alexandra's mind as her cab pulled up in front of the modest whitestone church. She struggled with payment, an umbrella, a plastic clothing bag, and the door as the persistent old wives' tale lingered. Alexandra swore to herself she wasn't the least bit superstitious. Still, she hoped it was nothing more than this myth that nagged at her today.

The rain poured down steadily, as if taking revenge on the earth and its occupants for some infraction against Mother Nature. It was not supposed to rain today. It should never rain on anyone's wedding day, Alexandra thought, as she pushed the cab door open and was met by a gentle sweep of cold, damp air—but then, forecasters were notorious for being wrong.

Alexandra swung her legs cautiously out the cab door and promptly stepped into the shallow puddle of water running along the curb. The displacement her step made sent a wave of water into her bone-colored sling-back pumps, making her toes curl with the icy touch. She drew breath sharply between her teeth in exasperation. So far, events did not bode well. If Grandma Ginny's tales had any truth to them, Alexandra was glad she wasn't the one getting married.

With her head lowered and the umbrella braced against the chilling spring winds, Alexandra dashed up the church steps and through the heavy doors, crashing with teeth-rattling suddenness into the tall, gaunt, bespeckled form of Pastor Nichols. The wind was knocked out of them both, and the pastor grunted as he was pushed off balance.

"Good heavens, girl! Where are you off to in such a hurry?" he asked, as he placed a bony restraining hand on Alexandra's shoulder to steady her.

"I'm sorry," Alexandra said, out of breath, trying to shift her clothing bag and attempting to collapse the dripping umbrella.

The pastor chuckled indulgently as he relieved her momentarily of her garment bag while she fought with the temperamental umbrella. "I know they say that girls are all sugar and spice, but believe me, a little rain won't make you melt."

Alexandra smiled as she finally closed the umbrella and retrieved her bag. "I was more concerned about being late, Pastor Nichols. I should have been here thirty minutes ago."

He folded his thin hands over his robes and shook his head gently at Alexandra. "There's really no point in tearing around so. We can't start without the groom, and he's not here yet, either." His eyes twinkled. The pastor now looked at her carefully, making note of the softly upswept hairdo, the sienna-toned oval face with its full, wide, curved mouth. And eyes so dark they were like black buttons in her youthful face.

"Do I know you?" he asked suddenly, wrinkling his brow.

Alexandra's wry smile and raised brows indicated what she thought of the man's memory. "We met at rehearsals last week. I'm to sing in the service this morning, remember?"

Recognition now brightened the pastor's myopic eyes as he gave Alexandra a toothy smile. "Ah, yes. You're the young lady with the incredible voice. I remember now. What a joy it is to listen to you."

Alexandra merely smiled her response, taking a step further toward her destination, concerned about the time, even if Pastor Nichols wasn't. But he detained her still.

"You know, I could sure use you in my Sunday morning choir," he hinted broadly.

Alexandra shifted uncomfortably, a guilty conscience reminding her that she had stopped being a regular attendant at church services, here or anywhere else, and that her already busy schedule would not allow for any more commitments. She was spared having to make an admittedly weak excuse when the pastor quickly changed subjects.

"That reminds me, I haven't yet instructed the best man as to his duties. He was the only one not at rehearsals last week. Has anyone else had a chance to speak with him?"

Alexandra shrugged. "I'm sorry. I don't know who the best man is."

"Well, no matter. His job is simple enough, and there's lots of time yet," he said benignly.

Alexandra managed a quick glance at the clock on the wall, and thought not. She took another step away. "Is anyone here yet?"

"Oh, yes, yes. The bride's family has arrived. She's

with her mother in that second anteroom off the far corridor." He pointed helpfully.

Alexandra was about to thank him and go on her way when the door opened behind her and a gust of March air blew raindrops on the backs of her legs and swept tendrils of hair against her cheeks. An instant later, someone plowed into her back, pushing her once more into Pastor Nichols. She glanced over her shoulder to find a man breathing down her neck, his hands grabbing her arms to steady her once more. His dark blond hair was damp and windblown, his cheeks a bit ruddy. His strawberry-blond moustache curved at the ends as he grinned wickedly at Alexandra.

"We have to stop meeting like this. What'll I tell my future wife?"

Alexandra rolled her eyes and laughed softly. She watched as Brian Lerner adjusted his black bow tie and smoothed his hair into place with his hand. Then he turned to shake hands with the man who would marry him.

"Hi, Pastor. Hope I'm not late."

The pastor chuckled. "Young man, you can't really be late. You just have to show up." Continuing to hold onto Brian's hand, he steered him into the entrance hall. "I think we should move away from the door. I'm not sure I can survive being tackled a third time."

While the two men laughed in appreciation, Alexandra took the opportunity to move away. "I've got to go get ready. I'll see you in about an hour," she said, and began walking to the room the pastor had pointed out. The long, thread bare red runner down the center of the floor quieted her footsteps as she moved, making Alexandra feel reverent. She might not attend church regularly, but she experienced a quiet, peaceful sense of being whenever she entered one.

Knocking gently, Alexandra opened the anteroom door. Inside, a slender young woman, a few inches taller than Alexandra but about the same age, was having a wedding veil adjusted atop her curly red hair. The short train of the ankle-length Victorian lace dress was being smoothed and arranged by the young woman's mother, at that moment down on her hands and knees. They both turned their attention to Alexandra as she stood smiling in the doorway, and greetings were exchanged.

Alexandra watched the young woman, trying to gauge in her eyes and movement what she was feeling. She found the pretty face flushed and the green eyes bright with excitement. "Well, Debby. This is it," Alexandra said, her voice suggesting that it was getting too late for the young woman to change her mind.

Debby continued to move the veil around on her bright curls. "I can't believe this is finally happening." She whispered, in such wonder that Alexandra knew she had no intention of turning back.

"You'd better believe it," Debby's mother muttered dryly. "After all you've put your father and me through the last six months, if this isn't the real thing, we want to know the reason why."

The two younger women giggled, and Alexandra came closer to examine the beautiful gown. Debby's mother put a hand on a nearby chair and hoisted herself up, shaking out the folds of her own pale blue gown.

"I'm glad I have only one daughter," she lamented. "All of these plans and details have really done me in." But her laugh was nervous, and her voice had a suspicious crack in it.

"Oh, Mom," Debby whispered, putting an arm

around her mother's shoulder and kissing her soft, warm cheek. For the moment, the two of them were locked in an intimate moment that no one else could intrude upon.

Alexandra watched the exchange with warmth and a kind of detached envy. She herself had no immediate thoughts of getting married, although a very youthful fantasy still played itself out in her daydreams from time to time—the one in which she'd seen herself in a white dress and veil, about to walk down the aisle and be married to the man she loved. She'd even had a very specific man in mind, bringing the fantasy an inch closer to reality. But a fantasy was all it had ever been. It was safe, the dreaming, and filled a long-ago ache.

That same youthful anticipation had allowed her to realize too late that dreams didn't always come true. That one failed romance was to have other effects on her life. It was to touch on her relationship to her family and on what Alexandra herself wanted to do with her life. Sure, it had all been disappointing and unbelievably painful at the time. But not the end of the world. She had survived and grown up.

Alexandra watched also the genuine love and tenderness that was exchanged between her friend and her mother and noted another emotion: a sense of emptiness. Her own mother had died when she was fifteen and her younger sister not yet ten. That had been thirteen years ago. She had adjusted to the loss long before she'd reached maturity. Alexandra knew now, as she watched Debby with her mother, that there were certain to be special days when her own mother would be missed a lot.

Alexandra thought how young she'd been when she'd first begun to lose things and people in her life. How young she'd been to take on the responsibility of the family, of others depending on her, inadvertently and helplessly drawing on her strengths and caring until sometimes she felt she'd given it all away and there was little left just for her. In some ways she felt as though she'd grown up too fast. In some ways, she suspected, she had not grown up at all.

Alexandra felt her hands clasp together under the garment bag folded over her arms, suddenly feeling her losses again of having had so much taken away against her will: loved ones, dreams, princes. There were few things she wanted anymore, and these she held onto tenaciously, greedily, to protect them and herself. Alexandra let her tense body relax as Debby's mother spoke.

"Come on, now. Let's not fuss so. After all, you're only getting married, not leaving the country," she said, gently pushing her daughter away. "I'm going to try and find your father, and see if everyone else is here. No doubt he's in Pastor Nichols' office, being fortified with the sacramental wine."

Alexandra and Debby chuckled as the older woman disappeared through the door, leaving the two of them to the last few private moments when they were exactly the same, young women who shared the same interests and were friends. Alexandra had met Debra Geison at the university, where they'd both studied music. It had been Debby who'd willingly tutored her in music theory in exchange for having a steady companion to attend concerts with. Later they'd both begun to teach at the university's conservatory. Alexandra had gone on to give lessons to particularly talented but underprivileged children recommended through a scholarship program by the public school system. The children were all bright, but raw and undisciplined, their attention quickly diverted, and it had taken creative and ingenious steps to make the repetitive lessons fun. Alexandra enjoyed working with children most of all. She and Debby had both been young and idealistic, thinking they could make a difference in children's appreciation of music. Of course, that was before they both realized they were competing with the creative flamboyance of Michael Jackson and Prince. It was before they'd both had their first taste of love, which would change both their dreams and their lives.

For Debby, it had come to a perfect natural conclusion. She was marrying someone who loved music as much as she did, and they both very much loved each other. Another twinge of regret crept in around Alexandra's heart, but quickly dissolved. Alexandra let the true affection she felt for Debby soften her dark eyes with joy for her now.

"Well . . . how do I look?" Debby breathed out, pivoting around much too quickly for Alexandra to see anything.

"Debby, you look beautiful," she responded honestly.

Debby grimaced in mock disgust. "Is that all? Just beautiful? All brides are beautiful. I want to be so stunning I'll knock Brian clear out of his *socks.*"

Alexandra laughed as she put her things down and shrugged out of her coat. She hugged an arm around her stomach and braced the other elbow on her wrist. Leaning her round chin on her fist, she pretended deep contemplation of Debby's appearance. "Okay. Maybe you're more than just beautiful. I personally think you knocked Brian out of his socks a long time ago. He's going to find you stunning no matter what you wear today."

Debby gnawed her bottom lip. "Do you think so? I'm not sure about my hair . . ." she said, frowning slightly, and turned away to pat and fuss with the glossy curls in an ornate mirror behind her.

Alexandra smiled as she recognized the eleventh-hour nervousness that was attacking Debby with doubts and last-minute questions. Gently placing her hands on Debby's shoulders, Alexandra forced her down onto the vanity chair in front of the mirror. Just as gently, she removed Debby's hands from their blind marauding and once again straightened the filmy veil and train.

"There is nothing wrong with your hair. Everything is just perfect," she voiced softly, and smiled at the suddenly pale reflection of Debby in the mirror. "Are you a little nervous?"

Debby nodded, "Yes, I guess so. This is a pretty bad time to be wondering if this is the right thing to do. Is it what Brian wants to do?" Suddenly, Debby's eyes flew open and she looked positively stricken. "Oh, my God! What . . . what if Brian doesn't want to get married? What if he's only doing this for my sake, and wished he hadn't canceled out on that European tour with his band?"

Now Alexandra did allow herself to laugh. "Oh, Debby, stop it. You're scaring yourself to death for no good reason at all. You know very well Brian adores you. Getting married can't be compared to a European tour. And don't forget, you turned down his proposal twice before accepting."

In an almost comic turn around, Debby blinked at the reminder, considering it. Finally, she began to relax, and squinting, smiled back at Alexandra in the mirror.

"That's right. I did, didn't I?" she remembered gleefully.

Alexandra nodded sagely. "And you also told him you wanted to continue teaching and playing in the orchestra at the Kennedy Center, and he agreed."

"Yes!" Debby brightened even more, her green eyes large and happy again. With her confidence quickly restored, Debby's eyes became coquettish in her pretty face. "As a matter of fact, all things considered, Brian's pretty lucky to be getting such a talented, gorgeous creature!" she continued.

A quick frown passed through Alexandra's dark eyes and then was gone. A thought, a voice, a memory shook her, sending a shiver of feeling all through her body that was unexpected. "Talented, gorgeous . . ." She'd heard that before. Old wives' tales were one thing, but now she was getting waves of premonition that were unsettling; something that would affect *her,* not Debby. Deciding she was being fanciful, she sighed and withdrew her hands from their unnecessary but soothing chore at the elaborate lace headdress and smiled at Debby again. "Oh, I think Brian is well aware of how lucky he is. You both are lucky," Alexandra added, and stepped aside as Debby stood once more to face her.

"Thank you," Debby said in a soft, sincere voice. "Thank you for the pep talk, and for being here, and for taking my classes while I'm on my honeymoon . . ."

Alexandra uncomfortably brushed the words aside. "Don't be silly. That's what friends are for. Besides, I know you'd do as much for me."

"Of course," Debby said at once, checking her makeup yet again. "I don't have the voice that you do, but I'm looking forward to performing at *your* wedding one of these days."

A thought twisted Alexandra's mouth, and she chuckled soundlessly. It was on the tip of her tongue to utter *don't hold your breath* when she realized she'd have to explain her remark, and she didn't want to; but she also didn't want Debby to feel her offer was taken lightly. Yet Alexandra knew with a certainty that she had no intentions of marrying. That idea had been discarded in favor of doing other things with her life. In one way the decision had already been made for her.

Debby turned from the mirror. "Well, that's the best I can do with what I have. Ready or not, Brian, here I come," she laughed lightly. "I decided not to wear my glasses. Pastor Nichols could marry me to the best man and I'd never know it."

At that moment, Mrs. Geison opened the door and stuck her head in.

"For heaven's sake, you two. Everyone's almost ready. Come along, Debby. The pastor is ready for you to take your place."

Debby quickly gave Alexandra a hug. "I'd better let you change." She stood back and stared at Alexandra. "Do you realize that in twenty minutes, I will be Debra Geison-Lerner?" Before Alexandra could respond, Debby giggled joyously and went through the door, her train like gossamer behind her.

The amused smile on Alexandra's face lasted another few seconds before it slowly faded, and she stood alone and somber in the suddenly quiet room. Automatically she took out her gown from the garment bag, and went about quickly changing from her street clothes. She applied a teak blusher to her cheeks and chin, mascara to her dark, thick lashes, and gloss to her lips. She recaptured a few wayward strands of hair on her nape, and tucked them back into the bunched curls pinned high on her head in an arrangement with seven pale pink rosebuds. There was a quiet thoughtfulness to Alexandra's features, as if she always had a thought in mind. Her eyes were large and dark and sometimes sad, people had told her. Alexandra mentally compared her face to that of her younger sister, Christine. Sighing, she knew there was no comparison. Christine was without a doubt the real beauty in the family.

Alexandra could never see her true image in the mirror

and didn't recognize the attractive, poised woman of twenty-nine she'd grown into from the thin, gawky, all-knees-and-elbows, large, chocolate-eyed girl she'd been. She had also convinced herself that beauty gave a person many more advantages than being talented did. Having watched most of her life as a younger, capricious Christine got her own way just about every time had led Alexandra to believe that she herself was in on a pass.

A young man named Parker Harrison had once promised Alexandra that she was like a swan that wouldn't reach its full glory until after it was fully grown; like a wine that ripens slowly, a flower that blooms late, but then is the most magnificent of all. Romantic claptrap, Alexandra thought airily . . . it wasn't true then, and it wasn't true now. But at nineteen she'd been romantic, and young enough to believe the silken magic words of a man she'd thought herself in love with. Parker had seemed so sincere and had been so convincing that now, without him in her life to provide the image, to believe in it and enrich her, it all seemed to have been nothing more than mere fantasy, only pretty words.

Alexandra never believed she could possibly be pretty enough to hold a man's attention. But she had something else: a beautiful voice. And with her voice, the one thing that was purely her own, Alexandra was ready to set the world ablaze with her music. With it she had a career and life already mapped out. She was reaching for much more than singing at weddings.

As for the romance in her life, she had been only nineteen, but Parker had given her her first real and strong taste of love. It had helped her cross that mysterious invisible boundary between innocent teen and young woman. It had given her a soft feminism from the angular youth of inexperience, and had nearly broken her heart and left her cold.

He had given Alexandra just enough that it could not be mistaken for promises and commitments, and he had taken enough to make her wary and selective. She knew there was never any love like the first one; the next can only be second best. So Alexandra had turned completely to music and teaching it to children who hadn't yet realized their own potential. Teaching might be a poor substitute for love, but at least it was something she was sure of.

In the mirror, her large, dark eyes lacked a glow of total happiness. Her well-shaped, full mouth smiled frequently with warmth, but her smile lacked a certain depth. And her pretty brown countenance often spoke of a certain wishfulness. She was like a sleeping beauty, waiting.

Hearing the bracing cords of the church organ finally changed Alexandra's pensive expression to one of quick surprise. She was going to be late.

Hastily putting her street clothing away in the garment bag and getting things in order, Alexandra grabbed her music, pulled open the door, and rushed out. She ran lightly down the corridor toward the choir room, where she'd join the church members asked to sing during the short wedding service. The thought that she might cause the delay of her friend's wedding caused her to gnaw on her lips as she tried to remember which of the four doors on the adjoining hallway was the one she needed.

Suddenly, as she reached the junction, someone rounded the corner and Alexandra slammed right into a moving blur of black and white. The air was knocked out of her, forcing out a surprised gasp. She was bounced back several steps with the force of the impact. Her music sheets, shaken loose from her hand, drifted to the floor around her. A pair of strong hands immediately reached out to grab her arms and steady her.

"Hey! I'm sorry. Are you all right?" a concerned, masculine voice sounded in Alexandra's rattled brains.

She blinked rapidly to clear her vision and raised both hands to hold on to her sudden source of balance.

"I . . . I think so," Alexandra murmured, and then shook her head ruefully. "I've been bumping into people all morning. I'm not usually so clumsy . . ."

The man, somewhat taller than her five feet six inches, released her and bent to retrieve the scattered pages. But as he stood to face her once more, the rest of Alexandra's words were left unspoken as she stood gaping openmouthed at him. Blindly she accepted the sheets from him even as she continued to stare in disbelief.

"I just hope I didn't hurt you. We collided pretty hard, and I . . ."

"Parker!" Alexandra breathed, her heart feeling like it was flipping over and over in her chest. "What . . . what are you doing here?" she asked.

The man frowned at her, stared, and slowly began to shake his head. His brown eyes were intent and careful as his gaze searched her face. But there was no sign of recognition. A curious smile lifted a corner of his square mouth as he continued to frown.

"I'm sorry. You have the advantage," he said apologetically.

Alexandra blinked at him and the sudden involuntary light that had lighted her eyes faded, along with her initial shock. He didn't remember her. He had no idea who she was, or what connection they might have. Her voice completely failed her now.

A door opened and a buxom, middle-aged woman dressed in choir robes stood in the doorway, looking up and down the hall until she spotted the two people staring rather fascinated at one another.

"Are you the soloist?" she asked urgently.

Alexandra pulled herself back from the past and looked at the woman. "Yes, I . . ."

"Well, come on, come on!" she gestured impatiently. "We're waiting for you!"

"Oh . . . yes," Alexandra said vaguely, feeling herself caught in an odd sensation of time-warp. Her eyes, still round and bright, looked back to the man, who apparently still hadn't glcancd any insight into her identity, although his interest was obviously caught now. "I'm sorry. I've got to go . . ."

"But wait . . ." he began calling after her.

But feeling foolish, and beginning to experience a crushing, heavy sadness, Alexandra hurried into the room away from him.

Alexandra knew a kind of piercing breathlessness. The man who'd changed her life nearly ten years ago had no memory of her at all. It made her feel insignificant, unimportant. It made everything that had been between them seem a mere chance passing, and the crushing tension now in the pit of her stomach told her that perhaps for Parker, that was all it had been. But her own memories recalled that time as more special than mere chance.

She had no time in which to recover her shattered senses. The processional began and the choir, with Alexandra in the lead, headed out a side door that placed them eventually to the left and rear of the altar, facing the wedding party and the congregation of guests. Her stomach muscles began knotting alarmingly, and a sickening swirl of emotion rose to her throat. She felt hot and cold at the same time. Numb . . . and also alert.

Alexandra felt her eyes searching the seated guests,

quickly scanning for the familiar head and face. She found Parker in place as best man next to Brian. Alexandra irrelevantly remembered Debby's recent words about being married to the best man without benefit of her glasses to tell the difference, and a short, hysterical giggle escaped her. Debby would have to be stone blind not to know the chiseled brown features of Parker, a night-and-day contrast to the fair and blond Brian.

Parker was pursing his lips and staring thoughtfully into space when the eight-person choir reached their elevated spot in a balconied tier behind the pastor. His eyes caught the movement, he found Alexandra in front, and their eyes locked and held.

Alexandra swallowed hard and felt a breath catch in her throat as she returned his look with frank, unavoidable curiosity of her own. Her lips parted somewhat in awe at the handsome picture he made, dressed for this auspicious occasion. The stark white of his formal dress shirt contrasted richly against the tobacco brown of his skin. The black of the tuxedo made his slender six-foot frame sleek. His hands were crossed over one another in front of him, his legs braced a little apart, and he gave a virile image of a man totally in control. Alexandra raised her attention to him again, wondering if he really was. Certainly, he didn't appear to be as shaken as she had been by the brief encounter in the corridor.

Alexandra had a momentary sense of surprise that she had been anything at all to this man in the past. The fact that their lives had touched in every imaginable way for a period of three months now seemed some odd dream that she'd made up. She clearly remembered every second of their romance.

Parker had moved on to fame and fortune. There was no need for Parker Harrison, successful composer and songwriter, to look behind him to the young girl whose life he had stepped in and out of so quickly.

Alexandra gathered her wit, made a determined effort not to look at Parker again, and gave her attention to the service. She led the choir through the ceremony, her rich alto soprano voice clear and melodious, drawing an emotional response from the listening guests. She knew she'd been blessed with a strong singing voice, but she was generally unaware of its effect on people. She didn't take her abilities for granted, but she was more aware of concentrating on simply singing well. She listened to her own sounds, always wanting them to be the best she could produce.

Hearing Debby and Brian exchanging their vows, however, brought unexpected tears to her eyes. As of that moment, a new life started for both of them. Alexandra hoped their lives together would be everything they wanted. She hoped their love would last.

Then the organ began its final introduction and Alexandra softly launched into "The Lord's Prayer." She closed her eyes to feel it as she sang. The classic version of this hymn had always been a vocal challenge because of its sweeping climbs and drops in octaves. It never failed to move Alexandra, never failed to make her believe in the existence of something greater than herself which filled her with joy and gave her peace and hope. It was to this that she raised her splendid voice in song gratefully, as much as it was to celebrate the joining of Debby and Brian.

There was an eerie silence when she finished, and the chords of the organ finally faded away. Pastor Nichols's voice finally broke into the near-reverent silence to finish the service. Alexandra missed the final words, the final benedictions, as she was acutely aware of Parker's gaze on her. She suddenly found it difficult to breathe evenly, and she resented that she felt so uncomfortable and unsettled.

The guests and wedding party filed out of the room and crowded into the church vestibule. Because of the rain, pictures of the happy couple could not be taken on the steps of the church. Instead, the service was reenacted to allow the photographer to record it. Alexandra hung back, watching the photography session, since she only knew the bride and was only recently acquainted with the groom's immediate family. The other members of the choir had departed for the reception, leaving her now alone.

From a distance, she indulged her desire to observe Parker Harrison covertly as he was photographed with the rest of the wedding party. Alexandra sat in a pew quietly, still dazed by his presence.

Belatedly, Debby realized that she'd not been included in the photo session, and spotting her, exclaimed, "Oh, there you are! I wondered where you'd disappeared to. Come here, I want you in the pictures, too."

Debby grabbed her hand and unceremoniously dragged her down the aisle to the waiting group. Alexandra had no time to protest or demure as she was suddenly conscious of Parker silently watching her approach, his gaze more intent on her now than before. As a matter of fact, he was openly staring. She ignored him, however, and walked over to Brian. Placing her hands on his shoulders, she tiptoed to kiss his cheek.

"Congratulations," Alexandra said stiffly, trying to smile. Brian rested a hand on her waist.

"Thanks. Come over here. I want you to meet someone. You've probably heard of him," he teased coyly.

Alexandra felt her stomach knot as Brian gently swung her around to face Parker, who was standing to the side.

The warmth drained completely from her body, and her apprehension raised gooseflesh on her bare arms. Right now, she'd be just as happy if he never remembered who she was. But she raised her chin proudly, and looked squarely at Parker.

His gaze upon her this time was different. The curiosity was still there, but it was mixed with a kind of soft probing that thoroughly examined her. Whatever he saw he found pleasing as one dark, straight brow quirked and a lazy, appealing grin shaped his mouth.

For a quick instant, Alexandra lowered her gaze, then raised it again. She'd never before gotten that kind of look from Parker. In a way, it was flattering, because his eyes and mouth were flirting with her, liking what he saw in her. Alexandra hid a smile, perversely enjoying the knowledge that they knew each other far better than he realized.

Parker's jacket was unbuttoned for the moment and forced back as he stood with his hands in the pants pockets, watching her approach.

"Hey, man . . ." Brian began, slapping Parker on the shoulder. They were about the same height, but Parker was decidedly more slender. "I want you to meet the pretty lady behind the pretty voice. This is Alexandra Morrow. And this . . ." he smiled cheerfully at his friend, "is the famous Parker Harrison."

"Or infamous, as the case may be," Parker said in a quiet, deep tone as he continued to look at Alexandra. "Hello," he said, putting out a long, slender hand.

Hesitating, Alexandra put her hand into his and felt his fingers close warm and firm around her cold limb. She could tell he was aware of it as he tilted his head and gently squeezed her fingers.

"I'm aware of Mr. Harrison's reputation in music.

Hello," Alexandra said softly. She was proud of the poise she could command, even as her insides knotted with tension. She frowned askance, however, as Parker just held onto her hand, not allowing her to pull away. She looked at him only to find that he was once more scanning her face thoughtfully.

"Parker and I played in a tour together across the country for a couple of years," Brian explained, with obvious pride at their friendship. He slapped Parker's shoulder again. "While Parker here went on to become a household word, I went on to get married."

"You didn't do so badly," Alexandra scolded him softly.

"I agree," Parker voiced caustically, finally releasing Alexandra's hand, and turning his head to Brian. "As a matter of fact," he said in amusement, "anyone who can put up with a temperamental musician deserves sainthood."

"I'll drink to that."

They all turned to see Debby moving between them. She slipped her arm through that of her new husband and hugged it. "Not even married a full hour, and already I'm deserted."

"All for a good reason, Honey. I wanted Parker to meet Alexandra."

"Yes, and that reminds me," Debby said sheepishly, turning her appealing green eyes to Parker, "Would you mind very much bringing Alexandra to the . . ."

Realizing what her friend had in mind, Alexandra stopped her.

"Oh, come on. I can go alone. After all, Mr. Harrison might have other plans later this evening," Alexandra tried to excuse Parker. She wasn't sure how much longer she could claim anonymity.

He turned his dark, piercing gaze on Alexandra, and his eyes sparked. "Parker," he insisted. "I'll be happy to bring her," he interrupted Alexandra, directing his comment to Debby. He looked at Alexandra, once again amused, "Unless Ms. Morrow really objects to being in my company."

They all waited for Alexandra's answer, Debby's expression making it clear she would be out of her mind to refuse. Alexandra knew there was only one response left to her.

"N-no, of course not," she said lamely.

"Good! Now that that's settled, Brian, the photographer wants a family shot." Keeping her hold on his arm, Debby led him away. "Don't go anywhere," she whispered over her shoulder to Alexandra before she was out of earshot. "I still want you in some of these pictures."

Alexandra followed more slowly behind them for a short distance and stood by a pew, feigning an interest in what the photographer was doing. But her heart was racing in her chest, and her body was trembling with the anxiety of the last few minutes. She was still stunned that Parker was right here in the same space, together with her after all these years, and didn't remember who she was. And as much as Alexandra tried to deny it, it hurt that he didn't. Alexandra tried to let her spine stiffen with resolve. She had obviously left no lasting impression on Parker Harrison; she'd been completely forgettable.

She hadn't counted on Parker moving closer to her just then, so close that she could smell the faint, pleasant chemicals of mothballs from the recent storage of his tuxedo, and the clean, starched scent of the professionally laundered shirt.

Alexandra's body stiffened and she held her breath. Her back was to him, but she almost felt that at any moment he would reach out a hand and touch her. Was she waiting for it? What finally touched her, rasping on her nerve ends and sending a chill quivering through her, was his deep, low voice.

"Hello, Alex," he murmured.

Chapter Two

Parker's memory of Alexandra was almost ten years old. She had been barely a young woman then, truly still a girl. She had been incredibly young and endearingly naive. With him, she had had her first encounter with a man who wasn't her father, a teacher, or a friend. In many ways he had been all three.

Parker allowed his eyes to travel from the appealing angle and slenderness of Alexandra's neck to her shoulders, which were straight and erect, unlike the uncertainty she'd shown physically at nineteen. There was a discreet dip to the back of her formal gown, showing smooth skin and subtle curves, down to a small waist and narrow hips. He smiled appreciably to himself. There was at least one way that Alexandra Morrow had grown up. Parker felt painful regret and sadness and impatience overwhelm him. Damn it! She *had* been too young then. He felt a terrible crush to his gut that he had not recognized her right away, although he could not be blamed completely. Alexandra Morrow had finally come into her own.

It wasn't until she'd stood behind the Reverend Nichols. It was in the church light's diffused glow spotlighting her; then it came to him. And then Parker had been spellbound. Against all reason. Beyond mere surprise. Deeper than shock. For seeing Alexandra Morrow so suddenly had swept him back to a time in his life when he, too, had been too young.

It was a long, poignant moment before Alexandra could bring herself to turn around and face him. In a matter of seconds, she had to recover from the shock and disappointment of his not knowing right away who she was. And she had to show, just as she had moments ago, seeming indifference to him and to the past.

When she turned, Parker's gaze roamed over her face with memories as well as recognition reflected. There was wonder and surprise, curiosity and thoughtfulness, and as the seconds swept silently by, the slight smile on his mouth was mixed with sadness, shaping his mouth with irony as well as warmth.

Alexandra could see now, however, that their meeting again had been just as much a shock for him.

"I didn't think you remembered," Alexandra said honestly, meeting the steady gaze, alert to his every movement and reaction to her.

"No . . ." Parker said vaguely, his eyes not finished with their inventory of her yet. "That wasn't it. I didn't recognize you," he admitted.

"Oh," she murmured, feeling let down somehow. But it should not have surprised her that a man of Parker's experience should have forgotten a wide-eyed teenager with big dreams and innocence, an inexperienced teen who'd hung on his every word, every musical chord, as though he were a prophet. She didn't remember Parker ever having been impressed by adoration, but not to recognize her . . .

"That is, not until Brian said your name and I saw the freckles."

She glanced up, a hand self-consciously reaching to touch her face where a handful of brown dots dusted the bridge of her nose. Parker quickly cut short the movement by touching her hand and pulling it down. He looked down at her hand caught in his, running his thumb over the smooth, soft back. Her hand was still delicate and slender, although for the moment, she left it limp in his.

"Your hand is still cold. Were you wondering when I'd figure it out?" he asked in wry amusement.

"I think I was hoping you wouldn't," Alexandra stated evenly, extracting her hand, too aware of the warm strength of his fingers. But Parker raised a brow at her withdrawal. "It . . . it would have been too difficult trying to explain how we knew one another," she said.

"Oh, I can recall that," Parker said easily, with a slow smile, and it brought the heat of embarrassment to Alexandra's cheeks as she also wondered if he recalled how well and deep the knowledge went. Suddenly, she felt both the pain and exhilaration of having been so young.

Parker read both her expressions, and it surprised him. It had been a very long time, but was it possible Alexandra had not forgotten? Certainly part of the proof was in her easy and quick recognition of him. But it was too hard to think of more than that.

Parker half squinted an eye closed and tilted his head. "Let's see. It was seven years ago . . ."

"Almost nine," she corrected, without thinking.

He nodded, conceding the point. "You had an apartment down the hall, and liked my piano." His eyes took in the rest of her now, in her peach formal dress that flattered her slender form. The appreciation and surprise were back again in his gaze. It was new to Alexandra.

"I remember that you were studying music. You were

going to become rich and famous," he said, lifting a brow, his mouth in a smile.

Alexandra couldn't tell if he was teasing her or not, but even the thought that he might be added to the mixed emotions tumbling through her system. She had overcome too many past adolescent heartbreaks to stand and have Parker make light of her youthfulness of years ago. She didn't want him to turn his scant recollections now into an easy laughable account that might hold no meaning for him beyond this chance encounter. Because that was all it was. It had taken Alexandra a long time to come to the conclusion that what they had been to each other had been important only to her. For Parker, it apparently had held no significance beyond that point and space in time. But since he was here before her now, she wasn't going to let it change anything.

"I still plan to," Alexandra bantered lightly, and a frown settled on Parker's brow.

"Yes, I can see that," he said absently, knowing she wasn't just making conversation, she was still serious about that.

Parker turned his head to see how the photo session was going, and seeing that the photographer was going for every angle and shot possible, he sighed and faced her again.

"Look . . . I could use a cigarette. Do you think I'll be excommunicated if I smoke in the foyer?"

"I think your soul is safe for now," Alexandra chuckled softly.

"Good," he tilted his head to the left. "Come keep me company." Parker began walking toward the end of the aisle leading to the foyer, and a little reluctantly, Alexandra fell into step beside him. The light touch of his fingertips on the back of her waist guided her to the one lone wooden bench along the wall, and they sat down together, Alexandra making sure that there was some room between them. Only the filmy fabric of her dress floated and rested against his thigh.

"I'm convinced there's a church ordinance which dictates that there be only hard wooden benches to sit on," Parker said dryly, and Alexandra laughed softly, letting him charm her all over again with his easy ways.

"It's just to make sure your mind stays where it should," Alexandra said, rolling her eyes heavenward.

"No doubt," Parker murmured.

He was staring at her again, but this time Alexandra found it more disconcerting. She couldn't imagine what held him fascinated, what he looked for in her oval face. Parker reached for his cigarettes, never taking his eyes off her while he slowly lit one. A crooked smile formed around the burning cigarette held in his firm lips. A deep slash was revealed in one cheek, a masculine groove that was attractive and added a rakish air to his handsome face.

What he saw was a face that had filled in with feminine maturity and softness. Gone was the stubborn little ball of a chin Alexandra used to possess. Gone were the too-thin hollow cheeks, and the eyes that seemed too large for her face. But one thing remained; it was true then and it was true now—Alexandra possessed a calm, comfortable prettiness that made him want to smile.

Unaware and unashamed of her own staring, Alexandra reacquainted herself with Parker's face. His hair was curled into a short, even cut that defined the shape of his head. He didn't seem to have changed physically. Perhaps the face was more filled out and mature, the eyes a bit more worldly and thoughtful in their gaze; there were two parallel furrows across his forehead. He had always been capable of deep intensity. The wide, square mouth was more experienced. Alexandra lowered her gaze, and her wayward thoughts. He seemed the same, but she knew he couldn't be.

"Almost nine years. That *is* a long time," he said, removing the cigarette and expelling smoke. His voice was a disturbing, distinctive drawl. It was too caressing—a unique way, Alexandra remembered, he had of using his voice. It could make him nonthreatening, pleasantly friendly, unintentionally seductive, intentionally soothing.

"So . . . how have you been?" she asked rather stiffly, still feeling as much on guard with him as she was with herself. There was a part of her that wanted Parker to see how much she'd matured, how self-possessed and grown-up she was. She wanted *him* to be impressed and overwhelmed this time. But again, in view of his life now, she wondered if he'd care.

Parker chuckled silently, noticing an aloofness in her again. He could well imagine what was the basis for it. The past, and him. He slowly shook his head. "I'd rather talk about you. How have *you* been?"

Alexandra shrugged indifferently, lacing her fingers together. "Okay, I suppose. I teach now, I study music, I sing . . ."

"Anywhere besides church?" he teased.

"I sing at The Outer Edge," she stated confidently.

Parker's brows raised, and he nodded, taking another pull on the cigarette. "I've heard of it, but I've never been there." He tilted his head in question. "But I remember that you wanted to sing light opera . . ."

"That's true," Alexandra said, looking away from him and down the corridor. She knew they were both thinking that her opera career should have happened by now.

Alexandra's opportunity to do so at nineteen had been lost when Parker had suddenly and mysteriously departed from her life, leaving her emotionally devastated. At the same time, her father had been diagnosed as having a weak heart, an additional emotional burden for her. Christine, who'd felt restrictions upon her time and activities as a result of their father's condition, was frequently uncooperative. Alexandra had lost precious weight and sleep; she hadn't been able to concentrate on anything for months, least of all, the demanding practice and preparation necessary for the prestigious audition.

Alexandra had been determined to go to the audition anyway, but after the second required movement, she had disqualified herself, claiming illness. But the truth of the matter was that in that moment, standing on a brightly lit stage in the presence of peers, of stiff competition and strict censoring judges, she had been on the verge of embarrassing herself by collapsing into tears. In that instant, she didn't care about the competition, only what was happening to her father, and what had happened to cause Parker to leave.

It was only much later, as she began to pick up the trail of Parker Harrison's rising career, that it had come to her. Like the song, they had been strangers in the night. Meeting, touching, passing briefly, until his dreams and ambitions took him elsewhere.

A sudden bewilderment made Alexandra's hands clench together, and a sense of injustice turned her eyes bright and sparkling. He had no right to do that, she thought, as her throat threatened to close tight around the emotion of indignation. He had no right to make her care, and then to just walk away.

Alexandra stood up abruptly, and she knew that Parker's frown deepened at her sudden motion. His questioning eyes followed her as she walked to a small leaded-glass window. She looked out absently at the rain still falling on the streets of Washington, D.C., the slick surface distorting images, colors, and shapes. She was shocked to find that a mere half hour in his presence could revive so many feelings she'd thought were done and gone. Alexandra took a deep breath, and turning slowly, once more composed, she walked back to where Parker sat forward, resting his elbows on his knees, watching her.

Parker could tell that for whatever reason, Alexandra was angry with him. He could feel it. He wondered if it had anything to do with what they both had in common—music. It was true that he had gone on to incredible recognition, more money than he either wanted or needed, and the supreme satisfaction of knowing that his music was heard everywhere. Obviously, Alex had not achieved such lofty levels yet. But who was to say which of them was to be envied? Whose life was more normal? It seemed to be a question of a private life versus a public one. It didn't seem all that clear to Parker.

There was a sadness in his eyes, which he quickly shielded when she turned to face him. Parker took a final drag on his cigarette and flicked the butt into a nearby trash bin.

"You have a beautiful voice," Parker began, to break the silence. "It's grown strong."

"I think it's good enough. I still hope to be accepted by the Light Opera Company here in D.C."

"You probably will be. You seem . . . determined." Parker said.

"Oh, I am," Alexandra said, raising her chin in a stubborn, defiant manner.

In the past nine years, she'd fought down her pain and hurt to go on to other things in her life. She'd once given her all to Parker, but there was no more she intended to give of herself to him or the past. She had her music. Slowly but surely she had her future; she had her own dreams.

"I remember you could accompany on piano . . ."

Alexandra shifted her face from his scrutiny. "I don't play piano very well," she demurred. "It's not one of my strong points."

Parker stood up now, tall and straight, to look down at her. "That's all right," he said softly. "I seem to recall you had many others." He rebuttoned his jacket and checked to make sure his satin bow tie was straight. Then he smiled at her, charming again, and so appealing. "I promised my first dance to the bride. Will you save the next one for me?"

She was surprised. She'd expected him to probe deeper into the past nine years, to ask more questions. She'd expected that somewhere along the way would come unnecessary excuses and apologies and explanations. And Alexandra wasn't sure if she was relieved or frustrated that he wasn't going to offer, either. Perhaps it was best not to. What they were to each other only had to do with now—today.

Her sense of humor slowly began to return, and she could feel herself gaining both confidence and control. Parker Harrison was attractive and accomplished, and he was her escort for the day. She would enjoy it for what it was—no more, no less. She smiled now, her eyes softening, brightening her face. "Thank you."

Parker bent an elbow and held it out for her. Alexandra curved her hand around his arm. "You realize that this whole thing was a set-up, don't you?" he said, in mock seriousness.

She looked at him. "You mean Brian and Debby wanting the two of us to meet?"

"Umm-hmm."

"It *is* a bit embarrassing," she said ruefully. "I was hoping you wouldn't notice."

Parker laughed low, showing his strong teeth in a flashing grin. "So were they," he commented dryly, as he escorted her back to the group.

"Maybe I should make it easy on them and explain that we've . . ."

"No, don't," Parker objected firmly. He stopped for a moment to look at her upturned face with its questioning eyes. "Let's continue to pretend this is the first time we're meeting and we're getting to know one another."

The request was made so quickly that it surprised even Parker; it had come out of nowhere. Well, maybe his subconscious. Some of the past memories were distinctly uncomfortable, but he didn't want them to spoil today. Alexandra Morrow had popped back into his life, and he found her so attractive, so intriguing now as a woman, that he wanted a chance to know her again. It was also an opportunity to settle a few things.

"All right," she agreed reluctantly, feeling caution come into play again, as Parker gave her another warm smile and they walked on.

"So far, I like what I see," he drawled.

But if he was pretending that they could start over completely, Alexandra thought tightly, then he was in for a big disappointment.

The ride to the reception hall began in uncomfortable silence, at least for Alexandra. Parker seemed to be concentrating on the wet, slippery roads and the traffic through Washington D.C. But Alexandra was concentrating on him.

She'd half expected that Parker would have some kind of entourage at his disposal—waiting in the wings, for a word or signal, to do his bidding. But there was none. When they'd left the church, everyone heading for a car for the drive to the reception, Alexandra had found herself alone with him. She assumed that his car would somehow reflect his enormous financial success, something totally obvious and flashy. But it was a white Volkswagen, a well-preserved convertible Karmen Ghia Champagne Edition, that he led her to. Although in very good condition, it was not a flashy car. It did not lend itself to chauffeurs or entourages. It was strictly a two-person vehicle, closed and private.

He deposited her things in the back seat and carefully helped her into the front. In the tight confines of the small car, Alexandra was suddenly aware of his manliness. Alexandra had allowed herself only a passing interest in the opposite sex over the last few years, and disappointingly, their interest in her hadn't extended much beyond sex itself. She had convinced herself that involvement of any kind could not possibly work to her advantage. She had only once allowed herself a brief flight of fancy, and it had very nearly destroyed her. What she had in mind for her life now did not require a man or love. She would fulfill her life on her own, alone. Yet it was a surprise to find that she could still remember, still be moved by the maleness, the warmth that Parker emitted sitting in the driver's seat next to her, unbidden images of delightful intimacy filling her mind and imagination as she wondered if he, too, remembered.

Parker was exuding a sensual quality that was almost tangible. Alexandra found herself squeezing uncomfort-

ably against the door of the car as if to avoid it, as if it
reached out to her.

Parker didn't seem inclined to talk, only asking a question or two for directions or making an innocuous comment about their surroundings. He was also busy remembering the places he'd been, the things he'd done so long
ago in D.C. with Alex. Parker's mouth curved into a slight
smile at the mental image of their youth. He remembered
how confused and unhappy he'd been with his life at the
time, even with his music. But Alexandra's presence had
been a surprise which, for a while, had made it all beara-
ble.

Alexandra found that she, too, was capable of only
meaningless conversation during the ride to the reception
hall. For a frightening heart-stopping moment, she wondered just how indifferent she really was toward Parker
Harrison. She wondered if she could actually be afraid of
his persuasive powers, coupled with the knowledge of
what they'd been to each other in the past. Was there any
possibility she'd forgive him?

From the moment they came through the door of the
restaurant, with a fresh cigarette pressed into the corner
of his wide mouth, Parker captured everyone's attention.
All afternoon he was politely but persistently besieged
with questions, requests for autographs, and adoration.

At one point, while she was sitting alone, Alexandra
absently twirled the stem of her champagne glass. She was
half listening to the laughing conversation taking place at
her table among people she didn't really know. At the
tables to her left and right were the immediate families of
the bride and groom. Behind her, at the fourth and last
table, were musician friends of Brian's, and Parker.

Alexandra had found herself seated next to him at the
reception table. But beyond the dance he'd claimed with

her after proposing a toast to the bride and groom, they'd been separated all afternoon, and he'd wandered from table to table, speaking with everyone.

She'd been asked to dance by Debby's father, and then by Brian, and then by a few of the musicians. Each time she'd returned to the table, Parker was somewhere else, surrounded by female admirers.

Alexandra grimaced in resignation. She supposed that when you were as well known as Parker, anonymity was impossible. But it was hard to ignore the constant outbreak of cheerful voices and laughter around him, hard to enjoy herself when she found herself surreptitiously following his movements, and feeling so left out. Parker sat like a king holding court, smiling amiably, and giving each member of his audience a slice of his time and attention. Alexandra had to admit, he handled himself well. He'd become quite polished and sophisticated in comparison to the Parker she remembered, with his many doubts and insecurities. Of course, those had to do exclusively with his music, his public life, and his questions about his career, now that he was beyond the stage of child prodigy. It was those concerns which had made it possible for them to meet so fortuitously when Alexandra was nineteen. Often over the years Alexandra had tried to convince herself that Parker had found resolutions to his questions and that those answers had taken him away from her. It wasn't really satisfying as an explanation, but it was all she had. There was always the possibility, however, that Parker hadn't cared enough about her.

An attractive blonde flirted outrageously with him now, but she was no more successful than the other women trying to be special in his eyes. It was easy for Parker to be gracious and charming. Much of it came naturally because, although not very gregarious, he was approachable and friendly. Some of it had to do with his being a performer. He was probably used to having an audience even when he wasn't on stage.

As friendly as he was in this moment, no one could detect Parker's desire to slip away and go back to his table, back to Alexandra. She astounded him. She was so much more than he remembered. The raw, youthful vulnerability was gone and had been replaced by . . . he wasn't sure what. Certainly she had matured. And she had grown more lovely than ever.

What also caught Parker's attention almost at once was Alexandra's apparent lack of attention to him. Actually, it bordered on indifference. It was a refreshing turn-about from what he'd come to expect from people, both male and female. The Alexandra he'd known before, in her youth and honesty, had kept him grounded, had reminded him that he had a natural ability in music, that he had a responsibility to it and to himself. He realized now, as he listened to the overly bright laughter of those around him, and catered to their expectations of him, that he'd missed Alex's honesty and insights.

A vision in intricate white lace suddenly blocked Alexandra's frowning contemplation of Parker, and she looked up to find Debby in his vacated chair. Alexandra at once gave her a warm, bright smile while disguising her own emotional confusion.

"So, do you feel any different now that you're married?" Alexandra asked.

Debby lifted a brow saucily at her friend. "I'll let you know after tonight."

Alexandra laughed. "That's not exactly what I mean."

Debby shrugged. "Mom used to always say, the first time you have a fight is when you know you're really married. You can't very well tell him to go away."

"I think she was only teasing you," Alexandra offered.

Debby tilted her head thoughtfully. "On the other hand, fighting can have its advantages. Think of all the fun we'll have making up."

Alexandra shook her head at her friend's outrageous line of thought. "I think Brian is marrying you just in time."

Debby sobered a little and shrugged a shoulder. "I think it was time. Being separated while he was on the road was hard on both of us. We spent a fortune on long-distance calls. Believe me, it's probably cheaper to be married."

Alexandra took a small sip of her pink champagne. She stole a thoughtful look at Debby over the rim of the fluted glass. "Well, now you're married, but Brian will still go on the road, won't he?"

"This is his last tour. He's applying for a seat in the Washington Symphony. I think he wants to follow Parker's example."

Alexandra felt a lurching of her heart in her chest. She stared at Debby. "What do you mean, follow Parker's example?"

"Just that Parker told Brian he was tired of life on the road himself. He doesn't have to prove himself anymore, heaven knows. I think he'd like to settle down in one place to pick and choose what projects he wants to do." Debby looked anxiously at Alexandra. "That's . . . sort of why Brian wanted him here today. What do you think of him? Isn't he something?"

Alexandra ignored the question and narrowed her eyes suspiciously. "And I suppose that Brian thought Parker could follow his lead and find someone, er . . . interesting?"

"Well . . ." Debby hesitated, seeing the stubborn, de-

fensive set to her friend's face. "Brian just thought it
would be nice if you two . . ."

"I knew it," Alexandra moaned. "Brian's playing
matchmaker."

"Well, not exactly," Debby hedged.

"Did he mention me to Parker before today?" Alexandra probed on.

"No, I don't think so. He thought you two should just
meet and let things kind of take their own course."

Alexandra's eyes grew stormy. It was on the tip of her
tongue to tell Debby that Brian's efforts had been wasted,
and that he was about nine years too late. Things *had*
taken their own course.

"Look . . ." Debby said soothingly, not getting the
response she'd expected and seeing the storm rising in her
friend. "I'm sorry if it seems like we interfered. But Brian
thinks the world of Parker, and I'm so fond of you that
. . ."

"That naturally you figured that Parker and I would
sort of hit it off and have a happy ending—just like you
and Brian."

Debby looked shamefaced. "I guess it sounds awfully
silly."

Alexandra knew at another time, under other circumstances, it wouldn't have been. And there was no way on
Earth for either Debby or Brian to know that. She smiled
with a reassuring effort and patted Debby's hand. "It's
not silly at all. And I'm touched at your concern for me,
but . . ." She struggled to find the right words to express
her sentiments now. "I'm busy with my own music right
now. And I'm sure Parker would like to arrange his own
life. I doubt if it's going to include me," Alexandra said
with a false lightness.

Debby sighed. "That's too bad. I was sure you two

were right for one another. Parker is successful and popular and talented. But I don't think he's all that happy. There's something in his past he doesn't talk about, something that hurts him." Again she turned her eyes hopefully to Alexandra, but already her friend was shaking her head adamantly.

"We all have hurts in our pasts, Debby. I'm sure Parker will survive his," she said rather coldly, even as she swept aside her own curiosity at Debby's observations of Parker's present life.

Debby shook her head sadly. "I was so sure you'd like him."

Alexandra felt the warmth drain from her face, neck, and bare shoulders. "I didn't say I didn't *like* him. I just don't think you should marry us off so quickly."

"You haven't exactly been setting dating records, you know. I've never met anyone as picky as you are. Some really great men have asked you out."

She stared blankly at Debby for a long, silent moment knowing that the word "like" was not nearly adequate enough to describe her feelings. There was no way, not enough time to do so, and in any case, it didn't matter. She wasn't going to let it matter.

A large hand settled on her shoulder, and Alexandra jumped. She looked up into the quizzical gaze of Parker standing at her side. Alexandra merely stared at him, lost for the merest second in the past, and recalling with crystal clarity how she'd once felt about him.

"Oh, you've come to ask Alexandra to dance?" Debby instigated, getting to her feet.

"As a matter of fact, yes," Parker said. He gave Debby his champagne glass and reached for Alexandra's hand, and pulled her slowly to her feet. He'd already learned very quickly that it was best not to give Alexandra too much time to reply because the answer would likely be "No." He wanted to change that. Parker never questioned why it was important that he make a positive impression on Alexandra Morrow. She was intriguing, even in her coolness toward him. Still, wanting to charm her smacked of wanting to redeem himself in her eyes. Parker knew that there was something he'd done in the past which continued to bother her deeply.

The warmth and strength from his fingers sent a quiver of emotion through Alexandra again and, with a feeling of panic and defeat, Alexandra realized that she'd always responded to being near Parker. *That* apparently had not changed in all those years.

Parker led her to the dance floor, where a light Latin number played. The beat of the music didn't really allow for body contact, but every now and then Parker would take her hand to swing her through a series of intricate turns, drawing unexpected cheers and applause from a small group of guests who followed his every move. Alexandra kept up with his lead, excited by their matched timing, synchronized as if it were natural. She kept her eyes focused on his loosened bow tie, just a zig-zag of black fabric draped carelessly around his neck, the top two buttons of his formal shirt opened as well.

When the number ended, Alexandra was breathless, her face warm from the exertion and her eyes bright. Unexpectedly she had enjoyed the dance. When she raised her gaze to Parker, she could tell he'd enjoyed it, too. And she saw that it wasn't over yet. He held out his hands, wanting the next dance as well, which was slow and romantic.

One hand slid slowly, sensuously, around her waist, drawing Alexandra in until thighs rested against thighs. The other hand threaded with her fingers intimately.

They moved in time to the music. Parker was deliberately careful in holding Alexandra to him. There was a delicacy about her, a lightness that required subtlety and slowness. Sudden moves and actions could easily spook her. Parker thought with some irony that he'd apparently done just that to her a long time ago, and never realized it.

It had been a while since Alexandra had been so close to a man; an age since she'd been so close to Parker. She had a sudden mental image of a dark, secret moment with them together, and convulsively she squeezed his shoulder. Parker pressed her waist, and Alexandra blinked and looked up at him to find his scrutiny dark and serious.

"Your hands are still cold. What are you thinking now?" he asked, in a low voice.

Alexandra studied him for a moment, seeing all the things that had ever made him attractive to her. "That you never answered my question before. How have things gone for you?" she evaded.

Parker lifted a corner of his mouth as if he found the question amusing. "Things have gone okay. I have few complaints." He turned her to the music.

Alexandra raised her brows. "You have some? I'm surprised."

"Why?" he asked puzzled.

"Oh . . . I don't know. You've done well for yourself. Some would even say you lead a charmed existence. What could there be to complain about?"

His eyes grew very dark and scanned her upturned face thoughtfully. "Maybe 'complaints' is the wrong word. I should have said I want for very little."

"There's something missing?" Alexandra persisted.

Parker didn't answer her, but continued to watch her, and move her to the music. He asked a question rather than answering hers. "Tell me, what do you want out of life, Alex?" he asked softly, trying to understand the slight edge to her voice.

Alexandra stiffened slightly, and she silently chuckled. "What you have," she answered firmly.

"Perhaps you know something I don't," Parker said cryptically. "Why don't you tell me what it is I'm supposed to have?"

Although Alexandra thought he was teasing, his eyes were still targeted on her, and his stare showed he expected a serious answer. It made her nervous suddenly. "Well, for one thing, your music is heard everywhere. You are paid well to perform, and you get to work with exciting people." She stopped and looked up at him. Parker seemed totally unmoved.

"Go on," he said flatly.

Alexandra frowned. He sounded disappointed. What more could there be? "You have the attention of hundreds of thousands of fans, record sales in the millions," she continued. "You have everything."

Again Parker lifted a corner of his mouth, but this time, without any show of humor. He'd heard all that before. The image of him was not new, but it was tired. It was almost as if people couldn't really see *him*, only what he did and what he had. It was all so superficial. And it was sad, because Alexandra used to know him better than anyone and now she apparently believed the misconceptions about his life. My, how the mighty have fallen, Parker thought wryly.

"No . . . not everything, Alex," he said evenly, and a muscle began working in his jaw. His voice became wishful and soft. "My apartment accommodates one person. Me. I come back to it after a road trip, alone. There are lots of people in my life, but not many friends, and no one person who's special." His hand moved slowly along her spine. "If I go out for a walk, to just enjoy a day like someone who leads a normal life, I can count on being recognized and surrounded by scores of people. Strangers. They'll all know my music, but not one of them will really know me. I found out how lonely it can be in a crowd," Parker finished, with a lift of his brows, and a soundless chuckle.

The music had stopped again, and the band was taking a break. But neither Parker nor Alexandra noticed. The lights dimmed on the dance floor leaving the two of them locked in semi-privacy. Behind them the wedding guests were moving among themselves and shifting chairs. Alexandra and Parker remained in the middle of the dance floor.

Alexandra stared at him. The Parker she remembered had been a solitary man, often plagued with self-doubts and insecurities. He'd been well known and respected even then, but for different reasons. Then, Parker had said he'd performed to please and to cater to everyone but himself. He'd suffered a period of not wanting to play at all. It was during that time, Alexandra knew, that Parker discovered he wanted to compose his *own* projects; play his *own* music.

When he'd suddenly left Washington, D.C., all those years ago, she discovered later, it was to pursue that music and develop his own unique style, which would take him to the forefront of the musical world for the second time in his life. The first time he'd followed the dictates of his parents and his instructors. The second time Parker had taken control of his career and his life. But Alexandra had to admit, Parker didn't seem all that pleased or happy about his fame, just as Debby had hinted at earlier. She didn't understand what more he could possibly want.

Suddenly standing in his arms, her hands pressed

lightly against his chest, Alexandra surprisingly saw in his face and eyes all the things that had brought her so close to him once before. Did he still have the need for approval and support and faith? Was he still uncertain whether he was any good? Against her will, she felt empathy for that part of his life that might remain empty and unfulfilled, but she fought against it. He had made a choice. He had a life-style to die for. If he didn't "have it all," he certainly, at least, had the next best thing.

"Are you saying that fame isn't all it's cracked up to be?" Alexandra asked softly.

Parker frowned and shook his head. "Fame was never what I was aiming for. I thought you knew that," he finished, just as softly.

There was an implied criticism, an implied disappointment that made Alexandra suddenly angry. Who was he anyway, to assume so much of her after so many years? "Maybe I did at one time," she said sharply. "But I was very young and believed a lot of things that weren't true. I don't believe everything I hear anymore." She dropped her hands to her side.

Slowly, Parker released Alexandra and stood back a step. He surveyed her lovely, lithe body in the peach silk gown, and looked deeply into her eyes.

"What do you believe in?" he asked. "What's important to you?"

"Myself," Alexandra answered without hesitation. "My ability to sing."

"Is that all?"

No, she thought, *I always believed in you.* But her large, dark eyes never wavered from his. "Yes, that's all."

Parker slowly took a deep breath and slowly let it out again. He slipped his hands into his pants pocket. "You've changed, Alex," he commented. A strange pain settled in Parker's chest. It was disconcerting, but familiar.

His regret immediately caused Alexandra's heart to turn over, her resolve to slip, her teeth to clamp tightly together to keep her eyes from misting with tears. He was wrong in ways she'd never let him know, so wrong that for an instant she forgot the pain of the past and was tempted to blurt out what was really in her mind and heart at that moment. There was a time when she would have settled for just having his love. She would have given up her own dreams of a musical career for that.

"No, Parker. I haven't changed at all. I've only grown up. And I've learned that we all have to be responsible for what our lives become; some people are lucky and get everything they want. Others have to work very hard."

"Are you suggesting that I didn't really earn my good fortune?" Parker asked, his eyes staring bright, angry sparks at Alexandra.

She shook her head. "No, of course not. No one knows better than I the cost of your success. But I also learned an important lesson from you: never let anything stop you from getting what you want in life."

Alexandra turned and walked slowly back to the cheerful gathering, swallowing the tension inside herself. She was chilled and shaking with emotions, sorry that she'd let her feelings get away from her, but perversely glad that she could get them out.

By the time she'd pulled herself together, the wedding party and the guests were grouped for the next ritual in the afternoon's celebration. A chair was placed in the center of the floor and with great ceremony and applause Debby was led to it and seated by Brian. Brian bent to one knee and lifted the hem of his wife's wedding dress, exposing a comely turn of silken leg. There were whistles and cat calls as Brian slowly slipped Debra's "something blue," a lace garter, down and off her leg. Then he stood on a chair with his back to the group as the men gathered closer. Twirling the garter risquély around a finger, Brian let it go, flinging it into the crowd.

It was caught by Debby's school administrator, a timid, scholarly man in his sixties who gingerly examined the lace confection as though it was a curious insect. He turned beet red at the laughter around him and, with a sheepish grin, hastily stuffed it into a pocket.

Next, Debby was helped onto the chair as she, too, presented her back to the group while holding onto her floral bouquet. Alexandra continued to hang back on the edge of the group, her mind still on the conversation with Parker, and only half attentive to the rollicking. She wasn't in the mood right now to participate, but she made the effort to be part of the group.

At the boisterous count of three, the bouquet was flung up and over Debby's shoulder. Hands flew up and there were squeals and laughter. But Debby's arm strength was a lot better than her aim, and the flowers flew over everyone's head.

It was a fast second before Alexandra realized the flowers were headed straight for her, and all she could think to do was close her eyes and duck her head out of the way.

There was a surprised gasp and then a roar of more laughter. When Alexandra opened her eyes, it was to turn and find Parker holding the bouquet with an embarrassed grin on his handsome face. Everyone applauded. For a moment Parker turned his attention to Alexandra. Something fleeting and electric passed between them, causing Alexandra to quickly avert her eyes. Forgetting her anger at Parker, Alexandra remembered another of Grandma Ginny's tales: that the one to catch a bouquet at a wedding would be the next bride. There was an immediate appeal to the idea that was just as quickly dismissed in her mind.

He was tempted to give the bouquet to Alex, and he could see that she dreaded that he would. She had done a very good job of putting him on the spot all day whenever they were alone. Maybe it was even deserved, but Parker couldn't help wishing Alexandra had been a little more forgiving. Parker also knew she hadn't intended to be spiteful, but it did speak volumes for the way she felt toward him. He wasn't going to go tit for tat. Revenge could be wreaked in much more pleasant ways.

Parker walked past Alexandra and over to the six-year-old flower girl, who was also Brian's niece. The little girl's face lit up when she was given the flowers, and she rewarded Parker with a childish wet kiss to his cheek. There was additional applause.

Alexandra was pleased and soothed that Parker had handled the situation in the best way possible. It was further proof of the tenderness she recalled, and it made Alexandra feel all the worse for her petulance of a moment ago. But she had no intention of apologizing to him.

The reception soon broke up and the bride and groom made another receiving line to make farewells to their guests.

Alexandra thought to escape alone and quickly. Saying goodbye to Parker was going to be as awkward as saying hello had been, and she suddenly had a panicky feeling that she couldn't handle it. While everyone else was kissing each other goodbye and making hasty plans for future gatherings, she slipped away to the coat room unnoticed. She had her coat on and was actually at the restaurant door, ready to leave, when she realized that everything, her garment bag, her umbrella, was in the back of

Parker's car. Of course the car was locked, so she couldn't quietly get her things. As she stood wondering the best way to solve this latest complication, Alexandra became aware of someone behind her. The hair bristled on the back of her neck. With a fatalistic sigh, she realized that the rest of this evening had to be played out with Parker to the bitter end.

Slowly, Alexandra turned her head to look over her shoulder. Her large, wary eyes encountered Parker standing a few feet behind her. His eyes were dark and cold. His mouth was no longer sensuous and mobile, but hard and tightly closed. There was a purposefulness in his stance, in his stiffly held body, that made it clear to Alexandra a reckoning was coming. She thought to avoid it. But as she opened her mouth to speak, she was abruptly cut off.

"I'm taking you home," he stated firmly, eliminating any possibility of argument. And then, not bothering to put on his top coat against the cold, he headed out the door.

Chapter Three

"I can sense this day taking a turn for the worse," Parker said stiffly.

"It doesn't have to," Alexandra said. "You can still let me go home alone."

Parker shook his head. "It's not over yet." He didn't want the day to end with him feeling remorseful and guilty, with the resurgence of so much regret. He knew the decisions he'd made years ago were the only ones open to him at the time. Any alternative would have doomed him to failure. He'd hoped that Alexandra would have understood. But how could he expect her to? She didn't have all the facts he possessed about what had really happened.

They stood like combatants outside the restaurant's reception area, squaring off stubbornly, each wanting to have his way. Grimly, Parker realized he couldn't force the issue. Alexandra was going to win.

"Wait . . . wait!"

They both turned at the sound of Debby's breathless voice behind them.

"I thought you and Brian began your honeymoon ten

minutes ago, when you said goodbye to your guests," Parker said in amusement.

Debby grinned sheepishly. "It begins when the plane takes off from Dulles. I just wanted to make sure Alexandra would get home all right. I didn't want to leave her stranded in Maryland . . ." Debby's voice faded as she saw the mutinous transformation on her friend's face.

Alexandra did an admirable job of containing her annoyance and ill humor. She tried to remember that this was Debby's special day; she had no right to be difficult. She remembered that Debby only thought to see after her welfare. And finally, she remembered that Debby had no knowledge—how could she?—of Parker's past relationship to her. Alex took a deep breath.

"You know, it wasn't very fair to make me Parker's responsibility all day. He shouldn't have to be a chauffeur as well. What would his manager think?"

"I didn't mind," Parker said tightly.

Debby looked silently and wide-eyed from one to the other, hoping for redemption from either one.

"I wouldn't have missed this afternoon for the world," Parker said wryly, but took little satisfaction in watching Alexandra's discomfort. He reached for her hand, raising his brows at her still chilled fingers. Parker gallantly bent over the hand and kissed it lightly. "I'm looking forward to taking Alexandra home."

Alexandra averted her gaze and stood stiffly. She let him hold her hand. She could hear Debby's relief.

"Oh, thanks, Parker. You're a prince and a gentleman."

Parker chuckled, still holding Alexandra's hand. "It's a matter of opinion."

Alexandra forced a smile and looked at Debby. It became warmer when she saw Debby's obvious confusion.

"I'll be fine." She gave Debby a quick hug and pushed her away. "Go on. Brian is waiting."

"Impatiently, I hope," Debby giggled, then turned and ran.

The sudden quiet turned chilly again, and Parker released Alexandra's hand. With a further flourish, he stood aside for her to precede him. Alexandra pulled her collar up around her neck, wishing that at least Brian and Debby had decided to marry in June, like other normal people.

As though informing a cab driver of her destination, Alexandra, as impersonally as she could, gave Parker her address, and then sat back to gaze stonily out her window. She was so deep into her own reflections, wondering how she was going to handle Parker once they reached her apartment, that when he spoke his voice made her jump.

"You know, I get the feeling you don't like me very much," Parker said, in a tired, reflective tone.

Alexandra's eyes widened, and she cast a quick, surprised glance his way, before once again staring into the dark, wet night. "I'm sorry," she said softly. "I didn't mean to give that impression."

"Oh? Just what feeling were you trying to give me?" he asked, puzzled.

Alexandra bit her lip. "None at all, Parker. I mean . . . what is it you want me to say? We haven't seen each other in a very long time, and we only knew one another for a few months." She shrugged nervously. "There just doesn't seem to be very much to say."

There was a small silence, and then, in the quiet tenseness of the car, Alexandra heard him sigh. In it she heard exasperation, impatience, even defeat, as if he'd hoped and tried to elicit another reaction from her. She had been surprised and unprepared for seeing him again like this, but she hadn't forgotten that he'd been the one to walk away.

"I remember those few months as being pretty terrific in lots of ways. I thought we got to know each other real well. I have good memories of that time, Alex." His eyes searched her profile briefly before returning to the road ahead. "We shared a lot. We were good together."

"But you left," Alexandra whispered in a small voice, hoping none of the bewilderment showed. Again she bit her lip and clenched her hands. She hadn't meant to say that. It was too much like an accusation. She sounded too hurt.

"You always knew I would."

She swung her head sharply around to him. "I *never* knew that. I always thought if you left, I would . . ." Alexandra closed her mouth to stop the confession.

"In the end, I had to leave, Alex. But I didn't . . ."

She didn't allow him to finish. "Yes, and now it's all history," she said, taking a deep breath, closing her eyes momentarily and opening them to stare out the window again. "Why don't we just leave it at that? Tell me, how long will you be in D.C. this time?" she asked quickly, to change the subject. "You must have lots of commitments. Are you staying for long?" she asked, unsure of which she hoped it would be.

"I haven't decided yet," Parker answered. "I may drive up to Philadelphia to see my folks. Or I might hang around Washington for a while. I forgot how much I like it here," he answered, glancing at her briefly. Did she remember the fun they used to have? The good times that had been of her making, though he'd been too serious to relax and enjoy them?

"Are you staying with friends?" Alexandra asked carefully, again trying not to be too curious. She wondered if there was a current lady in his life. She was annoyed with herself for even thinking it, and dismayed to feel a brief twist of jealousy grabbing at her.

In the darkness of the car Parker lifted a brow and pursed his lips as he considered her innocent question. It told him instantly so much. It was a facet of Alexandra's personality which remained that he'd always liked. A certain natural naïveté that peeked through the young woman then, the adult woman now. It was a kind of youthful hopefulness and eagerness maintained for all things, despite the need to be seen and treated as mature and worldly. Alexandra *had* changed in nine years. But not as much as she thought.

"I'm staying at the apartment of my manager. He and his wife are in Europe, making a tour arrangement for another one of their interests. It's for my use for as long as I want. Or until the middle of April, whichever comes first."

Alexandra looked at him. The car turned slowly onto a residential street of row houses in northwest D.C. "What happens then?" she asked.

Parker squinted through the streaked window, trying to find her house number as he drove slowly. "Then I go to New York. I'm doing a benefit concert for the United Negro College Fund." He pulled the car into a spot in front of the line of nearly identical buildings, and turned off the windshield wipers.

"You did a benefit concert several months ago for UNICEF," Alexandra stated.

"That's true," Parker said, now turning off the engine, and swiveling a little in his seat to face her.

"How nice of you," she said stiffly, just a touch of sarcasm in her tone. She looked at Parker's face without being able to see the details. The shadows showed the twitching of a jaw muscle, the high, prominent line of his cheek, and the corner of his mouth. Only bits of nighttime light reflected in his eyes, and they shot off sharp sparks in her direction. He was annoyed.

She was being difficult, and she knew it. But Alexandra couldn't seem to help herself. It was as if some angry, enraged super-ego had taken possession of her, and was determined to be unpleasant, uncommunicative, unforgiving. She baited, pushed, and dared, thinking that her cold, ungracious demeanor was justified and would hurt him deeply, before she left him for the night . . . or for eternity.

Gone were all elements of the warm, even-tempered young woman she was normally. Invisible was the ready smile that brightened her eyes and face and made her a pleasure to be with. Hidden was the empathy she was capable of, that often allowed her to consider someone else's feelings and needs above her own. Alexandra didn't know herself, and she didn't like at all what she was as she sat opposite Parker. The humidity began to fog the car windows, closing him and her in an eerie pocket of silence as they sat like adversaries. The entire day, indeed their pasts, hung between them. It didn't seem possible to get past it.

The one-word question "Why?" had sat on her tongue all day long, needing to be asked of Parker, but her pride prevented her from asking it. What had gone wrong? What had *she* done? It had always infuriated her that she thought herself to have been at fault; after all, Parker had been the one to walk away. The question and the need for an answer had remained. Yet she wouldn't ask him; she couldn't. Alexandra felt so righteous in her anger, and she knew instinctively it would be a poor, unworthy victory.

"Doing free concerts has nothing to do with 'nice,'

Alex," Parker finally said, interrupting her thoughts. "It's my way of saying 'thank you' to all the people I'll never meet who believed in me, and who put me where I am today."

His voice was low and caressing, as if he was explaining something she should have understood. She was sure there was a sad note of regret in his tone, as if he shouldn't have to explain to her, of all people. He had always been sensitive to the wishes and needs of others, and she well remembered how torn other people's wishes had left him years ago. Which made his abrupt desertion of her, for that was the word, so unreal and so painful to bear. He had not shown much care for how *she'd* take his departure. Didn't her feelings count, too?

She lowered her head and fought to control the trembling of her lips. *What is the matter with me?* Alexandra wailed silently to herself. She felt like she was coming apart, wanting to forgive him, whatever his reasons, and wanting to strike back in retaliation.

"I'm sorry," she said, in a broken voice. "That was unnecessary of me. I . . . I don't know why I said that," she finished helplessly.

Her head was still bent, and she saw one of Parker's hands reach over to cover both of hers clenched in her lap. But she couldn't bring herself to look at him, although she suddenly wanted to grab and hold onto his offering.

"Alex," he said to her, *"I* know why you said it."

Now she did look at him, but she could read nothing in his expression. It was controlled, and *in* control, and Alexandra recognized what she hadn't allowed herself to see. Parker had changed, too. The earlier flicker of doubt was gone from his eyes. He was much more self-possessed and confident. He seemed to have made peace with himself, while her own peace of mind was shattering virtually before her eyes.

He closed his fingers around her hands and squeezed. "Your hands never did get warm," he said. "I'm hoping that means you still have a warm heart."

Before she could respond Parker released her and turned to open his door to climb out. He quickly came around to her side and helped her out as well before retrieving her things from the back seat. Placing his hand beneath her elbow, he led her firmly toward the brightly lit entrance of her building.

Alexandra had the entire second floor of a three-story limestone townhouse, and when they reached the top of the stairs, she had regained some command of herself. She dug her keys out of her bag and silently took her other things from Parker.

He knew that if he asked to come in, she would refuse immediately. It would be just another way for her to deny him as she'd done all day. But Parker also knew with a certainty that unless she could get beyond the anger of their past before they said goodnight, he might never see her again. He didn't want that to happen.

"It was nice seeing you again, Parker," she said formally. "You look well, and I'm glad you're so successful." She held out her hand awkwardly for him to take. She felt so foolish. This was the man who had taught her about love, and she was now about to shake hands with him as if they'd never met before. "Thank you for driving me home."

Parker suddenly leaned against her door frame, ignoring the hand, watching the play of emotions on her smooth countenance after a long afternoon of trying to control them. "Did you ever get your piano?" he asked quietly with a smile, out of left field, but it succeeded in diverting her for the moment.

Alexandra blinked at him. When they'd first met, she'd been very envious of the grand upright he owned. "Yes, I did," she finally answered.

Then Parker held out his hand. After a moment's confusion, Alexandra placed her apartment keys into his palm. Silently, he opened the door and turned the knob, letting the door swing open into the interior. He waited, and finally Alexandra preceded him into her apartment. She flipped on a wall light as he closed the door, and continued through the small foyer to a darkened room to her left. Another light switch was turned on and she stood at the entrance waiting for Parker to catch up to her. He stopped next to her looking at the baby grand piano which dominated her living room.

A low, appreciative whistle came between Parker's pursed lips. "For someone who says she doesn't play so hot, you sure went all out."

Alexandra couldn't help but be pleased that Parker thought she'd chosen well. She'd saved for two whole years to be able to afford this one. Parker walked over to the piano and automatically turned on the small reading lamp positioned over the sheet music stand. Idly he fingered the keys. Alexandra felt herself go still inside, and she just stood and watched. She felt time slip slowly away.

Parker, his attention totally on the beautiful instrument, slipped off his coat and dropped it over the back of a nearby chair. He sat down at the keyboard and was contemplative before he lifted his hands, and the long, masculine, well-trained fingers touched the keys.

Parker surprised her by starting with a classical fugue as he became familiar with her piano. He then played several short classical pieces with such concentration that he might have been totally alone. His eyes closed as he tilted his head to catch his own sounds. His mouth moved and pursed with inner reactions and emotions, his jaw tensing, brows furrowed.

Alexandra knew that Parker did not often delve into his classical background anymore—at least, not in public. He did not often search among the keys for the music that had begun his auspicious career when he was just a child. But it was obvious he still loved it. Alexandra knew that this, too, satisfied his joy of music.

Parker himself had said he never fully understood where the love had come from. At what point did he begin to *feel* music in his bones, to absorb it into his soul so that he felt nourished and fulfilled? When did he know that this would be his life, playing and creating music?

Alexandra had met Parker in a period of transition, and had learned quickly that he wanted more from his talents than performing just the classics. She'd always assumed it had been in pursuit of recognition, but words he'd spoken to her earlier in the day echoed softly through her head, and she realized with a small shock that there were many things she didn't know or understand about him.

Then Parker switched to something by Aaron Copeland, and moved briefly into a jazz piece she didn't recognize. Without consciously being aware of it, Alexandra put down her things and shrugged out of her coat, and, as if mesmerized, her eyes followed Parker's sure hand movements and her ears filled with the sounds of his music. Her heart remembered well the wonderful presence of him, the admiration, joy, shyness of being near this extraordinarily gifted and handsome man.

She stood just behind him and nearly held her breath as the music floated like magic on the air, and all her first young emotions were reborn.

"Do you remember this one, Alex?" Parker reminisced with a smile. He launched into *All Because of Love,* and then *Memories.*

Her throat started to close, and she swallowed hard. Oh, yes . . . she remembered.

Parker's glance bounced off her quickly. "Sit down," he said as he switched melodies and, with a knowing look at her, started with something fast and intricate and breathtaking, the movements across the keys requiring skill as well as a sense of feeling for the piece. Alexandra smiled.

Instinctively she lifted her slender hands, and at the right moment, came into the piece with Parker, their duet in syncopation; a smile curved her lips as the near-forgotten became instantly familiar again as she and Parker played a piece they'd improvised together during that time he was helping her to improve her skills. It had been so much fun.

Now Parker added some chords, instantly new, and Alexandra kept up the harmony, sensing rather than actually knowing the way of his mind with the music. But she'd always understood his music.

He nodded. "Hey! Well all right, now!" his brows raised in surprised pleasure. "You've been doing a bit of practicing, Miss Alexandra Morrow," he crooned over the piano music.

Alexandra felt at once elated and then, just as quickly, wanted to pummel the keys in frustration. It shouldn't matter what he thought. His praise should mean nothing . . . *nothing.* But her music was better because of all the time Parker had spent with her at the piano, *his* piano, teaching her about rhythm and pacing and how to touch the keys. Her musical ear and the touch of her fingers had become more sensitive because he'd told her not to think so much, but to feel how her fingers moved when she played. *She* had become more sensitive, because of Parker.

With eyes bright and large, Alexandra looked at him, and caught his scrutiny. Her hands faltered once, and then again. Suddenly she stopped. Parker's fingers continued for several more chords, and then he stopped as well.

They looked at one another and Alexandra knew that the pretense had come to an end. The natural joy of just a moment ago became a sadness that began to weigh heavily within her. Alexandra felt confused again, betwixt and between, no longer sure what she was feeling, or what was real. But she knew that the longer she remained in Parker's company, the less sure she became.

"Stop. That's enough. I . . . I think you'd better leave," she said, in a shaky whisper.

"Alexandra . . ." Parker said hoarsely, using her full name for the first time. Hearing him say her name with his own unique enunciation always made her feel she belonged with him. He used her full name to get her attention, make her listen and to make her believe what he said.

Alexandra stood up abruptly. "Please! I want you to go."

"I never meant to hurt you." He let out a harsh chuckle. "I swear, there were times years ago when I didn't know if I was coming or going. Don't you remember how confused I was?"

"Well, I guess you decided you were going. So fast, as a matter of fact, you never bothered saying goodbye." Alexandra marched over to the chair and yanked up Parker's coat. "Here," she said holding it out to him. Her hands were shaking.

Parker stood up and slowly advanced toward her. He

ignored the coat. "It was best that I did that, Alex. I was no good for you then. Hell, I could barely keep myself together. I had a lot of things to work out," he explained angrily, his jaw and mouth taking a proud and stubborn line. He saw her struggling with tears, saw her soft hair loosening under its pinned restraints, and the tendrils adding a lost, vulnerable, wary look to her face. "Alex, I needed you. But if I'd stayed I might have taken everything from you and left nothing in return. I wanted you to have your music, your chance, your own life."

"How noble of you. You should have told me that before I cared so much," she whispered brokenly.

"I cared," he said clearly. "But until I got my head together, it wouldn't have worked," he said softly. "It was harder for me to leave than you think. Believe me, I was only thinking of you."

She shook her head. More curls came loose and lay against her neck. Her vision was blurred with tears. "You were thinking of yourself," she said angrily. "You probably had a good laugh because this silly teenager was so infatuated with you."

"Alex . . ." he began coaxingly.

"Take your coat." She thrust it into his chest, but Parker grabbed her wrist, holding her still for a moment.

He plied his cashmere coat from her rigid fingers and carelessly tossed it back on the chair. Then his hands wrapped around her arms and slowly began to pull Alexandra toward him. She braced her hands against his chest as fear clutched at her heart.

"I never laughed at you, Alex." He slid a hand around her back and down her spine, drawing Alexandra in closer until his thighs and hips were tight against her own. There was a gentle trembling in her entire body, like that of a small, frightened animal that has been trapped and cornered. Parker knew he'd have to be careful and prove to Alexandra that he wasn't going to hurt her. Not again. He wasn't even responding to the past, but to the now.

Alexandra felt wholly feminine and fragile in his arms. It seemed so sudden, so inappropriate. But it was instantly exciting to feel that physically she affected him the same as when he'd last seen her; that emotionally no one else seemed to have gotten next to her the way he had.

Alexandra leaned back, vowing not to give in to Parker. Her chest rose and fell with the extent of her emotions and she no longer had the ability to hide them. A tear slipped down her cheek to the corner of her mouth. She felt the start of a sudden quivering heat from inside. She was frightened. She was angry. And she was responding to the mere closeness of Parker.

"Li-liked you? *Cared* about you?" she mouthed blankly. Her elbows bent, and her hands were flattened on his chest as Parker finally closed the distance. "Oh, Parker . . ." she moaned brokenly, her emotions winning out. "I was foolishly, hopelessly in love with you," she confessed plaintively, and let the distance close between them.

Parker kept one hand around her waist, and with the other he automatically tried to brush the tears from her cheek. "I know," he whispered gently, and bent to ply a feather-light kiss from her lips.

It was over before Alexandra realized it had happened, and belatedly she registered the firm, sensual width of his mouth on hers, the fleeting warmth of his breath, and the intoxicating power of being held by him again. But it was just enough to involuntarily trigger all her senses to another response, one that made her breath catch with surprise. A sensation of melting assailed her system. She was suddenly terrified of what was happening between them.

"It was the most wonderful gift anyone had ever given me, Alex. Absolute faith and all your love." His head was still bent over her, and his words melted all resistance in her. He had always known that Alex loved him; it was hard to miss. He'd left not because he'd been afraid of her love, not because he didn't return her feelings, but because the timing was all wrong. Had he stayed with Alexandra, he truly believed neither of them would have grown. Each had to become his own person so that they'd know for certain what they shared between them. Had he stayed, he would not have realized his music and she would have been disappointed in him. He would have disappointed himself.

Was it unfair, then, to hold her now after all these years, to use the moment to say how sorry he was?

Alexandra rested her forehead against his chest. She'd just admitted she'd loved him. She hadn't known how to handle it at nineteen but had hoped that eventually Parker would tell her first that he loved her, too. Then she would have been free to express her feelings. But he'd known all along how she felt and had never said a word.

"You were the best thing that ever happened to me," he said, with such force and seriousness that Alexandra held her breath and stared at him as though she were nineteen again.

In slow motion Parker bent his head to kiss her; Alexandra watched his features until they blurred and her eyelids naturally drifted closed. When she again felt Parker's lips, they were slightly parted and settled purposefully on her own. He pursed his mouth and gently pulled at hers until her lips parted, too. Then she felt his tongue gently explore. Without another hesitation, she gave him entry, and became pliant against his firm length. Another tear trailed down her face as her body surrendered to the gentle passion. Parker's hand squeezed her tightly around the waist, the other hand lay along her jaw, the thumb touching her bottom lip and urging her to answer his kiss.

Alexandra felt her senses spin. She had no strength to fight him or to deny the near-dizzying effect being touched by him had on her. She didn't care. She only knew the need to press her slender, trembling body closer to him . . . to let his kiss reclaim her as his mouth manipulated and moved eloquently until a moan deep in her throat escaped. She lost herself in the feeling. But slowly his mouth lightened the pressure, his lips teasing and nibbling until they separated from Alexandra.

Her fingers clenched in his shirt front. She could barely breathe; she felt weak. Parker's mouth trailed teasingly along her jaw, her cheek, until he reached her ear and gently bit the lobe, making her stomach muscles curl with the tingling sensation. Parker's hands stroked her back and shoulders as he whispered something into her skin. The words were hot and absorbed into her neck. She only wanted him to kiss her, hoping the intimate dance of their lips and tongues would ease some of the hurt, wash away the past, and finish what had been begun before.

"It was so damned hard to leave," Alexandra heard him say finally, before she tilted her head back and turned it to meet his mouth halfway. A long, quivering sigh eased out as she allowed Parker's large hands to hold her head, while his mouth gently but thoroughly ravaged her own.

A shudder coursed through Parker, and Alexandra felt it in his tightened embrace, in the forward thrust of his thigh and hips against her, blatantly outlining his aroused state against her trembling body. She heard it in his deep moan, and gave no thought to what she was doing, only what she was feeling and needing.

Suddenly Parker literally tore his lips from hers and, on a deep breath, rested his forehead against Alexandra's. "Do you realize what we're doing?" he asked harshly through clenched teeth. "Do you know what you're doing to me?"

Alexandra opened her eyes. She wondered if there was a struggle going on in him, too, a need for her. Their emotions had escalated beyond belief. She knew that her whole being, body and soul, yearned unashamedly for Parker's complete caress. But she didn't know if she would be opening a Pandora's box of more problems, when the last ones had yet to be resolved.

"Parker . . ." she began in confusion, wanting him to make the decision.

"Look," he began, bringing his mouth to within inches of hers again, so close that she could feel his warm breath. "Maybe this shouldn't be happening. This afternoon, I got the impression from you that if looks could kill, I'd be dead," he growled. His mouth touched her cheek and rubbed along the silky surface, erotically coming back to within a hairsbreadth of her parted lips. "But right now," his voice grew low and hoarse, and he again pressed his lips to hers, "you feel so good to me."

Again his mouth took hers, the pressure of his lips taking the kiss deeper, forcing her to give him full access. Parker put his arms tightly around her, one hand smoothing over a hip, his fingers digging gently into her.

Alexandra was beyond a single clear thought. She was experiencing a pure joy, outside of reason, which made her feel she was right where she belonged.

Parker again released her mouth and Alexandra knew that the moment of truth had arrived. Parker frowned deeply, his eyes searching over her soft features, her dreamy eyes and moistened lips. He shook his head ruefully. "I don't know if I should make love to you or get the hell out of here," he said.

Alexandra looked clearly at him. "You didn't give me a choice last time," she responded quietly.

A slow, uncertain smile shaped Parker's mouth. "No, I don't suppose I did. There were reasons."

"*Your* reasons, not mine. I didn't want you to leave."

His thumb brushed over her lower lip as he continued to try and gauge her feelings. He moved his finger and began to kiss her slowly again. "Where's your bedroom?" he asked against her lips, making the decision.

It was then that a warning bell went off in Alexandra's head. There would be no turning back. Was she doing the right thing? She couldn't answer Parker's question and stood stiffly until he gently took her by the shoulders and turned her until her back was to him. There was a momentary rustling of fabric until Parker's arm swung past Alexandra to drop his tuxedo jacket and shirt on the cocktail table before the sofa. Then his fingers found the zipper of her dress and slowly opened it. Alexandra closed her eyes as the material drifted. His arms reached around her. Her breasts were firm but small and fit perfectly in the palms of his hands. While there were no callouses on Parker's fingers the tips were hardened, and their slow sweeping movement on Alexandra's heaving chest made her nipples instantly erect and sensitive. The motion raised gooseflesh of anticipation along her arms, but Parker's body emitted a stirring heat. Alexandra's senses became heated by the erotic stimulation of Parker's hand.

Parker's mouth descended to find the hollow in her neck and nuzzled at the skin to trail random kisses along the slim column until he reached her ear. Then slowly he released Alex, and walked over to turn off the wall light. They were left in only the tiny reading light on the piano.

It made crazy dark shadows in the room, and Parker seemed an almost ominous figure as he approached her.

To Parker she looked waiflike, her eyes large and uncertain. Her dress was slipping off her shoulders, but her gaze was riveted to his face as if trying to understand him, and the moment. He wasn't at all sure what there was to really understand. They wanted each other, and that was perfectly clear. He'd always been able to exercise good sense in matters concerning the opposite sex. But Alexandra was different. She'd always been different because she'd come of age with him. He had been her first lover. That also made her special.

Alexandra held her breath, and her gaze held his as he removed the rest of his clothing. Then he slowly began to remove the last of hers. The warmth of his arms closing around her and drawing her to his hard, lean body was electrifying. She wordlessly raised her mouth so that he could kiss her and love her again.

Parker lowered her to the sofa and neither mentioned the bedroom again. Parker stretched out his own body atop hers. He removed several of the pale rosebuds still pinned in Alexandra's hair, crushed earlier by his fingers. He placed them on the table with his shirt and jacket, and settled against her.

Parker looked into her eyes, searched over her creamy brown face for several long moments. Alexandra shifted her legs so that he was nestled comfortably between them.

"I used to dream about this," he said thickly, gently moving against her.

"What?" Alexandra asked, resolutely burying a rising anger beneath the onslaught of her desire. "What it would be like to see me again? To make love to me again? To have me so foolishly willing?"

Parker shook his head, and smiled sadly. "No. What it

would be like never to have. left. I feel like tonight is *our* honeymoon."

The words were a complete surprise. But his kiss once again distracted her. His lips held her captive, but it was just a prelude to stimulating the rest of her senses into molten desire. They would have been so much more comfortable in Alexandra's bed, but Alexandra wasn't ready for that step. No, not yet.

Parker rubbed his body against hers and Alexandra felt a twisting, grabbing need spiraling throughout her body. Her loins seemed to melt and soften beneath him, and his quick, sure possession of her eliminated the need for talk as they clung together to bridge the past.

Alexandra's mind was a blank. She wasn't at all sure what she'd done or what she'd hoped to prove in the last three hours with her and Parker entangled in each other's arms. She only knew she couldn't have pulled herself away. Whatever anger she'd held, whatever remorse Parker had been trying to overcome, had been forgotten in three hours of primal passion. Her body felt warm, relaxed, sated. Achy. His touch had been expert and sure, his caresses and kisses leaving her limp with a need for fulfillment. She loved, delighted in every moment. It was obvious that they were still perfect together as lovers. But it had not settled the past, it had not changed anything.

Parker was propped up against the sofa cushions, Alexandra lay against his chest. There was a long silence between them that was both strained and embarrassed. Parker was not the least bit sorry he'd made love to Alexandra. To him it had been more than just lovemaking; they had begun to reconnect, to find the spiritual and emotional kinship they'd once known. But now Parker suspected they were back to where they'd first been when they'd arrived at Alex's apartment.

Parker had located his cigarettes and was smoking, the smoke a pale gray veil over them. Alexandra, her cheek to his chest, listened to the small puckering sound his lips made around the cigarette as he inhaled. Her head moved with his chest as he exhaled. She was deceptively fascinated with his coordination of smoking and breathing. Anything to take her mind off the last three hours, and the emptiness she felt inside.

She'd wanted to make love with Parker but she didn't know why.

Parker had maintained complete control over their passion, tempering the pace when it seemed to spiral ahead too fast; picking it up when the ache in them both stretched out too long. He'd known—remembered how to touch her and make her respond at will; but then he had been the first to teach her how. They'd brought each other to a precipice and the fall over the edge into fulfillment had been sweetly torturous. After long moments of silent recovery, they'd begun it all again.

To Alexandra, the loving, instead of having brought them closer, seemed to have driven her farther away from Parker.

He finished his cigarette and put it out in an ashtray on the low table. He made a movement to get up, and Alexandra shifted to allow him to. She immediately felt bereft of his support and warmth. She watched as he retrieved his clothes and silently began to dress.

"Why did you let me make love to you, Alex?" he asked suddenly, the words not loving and seductive, but harsh and cold. He didn't even look at her, but sat on the edge of the sofa to put on his socks and shoes.

Alexandra's nakedness made her feel too exposed, too

vulnerable, and she quickly got up. She retreated to the bathroom for a floor-length robe, slowly returning to find Parker buttoning his shirt.

He stopped for a moment to stare at her. "Why?" he asked again.

Alexandra balled her hands and stuffed them into the pockets of her robe. "Because we both wanted it," she said softly. "It's been a very long time."

Parker began shaking his head as he resumed buttoning his formal shirt. "No, Alex. *I* wanted to make love to you. *You* were just looking to punish me."

Alexandra hugged herself, a flush of warmth flowing over her. "I don't see why you should feel that way," she began evenly.

"Don't you?" he said. "What were you trying to do, Alex, remind me of what I'd given up by leaving you years ago? You don't credit me at all for having made a real hard decision."

"That's not what I was thinking. I wasn't thinking much of *anything* a moment ago. But you're one to talk. It couldn't have been so hard for you to leave," Alexandra said stiffly. "I'll remind you again, you never said goodbye."

"All right, damn it. Never saying goodbye was a mistake. But if I'd tried, I might never have left. I *had* to go, Alex. For more reasons than you know."

"Reasons," Alexandra answered back. "Obviously, you didn't care at all how I'd feel," Alexandra angrily whispered.

He looked at her strangely, then, his eyes at first puzzled, and then only thoughtful. "I figured you'd get over it. You were very young."

Alexandra swung away from him, the quick motion

dislodging the rest of her hair and causing it to fall in a haphazard way around her face.

Parker walked over to her and grabbing her arm, swung her back to face him. His expression seemed incredulous. "And this is how you deal with men who've hurt you? You tease them into your bed, then let them go, with only memories?"

Alexandra pulled her arm free, and with the other brought her hand stingingly against Parker's cheek. He barely flinched, but his jaw muscle worked quickly, tightly, as he regained control of his emotions.

"I didn't want you to bring me home at all, remember?" she reminded him in a tight voice.

"I guess I deserved that. Except for one thing. I could have had sex with anyone, Alex. I didn't come here tonight for that."

"What did you expect? That everything was the same, and I'd just be here waiting for you?" she asked raggedly, ashamed, angry, hurt all over again.

"The past is over." He got his jacket and slipped it on. "I think tonight has taken care of that." He reached out his hand. But he thought better of touching her. "I wish to God things had worked out differently. But we can't change the past."

"The past is all we'll ever have between us, Parker. I *hated* you for what you did to me then. I hate you for making a fool of me now."

Parker calmly reached for his coat and threw it over his other forearm. "I don't know if you love me anymore, and I'm not sure if you really hate me, either. You can't have it both ways, Alex." He turned and walked into her hallway and stopped to regard her again. "It's either one or the other. And I mean to find out which it really is and what it is you really want."

Alexandra stood as if in a trance as she heard Parker let himself out, and the door clicked closed behind him. For another few seconds she stood like that until she gave way to the overwhelming sea of emotions that washed in waves over her. She collapsed on the piano bench and cried. She cried because it was already clear to her what she really felt for Parker, as she had known all those years ago.

Talk was cheap. Some things never change. She hadn't stopped loving Parker at all. And her vindication was a poor substitute for it.

Chapter Four

It was nearly dawn and the only sound from the bedroom, dimly lit by one bedside lamp, was the crackling of stiff acetate pages being turned in a photo album. Alexandra turned the pages slowly, her reddened eyes sweeping with familiarity over the layout of photographs and clippings, reviews and music sheets. It was fat and heavy and warm on her lap as she lay propped by pillows against the headboard. As she slowly turned the pages, surprised by some of the contents as if reading them for the first time, or smiling thinly at more familiar, dear pieces, she was amazed at the wealth of documentation that marked the public and very prolific career of Parker Harrison.

Attempts to sleep had been futile. After Parker had left, she'd cried herself into hiccoughs and exhaustion for a full hour. Later, Alexandra's immediate reaction was that she felt surprisingly better. The horrible tensions of the day and evening, the surprise elements that had forced her to maintain a control she was far from feeling, had been purged from her system. She felt calmer. And she was hungry. She realized, after Parker had left, that with the trauma of seeing and dealing with him all afternoon, she'd been unable to eat a thing. After taking a long, hot bath during which she reflected even further on their evening, Alexandra saw it as a healthy sign that she wanted to consume anything she could get her hands on in the kitchen.

As she sat eating French toast at midnight, Alexandra recalled Parker's prophetic departing remark, that he had every intention of finding out how she really felt about him. She recognized it as a challenge, and she grew excited by the prospect. Yet there was not even the smallest hint from Parker as to how he might now feel about her—except regretful. Nor had there been any suggestion as to how he would carry out his challenge. Alexandra did wonder, for a moment of make-believe, if Parker intended to kiss her into submission, force *her* to declare herself, or sweep her away by the sheer force of his desire.

She was old enough to know that men found her appealing. But it did occur to her that the very volatile consummation with Parker in her living room was new. It was intense and very physical. It was adult. Years ago, Alexandra would not have been able to handle the passion which had been generated so quickly and so thoroughly between them. The earlier innocence and naïveté of their relationship was gone. What happened definitely indicated unresolved feelings. But Parker had said he'd wanted more from her than mere sex.

After making herself French toast, Alexandra went to the bookcase in the living room and searched out three thick binders. One was a photo album, and the other two were scrapbooks. She'd taken the albums with her to bed and sat up the rest of the night reviewing the contents. When she opened the first one, several unsecured articles on Parker Harrison slipped out onto her lap. Alexandra read every word of every article, feeling both comforted and regretful.

Sadly, she had to admit that Parker had been right about one thing: she had hoped to punish him. She had hoped for instant retribution, vindication, but she also wanted a sign, not so much an indication of guilt, but of love. That he had loved her. The fact that they had been so easily, so quickly drawn to one another again, spoke of an affinity between them that had always been there. It had not happened all at once, such as the physical eruption of the early evening, but had taken time and youthful uncertainty and trust. Alexandra still resented that Parker Harrison had taken her trust lightly, that it might not have meant more to him.

She'd always thought that Parker truly understood her driving need for her own life, for her own music. Even her own father, with his music background, limited as it had been from lack of nourishment, had not understood what music gave her. Parker always had. Sometimes she wished she could have been more like her younger sister, Christine, who wasn't the least bit interested in music beyond whether or not she could dance to it. Besides, she and Christine were not remotely alike; Christine didn't have to want to *do* or *be* anything to get what she wanted. Opportunities fell into her lap.

Alexandra read the pages in the album, savoring each event of Parker's career which she'd preserved forever on the black pages. She felt pride in Parker's accomplishments because she had encouraged him and believed in him.

Alexandra lay back against the warm comfort of her pillows, feeling a perverse delight in having followed Parker's career and in realizing that her collection of memorabilia may have actually bridged the gap between the past and present, keeping her connected to him vicariously while she continued slowly to grow up and become

a woman. With a deep sigh, Alexandra recognized another truth: the past was indeed finished. Making love
with Parker tonight had not been so much for whatever
might be between them now, as for what was. It closed a
chapter; it said goodbye.

Again Alexandra's mind came back to Parker's words,
"I mean to find out." Did that mean he would stay? If so,
for how long? This time she would know for sure and not
indulge in fantasies that were impossible. This time, if
they were to start over, Alexandra promised, beginning to
recall the first time she and Parker Harrison met, she
would be careful how she loved . . .

Alexandra had been four months shy of her twentieth
birthday when she'd moved into her first apartment in
Washington. For the very first time she was on her own,
not responsible for a semi-invalid father, or a younger
sister who was annoyingly self-centered and capricious.
Sheer determination and singlemindedness to get out
from under the demanding home life had made her work
hard enough to win a scholarship to study music and
voice at the music conservatory of George Washington
University. Then she'd had to arrange for a local health
care provider to check in on her father two days a week,
although by then, her younger sister, Christine, was old
enough to bear some responsibility. Her father had been
proud of her and had wished her well.

Alexandra didn't have the sultriness or funkiness, as her
sister liked to remind her, to be a popular singer, but it
didn't matter, since she was aiming to sing light opera.

Her apartment outside of Georgetown was just a sublet
for eighteen months, long enough to eventually find
something else. Alexandra had been settled for only a few

weeks when one evening, after she'd returned from a voice class, the muffled strains of a concerto came through her walls from another apartment. She'd opened her door and stood trying to figure out which apartment had someone who played so beautifully. Then the music had abruptly stopped. Alexandra waited, hoping it would continue, but finally gave up with a sigh and turned back to her apartment. Suddenly the music started again.

Quickly she turned around, back into the hall, putting out a hand behind her to catch the door. But she misjudged the distance and made a frantic grab for the knob as the door swung heavily closed, automatically locking her out of her apartment.

"Oh . . . no," she groaned, grimacing in frustration. Futilely, she twisted the knob back and forth. Annoyed, she kicked at the metal door, and it sounded like a shot echoing around the narrow hallway. She quickly recoiled as a pain shot through her bare foot.

Alexandra didn't notice the music had stopped again as she considered her dilemma. She couldn't believe she'd been so completely careless. She stood there, her mind totally blank, as she wondered what she was going to do. How embarrassing to have to ring the bell of a neighbor who was a stranger, in her bare feet, and admit she'd locked herself out! Shortly, a door opened down the hall and a tall, very slender man stepped partway out, looking up and down the corridor. Alexandra protectively pressed back against her door. But the man, a lit cigarette hanging from his lips, couldn't help but see her.

A straight black brow arched up after he'd leisurely surveyed the stiff length of her. She stood dressed in ancient jeans and T-shirt and balanced on one foot as she favored the injured one. His dark eyes sparkled from his square face. He took the cigarette from his lips and exhaled as he lounged in his doorway. A smile slowly began to spread over his sharp brown face, and even in her embarrassment, Alexandra saw he was very good-looking.

"If you're trying to break into that apartment, kicking the door won't do it."

She stared silently at him.

"And you'll give burglary a bad name dressed like that." He was laughing at her.

"I live here," Alexandra said, examining him.

"Do you?" He crossed his arms completely over his lean torso. He was dressed in a pale blue shirt, at that moment hanging open outside his close-fitting faded jeans and exposing a slight, smoothly muscled chest. Alexandra was suddenly acutely aware she was braless under the T-shirt, as she watched the way his gaze traveled over her body.

"The best way of getting into your apartment is with a key," he teased. "Don't you have one, or did you lose it?"

Alexandra's mouth suddenly curved into a small smile at the absurd conversation he was having with her.

"That's better. Now, what happened?" he asked.

She lifted her shoulders in resignation. "I locked myself out."

"Not too cool," he said shaking his head. "How did you manage to do that?"

Alexandra liked the low timbre of his deep male voice. She self-consciously fingered her loose hair, wishing suddenly that she was dressed more attractively, wishing she didn't look like an adolescent. "It's actually your fault," she accused.

He raised his brows incredulously. "Me?"

"I wanted to find out where the piano music was coming from. I stepped into the hall for a second . . ."

"And the door closed shut behind you," he finished. "That's it."

He let out a sigh and stood straight, being careful not to close his own door completely. He walked to the incinerator and flicked the cold butt of his cigarette down the chute. "You have a real slim case, but I guess I'm partly to blame. Why don't you come in and we'll call the super to bring up a passkey?" He held his door open, expecting Alexandra to enter. But she didn't move, and he looked quizzically at her. "Hey, we can't do anything if you just stand there," he reasoned in amusement.

"I don't know who you are," Alexandra explained suspiciously, with a quick shrug of a shoulder.

He stared at her for a moment and laughed in disbelief. He scanned her vulnerable position and questionable dress and grinned ruefully. "Right. I'm Parker Harrison, your piano-playing neighbor. Now, come on in . . ."

"I'll wait here, thanks," she said stubbornly, feeling both absurdly young and foolish.

Some exasperation began to show on his face. "Look, I can't leave you in the hallway. And I promise, your body is safe with me."

His eyes were filled with amusement again as she continued to hesitate. Chewing on the inside of her bottom lip, Alexandra knew a moment of feminine ire as she realized he was sincere. She would be perfectly safe with him.

"Besides, if I bite, you can always bite back," he said wryly.

She grinned nervously then, but still felt butterflies in her stomach. She walked toward him, keeping her eyes down, and slowly entered his apartment. She had never been in a single man's home before, and she slid past him, avoiding any chance of their touching by accident. But a new warm sensation snaked through her body at her physical awareness of the handsome stranger. And she remembered once more that she had no bra on.

"The piano's in there." Parker pointed to a room at the length of the apartment. He walked past her into another room and she heard him pick up a phone and began dialing.

Shyly, Alexandra continued on into the front room, absently noting the framed posters and artwork on the walls. She spotted the piano at once. It was dark and shiny, an expensive Steinway baby grand. What also caught her attention, however, was the haphazard scattering of paper all over the room. On the piano bench, the floor, the piano top, the coffee table, lay sheets upon sheets of music. Fascinated, Alexandra moved to the piano stand to see what he played. She walked slowly about the room, tilting her head this way and that as she craned to read titles. She stepped over piles on the floor. The answer was, he apparently played everything. There was Chopin, Beethoven, Ellington, Bach, Satie, Rachmaninoff, Hancock. There were notebooks with notes and partially finished music. Alexandra was lifting a page, trying to decipher it, when Parker entered the room. He stopped for a moment in the doorway, then casually walked over to her.

"The super is on call somewhere in the building . . ." He gently took the notebook from her and closed the cover over the written page. "He should be up in half an hour or so." He looked down thoughtfully at the notebook in his hand.

Alexandra knew at once that she had not only breached good manners, but had invaded a part of this man which was private and sensitive. "I'm sorry. I didn't mean to touch your things," Alexandra began, noticing a tightness around his previously smiling mouth.

Parker shrugged indifferently, but Alexandra could sense the tension in his body. "No problem," he said.

But Alexandra knew he did mind. He threw the notebook carelessly on a pile and sat on the piano bench, facing her as she stood awkwardly in the middle of his papers. Alexandra watched him furtively, the silence between them stretching out as he slowly let his eyes appraise her. His mouth had lifted in amusement when he'd spotted her narrow bare feet, the toes curled under on the wood parquet floor. When his eyes again assessed the curving of her breasts under the T-shirt, Alexandra quickly and modestly crossed her arms over her chest. He made her feel so young.

Alexandra stood looking covertly around the minimally furnished room, dominated by the beautiful piano. On the walls were framed programs and photographs of Parker, but much younger and formally dressed. In one he was seated at a piano. There was another of him accepting an award of some kind. In none of the photos did he smile or give any indication of being pleased at the recognition accorded him. In none did he seem relaxed or proud, or exhilarated. Alexandra became fascinated by the sense of dissatisfaction that was apparent on the many different faces of this man. She somehow knew that it wasn't the recognition that irritated him, but his playing. He hadn't been satisfied. He hadn't felt he'd done his best. Alexandra felt a sudden kinship. She *understood* that look.

"So, what do you think of the piano?" he asked, his eyes scanning over her slender body thoughtfully once again.

"I didn't touch it," Alexandra disclaimed quickly, turning around to face him, her attention diverted from the gallery of pictures.

"You can," he shrugged indifferently, and moved to make room for her on the bench. "Come on. Try it. Do you play?" Parker swiveled on the bench to face the keyboard.

Alexandra smiled slowly at the invitation and she approached the bench somewhat in awe. "Not very well. Not enough practice. I'll probably sound terrible." She sat down and aimlessly played a few bars and exercise chords. Then, because he seemed to be expecting it, she tried something a bit more advanced, concentrating on her movements. She looked expectantly at Parker when she was finished, her sable brown eyes unknowingly seeking approval, her pretty brown face open and instantly trusting.

"Not bad. Where did you study?" Parker asked, drawing on his cigarette.

"I've only had two years of formal study," she said carefully, not adding that two years was all that could be afforded from the household budget. She had fought to get that much for herself. "My father taught me to play."

"Oh? And where did your father study?" Parker persisted.

"He didn't. He's self-taught," she said, shaking her head and continuing to move her fingers along the keys until the sight of his almost bare chest so near made her stop abruptly.

Parker nodded briefly. "If you learned that from your father, I'm impressed." Then he suddenly moved closer to her on the bench, squinting at her face.

Alexandra once again tensed at his closeness, as he seemed to be examining every square inch of her face. She could smell the tobacco smoke on him, but also the hint of soap on his skin from a recent shower or bath. There was still another essence, something that awakened Alexandra's senses to him as a man. She felt an unexpected tension and tingling in her stomach. There were stirrings, and the start of new physical sensations that felt good, but which were frightening. It was much too intimate a circumstance suddenly, and she felt threatened because she didn't know how to handle either her awareness of or her fascination for this good-looking, confident man.

"Well, I'll be damned! Should I call you 'Freckles'?" he teased in surprised wonder. He obviously wasn't reacting to her in quite the same way.

Alexandra was indignant and moved to stand up. "Don't call me that. I don't like it," she ordered softly, in a firm, noncompromising fashion.

Parker grabbed her arm and forced her to stay seated, then quickly released her again. "Then what should I call you?" he asked, ignoring her anger.

"My name is Alexandra Morrow," she responded primly.

Parker raised his brow and hid a smile. She was suddenly so correct and polite. "Alexandra," he enunciated each syllable carefully, making the name sound like a disease or a proclamation. He paused before slowly saying it again, this time lyrically, in such a way Alexandra loved the sound of it on his lips. "That's quite a mouthful for such a little girl."

"I'm not a little girl," she corrected. Again he'd seemed to ignore her indignation, and it seemed to Alexandra that he wasn't treating her seriously at all, that he was amused by everything about her.

"What do people call you?" he asked curiously.

"Alexandra," she said clearly, but it didn't have the least quelling effect on him.

"No, no, no," Parker said, shaking his head sadly. "It takes too long to say all that. Just Alex is enough," he decided. He put out his hand for her to shake.

"That's a man's name. And I don't like nicknames, either," she frowned. "Alexandra" had always made her feel older and more mature.

Parker shrugged. "I think Alex suits you. It's clear, precise, and strong. Some nicknames aren't very nice, it's true. But some are used out of friendship or love. Haven't you ever had friends or love, Alex?"

Again there had been that teasing glint in his eyes. Alexandra was about to answer honestly, "No." Instead, she merely looked away indifferently and shrugged a thin shoulder. Let him think what he wanted.

"Anyway . . ." Parker continued, swinging back to the piano and letting his right hand absently perform magic upon the keyboard. "I'll call you Alex. I'm sure no one else ever thought of it." He turned to regard her thoughtfully, his gaze warm and suddenly playful. "You don't have to tell anyone. It will be just between the two of us."

She knew that he was teasing her again, but she didn't know how to tease back. There had never been much time in her life for boyfriends and flirtations. Except maybe for Nathan, when she was in high school. She'd really liked him because he'd seemed as shy and serious as she had been. He'd gone away one summer after school was out, and had come back the next fall, older and more demanding. Alexandra hadn't been in love with Nathan. What he'd wanted from her in their junior year she hadn't been prepared to give him. Alexandra certainly didn't kid herself that someone as smooth and handsome as Parker Harrison was attracted to her. He might tease, and show indulgence, and some curiosity. He might recognize that she had a lithe, innocent beauty and a nice way about her, as her father used to say, but he wasn't going to be seriously interested in her. Yet Alexandra also felt that something had just been created between them which was going to be unique and different. It was going to be something for herself that she didn't have to share with her sister. She liked that.

"I wasn't making fun of you," Parker said earnestly.

Alexandra relaxed. "I'm sorry I got angry. I guess I'm too sensitive about them." She put a hand up briefly to her cheeks as if hoping to brush the scattering of freckles away.

Parker smiled kindly, drawing on his cigarette and finishing it, adding the butt to an already overflowing ashtray. "You shouldn't be. They are very attractive."

Alexandra felt uncomfortable with the gentle words and compliments, not used to them at all. Nervously, she got up and moved around the room.

"Where did you study?" she asked, using Parker's earlier question to bring the conversation back to safer ground.

Parker groaned and grimaced. "Everywhere," he said dryly, "since I was six years old." He didn't seem thrilled by the memory. "Private lessons, Juilliard, more private lessons, the Sorbonne in Paris."

"Paris," Alexandra sighed enviously, her eyes popping open.

"And more private lessons. I was what they call a 'wonder,'" Parker said, somewhat indifferently.

"Are you someone famous?" Alexandra breathed, again looking quickly to the framed photos on the wall.

He laughed out loud at her question. Alexandra smiled to herself dreamily, liking the rich, resonant sounds.

"Not at all. I could have been another Andre Watts, but . . ." he trailed off and shook his head.

"But what?" Alexandra persisted, leaning carelessly on the piano top and regarding him in near awe, forgetting that her breasts bobbed against the T-shirt.

For a moment, Parker's smile was warm and indulgent, his eyes scanning her face and seeming to enjoy the novelty of being unique in her eyes. Then, Parker got up restlessly, and frowned at the stack of music on the floor. He stuffed his hands into his jean pockets. "I wasn't interested. I got tired of concerts and recitals, limited engagements, and special appearances. I'd had enough," he ended impatiently.

"Your parents must have been very disappointed."

"You're right, they were. I felt very guilty telling them I wanted out. After all, they'd done everything to see that I got the best training and the best instructors. They told me that they understood how I felt, but . . . they were hurt. They had my future all planned out." There was a trace of irony in his words. "They'll get over it."

"Yeah. But will you?" Alexandra asked astutely. "If you were that good . . ."

"Why throw it all away?" Parker blinked thoughtfully, and his eyes became distant. His face, that of a man probably in his late twenties, was now curiously young and fleetingly uncertain.

"Because I'm sorry I missed going to regular school like all the other kids on the block. I missed Saturday morning football because of Saturday piano lessons. I hated traveling to different cities to give a concert, because I never knew anyone there. There were times when I just wanted to hide in a penny arcade and play pinball all day."

His eyes slowly focused and settled on her face. Alexandra had a fleeting glimpse of longing in his eyes, some distant vision or hope that perhaps he'd never really known. But it quickly cleared, and that derisive spark came back. He got up abruptly from the piano bench.

He moved to the coffee table and carelessly leafed through the music sheets. "Besides, I have my *own* music . . ." he tapped his temple, "up here. I didn't want to interpret and play the world masters; I want to *be* one.

"There's a lot of music inside of me, Alex," he continued, his words spilling out. "I have to try and work it out. Even if everyone, including my parents, think I'm crazy, I need time to work it out. All artists have their own style. Well, so do I."

Parker had looked over several of the composition sheets, his eyes quickly scanning the notes, and for a moment Alexandra knew he had music running through his head. For just that instant he was far away, in another world. She felt a jolt of understanding go through her. It was exactly how she felt when she was singing.

Alexandra was mesmerized by his energy and convictions. She found that she liked the shortened form of her name when Parker said it. It seemed so friendly and personal. It *did* make her feel very special.

"I'm going to be famous someday," she whispered confidently into the suddenly quiet room, unconsciously raising her chin at some unnamed objection or obstacle.

Parker raised his brows and looked at her, gently studying her for a long moment. "Is that what you want? To be famous?"

She nodded. "I want everyone to love my voice and singing. I want to sing at Carnegie Hall and at the Metropolitan Opera. I want to travel, *be* somebody."

Parker's eyes softened and he shook his head slightly. "Hey, you *are* somebody." Then his empathy changed and his expression became serious and fixed. "Be careful what you wish for, or you're likely to get it, Alex."

His tone brought her sharply back to the present, and the dreams that were going to come true suddenly became clouded by this new prophecy.

She shook her head. "No. I want to be famous."

The doorbell rang shrilly then as the super arrived with his passkey. Regretfully, Alexandra had to say goodbye.

"Not goodbye, just goodnight," Parker had said, walking her to the door. "Come and visit my piano anytime," he teased lightly. "And me, of course. I'll even give you some pointers on the keyboard, if you like."

"Am I that bad?" Alexandra asked.

Parker grinned. "Not at all. But everyone can be better. We'll work on it together."

She shyly thanked him for his kindness, but Parker grinned wickedly at her. "Don't thank me yet, Alex. I'll probably expect retribution . . ."

That had been the start. And retribution, when it came, had been the end of it. Quickly, mysteriously. Silently, without goodbyes or goodnights.

Alexandra slowly closed the album, running her hand over the smooth leather which protected the treasured contents. She put the albums away with a sleepy sigh, but the reminiscence stayed tenaciously with her, keeping her nervously awake. She turned off the bedside light and stared into the dark, her memories vividly alive. Parker, then and now, was different. Then, he was too thin and too intense, and had too much energy. Parker was still slender, but matured and confident. With a frown of concentration, Alexandra realized that he was a man fully grown, and rather different from the young man who had so captured her heart and attention. For all her memories, she had to admit this new Parker was more of a stranger. He had outgrown his uncertainties. He had outgrown his youth. He had outgrown much of the past, and perhaps her, too.

Reluctantly, Alexandra also admitted to finding him appealing in a way that stirred the woman in her and made her restless. It was confusing, because it was not as she'd remembered it from years ago. At that time, the feeling had been fantasy and dreaming—not based on much more than her awakening to her own feminine capabilities, and the flexing of her charms and innocence. Her reactions now were primitive and basic. She had some experience and memories behind her which allowed the ready response to Parker Harrison's kisses and embrace, which had allowed the precipitous lovemaking the night before.

Parker was calm and self-possessed. He had cooled out a lot with accomplishing what he'd set out to do. But what did he really mean, fame wasn't all it was cracked up to be?

Parker, years ago, had been indulgent toward her, teasing her playfully, much as one would tease a favorite younger sister. Except that Alexandra had quickly developed much deeper feelings than that. She was infuriated with him for not recognizing them, but never having been in love before, she hadn't a clue as to how one proceeded, or even how to deal with him and the knowledge of her growing feelings for him. How do you tell someone you love them when they treat you like a favorite relative?

Alexandra also remembered that Parker smoked too much, and often forgot to eat, causing her to assume the role of protector. He sometimes had dark, brooding periods. He frequently locked himself inside his apartment, burying his telephone under sofa cushions, disconnecting the answering machine, not answering messages slipped under the door while he worked with a vengeance on his music. Just as unpredictably, he'd call her to come and hear some work in progress, as if he was uncertain and needed her to act as a sounding board. He asked for input and suggestions, teaching her, inadvertently, what he needed from her. Once, Parker got her out of bed at three-thirty in the morning, excited and tired and fulfilled with a composition that had worked just perfectly. Alexandra smiled as she remembered him pounding on her door, telling her to hurry and get up because he had something new she had to hear. She became like a shadow in the hallway between the two apartments, floating back and forth between his life and her own.

Afterward, Alexandra would curl up on his sofa, offering sleepy praise and encouragement. She'd then fix breakfast and they'd talk about the music some more until Parker's energy was replaced by sheer exhaustion. He would kiss her cheek affectionately and go off to sleep for hours, leaving her to let herself out of the apartment where beautiful music was made. One of her greatest joys with Parker had been that he'd honestly sought her opinion and listened to her suggestions.

He was like a man possessed at times, switching back and forth between classics and Jazz, as if not sure what he really wanted to play, or as if choosing one could mean giving up the other, or as if torn between the need to take a risk with his life or seek the comfort and safety of an assured concert route. Many times Alexandra had come across telegrams crumpled among the debris of his studio. Telegrams from an agent, a concert hall manager, a professor begging him to return to the fold. But when even she, who saw how obsessed he was at times, suggested that perhaps he was being foolish to give it all up, Parker had only said flatly, "I can't go back." He had been dead serious about finding his true place in music.

When Parker had taken to disappearing for a day or two, Alexandra unexpectedly realized the depth of her feelings for him, and the fear that he'd never know. He'd told her from the start his stay was short. She always knew he planned on going elsewhere, wherever he needed to go to speak and play with new musicians, hear new music, get his perspective straight. He had only recently said he'd already stayed in the apartment down the hall months longer than he'd intended to.

"You're the only person who understands the music and what I'm doing," he'd often teased. "Sometimes, even I'm not sure it's worth anything."

"I believe in you." Alexandra had told him. Did he ever understand the depth of that belief?

Alexandra turned on her side and hugged her pillow. She closed her eyes against the subtle blue glow of dawn through the window blinds. She sighed sleepily. They *had* been so good together. And then it had gotten even better, as she recalled the first time he'd kissed her.

It had started out playfully enough, just after she'd run to him with the news that she'd been chosen to sing in a chorale at the Kennedy Center during a Christmas performance. The congratulatory kiss that had been a mere pressing of his lips to hers had changed things subtly between them. The woman in her was gently touched. She became aware of his masculinity, of the sleek hardness of his lean body, his wonderful deep voice, his beautiful hands. The safe, friendly distance that had existed between them was suddenly gone, and their awareness of each other grew into a sensual tension that was quite mysterious to her at the time. From then on, Parker would touch her affectionately, hugging her, holding her by the waist, holding her hand. It made her giddy with anticipation, made her yearn for much more from him, though she could not put the feelings into words. And she was afraid to actually admit to herself what that yearning might be. That early exploration had been in the first month. By the second month, curiosity between them had reached a vibrant, tantalizing peak.

Everything between them seemed to culminate right after Parker had written a beautiful new piece of music. It was a sweeping melody with romantic tension. In it, Alexandra could hear lovers' heartbeats, breathy excitement, and the anxious anticipation of being in love. She saw herself in it.

Several days later, Alexandra had surprised Parker with words to go with the music. After playing it through several times and changing a note here, a word there, it was finished—and absolutely perfect.

"That's it!" Parker said in wonder. "That is just what I wanted. Awright . . ."

He'd grabbed her and started kissing Alexandra all over her face, making her laugh happily. Then the kisses reached and stayed on her lips, becoming slow, sensual, and serious. For a breathless moment they stared at each other with the sudden excitement of their discovery changing their breathing, the heat of their bodies, the tension. Suddenly they sought the deeper embrace of each other's arms. They kissed and then kissed again, suddenly aware of the texture of each other's lips. Alexandra noticing that Parker's mouth was mobile, firm, teaching her how to kiss him. The kiss deepened, Parker expertly parting her hesitant lips to explore beyond the small white teeth and stroke against her tongue with his own.

Parker found the feminine curve of her lips and waist, felt the soft, delicate roundness of her breasts. When he'd hesitated and stared into her face with a thoughtful frown, Alexandra had hoped he wouldn't see her inexperience, but only her trust in him. She'd wanted him to take her beyond friendship.

Parker had cupped her face and smiled tenderly. The moment had become special forever.

"This is a love song, for you," he'd whispered.

Parker had taken her into his arms carefully, but she knew he must be feeling her insecurity. He'd kissed her sweetly to ease her nerves; had reassured her silently as his mouth started the sensual dance. Parker's hands roamed her body, eliciting soft gasps of surprise as he introduced her to physical love. In his darkened room he undressed her, uncrossing arms modestly protecting herself, allaying her fears with murmured words and tender touches. But the kisses were potent and searing, demanding a response that was impossible for her not to return. She kept her eyes averted from the undressing of Parker's own body. She was familiar with the expanse of his torso but had never touched him or seen it so close to her before so that she could feel the warmth of his skin. He had long, muscular, athletic legs, his hips narrow, the swollen male part of him sending eddies of apprehension and anticipation through her body, but in a dizzying, pleasurable way. She felt herself a mass of quivering raw nerve ends waiting to explode or burn out. Parker had led her slowly to his bed, and she had never considered not following or letting him pull her down to the quilted top, drawing her slowly into his arms as his mouth sought hers again. Alexandra had been surprised and awed by the incredible feel of his warm, naked body pressed to her with such intimacy, startled by the way they seemed to naturally fit together. She had been mesmerized by Parker's lack of inhibition in exploring and touching her skin, feeling safe in his knowledge and know-how.

Parker led her though an intricate maze of new sensations, one escalating on top of another, so exquisite as to leave her weak and breathless. His hands were a caressing joy upon her body, sensitizing her quivering skin, tickling the smooth surface into responding to him, and recognizing and satisfying her own raw needs. Alexandra felt herself waiting for the next wonderful sensation. But the apprehension returned when Parker lay his full weight on her body and maneuvered her legs apart. He poised over her before lowering his hips and thighs, and thrusting gently forward between her legs.

When it came, she was shocked into stillness by the unavoidable pain from him. But Parker had soothed her, whispering low and kissing her hot skin. He was slow and easy, until she became used to the total fullness of him deep within her body. She was lost for a moment in a combination of tingling pain and pleasure.

Parker had demonstrated such care for her, holding her against his long body, his movements oddly possessive and comforting. The stroking of his hands was sure and knowledgeable. She clung to him with total love. She trusted him completely. Alexandra marveled at the rhythm their bodies swayed into, rocking in union, the personal and intimate movements she'd never known until Parker reached some pinnacle still beyond her reach, releasing himself into her, relaxing on her.

Then, with all the time in the world, with a giddy sense of discovery and magic, they'd started all over again. Parker had shown her slowly, completely, what loving was like between a man and a woman, until finally she, too, had known the heart-stopping moment of fulfillment.

She'd stayed with him that night, the first of many in which they played and explored and loved each other with an affinity that neither questioned, but which Alexandra thought would last forever.

And then Parker had left.

Two weeks before she had an important audition.

Two weeks after they'd started a new song which went unfinished.

A month before her twentieth birthday.

Alexandra turned over restlessly in her bed. She threw the covers off, and then, two minutes later, reached to pull them up again. She felt again the familiar, horrible pain of betrayal and humiliation, thinking of the way Parker had just walked out of her life. She had gone over every detail of their last phone call together, and after all these years, had never been able to find any one moment that might have alerted her to what was about to happen.

They were going to spend the evening working on their song, although Parker had admitted he'd thought of nothing new for the melody. But Alexandra had called to say she had to spend the day with her father, who needed to be escorted to a medical appointment.

"Don't worry about the song," Parker had soothed her. "We'll get back to it later."

"But I might have to stay the night. And I have classes and a rehearsal tomorrow."

"Alex . . ." Parker had interrupted. "There'll be time for everything. Your father is more important now."

"You won't try and finish it without me?"

"It's our song. We'll finish it together," he'd promised. "Sooner or later."

Was that it? Had he hoped that she would know he'd

made a decision, accepted a band position, was going to leave immediately? Was she supposed to assume that of course he'd be in touch? And when he wasn't, how long was she supposed to wait before realizing the painful truth—that he had no intention of contacting her again?

The break had been quick and clean, surgical. She had always known Parker would move on. She would hope and pray for a romantic miracle, but she had yet to finish school, and he was trying to find himself.

She'd always known . . .

Alexandra had barely gotten through the rest of the semester. She had moved back home to her father's house to mope, cry, and function in a daze all summer as she sought to understand why. Thankfully, her father had asked no questions, but had made it clear that he was glad she'd come home. She, in turn, did not want to burden him with her heartbreak. Mostly, Alexandra wanted her father to hold her and comfort her.

Christine, on the other hand, had shown mostly disappointment at having her home again. Perhaps she had believed that with Alexandra on her own, she'd outgrown the need for a surrogate mother in the form of an older sister. But Christine was also curious about her life away from home. Christine had no sympathetic offerings to make, although, Alexandra was to admit later, her sister's voiced opinions held their own wisdom, borne of both innocent observation and awakening teenage conjecture.

Alexandra had been listlessly unpacking her things when her fourteen-year-old sister had come into her room, not heeding Alexandra's silence as a sign that she'd rather just be left alone.

Christine, who had long ago shown signs of being a beauty, was a full three inches taller than her older sister, and more self-possessed. Her near-black hair was thick with fat locks loosely curled and layered from her face to her shoulders. The budding feminine softness was completely misleading, hiding within it the hard determination of Christine that was often demanding and often got her her own way.

Christine had perched on the edge of the bed, idly watching as her sister removed things from her suitcase. She began to swing her leg back and forth against the mattress.

"So what happened?" she'd asked boldly.

Alexandra hesitated only a second in her chore, her stomach lurching with the sure knowledge that Christine was going to ask questions she didn't want to answer. She refused to meet her sister's gaze, pretending an indifference to the question.

"What do you mean, what happened?" Alexandra asked, carefully turning her back to open a dresser drawer.

"I mean," Christine sighed, "why did you come back home?"

"Aren't I allowed? After all, I do live here, too."

"Well, you were the one who wanted to leave, to become famous, remember?" Christine taunted.

Her recent disappointments flooded Alexandra, sending chills through her system and making her shiver. She had been so boastful, so sure of herself. She didn't respond.

"You sure didn't become famous since you left," Christine chided with a light laugh. "You don't look famous. I bet you never even tried to sing anywhere."

"Will you please stop?" Alexandra begged, in a thin voice. She didn't even have the strength to be angry, just hurt all over again.

Christine had suddenly stopped as if she could see the

genuine look of pain on Alexandra's face. It had always been easy for her to tease and goad her older sister, but Alexandra recognized that she'd never done so to deliberately hurt her. Shrugging at her sister's plea, Christine had gotten up from the bed and wandered over to Alexandra's bureau, poking idly among the few pieces of jewelry laying on top.

"Did you meet anyone interesting?" she had asked, lifting a bracelet to examine the design.

Alexandra looked furtively at Christine, hoping that her own face and expression gave nothing away.

"Of course, I did. There were plenty of people in my classes whom I got to know."

"No, I mean someone *special*. You know—as in falling in love," Christine patiently explained.

Alexandra's hands tightened around the garment she held, and she knew she couldn't lie, but she didn't know how to answer. It somehow seemed strange to be talking about a feeling like love or an emotion like hurt with a fourteen-year-old, when she was struggling so hard herself to understand what she'd been through. And as she'd never been in the habit of confiding in Christine the things that were closest to her, she found herself being cautious now, even though there was a desperate need to unburden herself. She decided, instead, to play it safe and tell a half-truth.

"People don't fall in love in just three months," Alexandra had responded, but the lie caught in her throat, and she'd wondered if her voice, or her overly warm face or clenched hands, would give her away. Apparently, that answer had satisfied Christine, who now dropped the bracelet noisily, and turned to regard her beautiful unusual features in the bureau mirror.

"Anyway, you can't fall in love and be famous at the

same time," Christine murmured, practicing the enticing arching of a brow, and pursing her full mouth this way and that.

Alexandra frowned at her sister, caught by the curious nature of her words. "What makes you say so?"

Christine wrinkled her nose quaintly and grinned at her image. Then she looked over her shoulder at her sister. "Well, you know, if you really want to be famous, you have to work real hard at it. You don't let anything or anyone stop you. *I* wouldn't."

Alexandra had believed this was true of her sister. It had been true of her until she'd met Parker, who'd left her not sure of what she wanted anymore.

"Christine, what do you want most? What do you want to do with your life?" Alexandra asked her sister, eager to know if she had any dreams, any ambition beyond being pretty and popular. Did she have any fears at all that life would just pass by without her having done anything with it?

Christine shrugged and giggled. "I just want to have fun. I want to have lots of friends and lots of money. Maybe I'll be a dancer or an actress."

"But what if *you* fall in love?"

Christine had raised her chin, showing surprising confidence. "I'm not going to fall in love until after I do what I want."

Alexandra chuckled grimly at the memory of Christine's words, which were a mixture of naïveté and inexperienced bravado. But she'd known Christine meant it. Christine was not the kind of person to let herself be overcome with grief. She would have shrugged her shoulders and quickly dismissed it as unimportant. Christine would have turned to the next adventure, the next admirer waiting in the wings. Life was too short for constant reflection.

Alexandra considered the coldness and odd truth of Christine's observation. But, she reasoned, if Parker had loved her, they could have worked it out, even though she couldn't see how. Would he have left her if he loved her? And how would it have affected his music? How would it have affected her own? But why did it have to be either love or success? Why couldn't there be both?

Alexandra sat on the bed. Maybe Christine was right, maybe she had to be single-minded with her music. There should be no distractions.

She had privately hoped all spring and summer that Parker would call, filled with remorse and with a desire for her forgiveness. Each time she'd return home after her job or a class, Alexandra would ask if anyone had called for her. After a while, it seemed that her father came to dread the question, and to dread having to tell her "no."

It had all been so confusing. She had been too upset to go through with her audition, but she had also been too scared; terrified that she was no good at all. Her confidence left the same day Parker had. She had been left to wonder why she'd backed down when the moment of truth was at hand. Had Parker's leaving been just an excuse?

"We make beautiful music together, Alexandra Morrow," Parker had once said to her.

They had.

The memories stopped abruptly, and Alexandra rolled onto her back feeling totally wrung out and incapable of shedding another tear for the past, yet recalling with a clarity that was frightening how much pleasure she'd known with Parker Harrison. It was very obvious that that, at least, had not changed. They'd made love together just hours ago and the magic was still there. But her pleasure tonight had been a mixture of seduction and revenge, although it was hard to decide whether it was worth it.

Alexandra no longer felt depressed. The day-long stress of being with Parker seemed like a catharsis. Right now, it no longer surprised her that after so many years she could still be moved by the emotions that had so affected her life at the time.

Alexandra had thought that with her maturity, her love and anger for Parker, the two extremes, would cancel each other out. But that had not been the case. She was finding now that the anger had become a need to question why. And the love had become a persistent, gnawing ache needing to be fulfilled.

Parker left Alexandra's apartment feeling angry and shaken. He had tried to deal with the unexpected encounter with her in a mature fashion. But the Alexandra Morrow he remembered from years ago had grown up with a vengeance.

He had carried with him a sweet memory of a pretty, talented young girl who'd clearly idolized him. It had been charming and amusing, but he'd never tried to play into that. It was only after they'd started a serious affair that Parker had realized Alexandra could easily fall in love with him and he could hurt her just as easily. One more reason for the decision he'd made.

Parker was shaken because the changes in Alexandra destroyed some of the memory he had of her which had been safe and romanticized. He was angry because he'd allowed his ego to be manipulated by Alexandra's cool aloofness toward him. He'd wanted to see that she was still the sweet, innocent wide-eyed girl he'd introduced to love, and who'd believed in him with her heart. Parker was angry because despite everything, he'd hoped not to hurt Alexandra, and it was abundantly clear that he had nonetheless. At the time, he had been deathly afraid of making a wrong decision for both of them.

The events for his leaving came back with force: the invitation to attend a creative artists' community for the following summer, the former mentor wanting to see and hear what he'd been working on incognito. Alexandra's father. Parker had thought the time perfect.

That day . . . that last day, with everything packed and him ready to leave, Parker had written a letter, but then had stood outside Alexandra's apartment, debating whether or not to slip it under the door. He'd desperately wondered if there was another way to do this. Why not be open and just tell her? Because it would have been too easy to have been persuaded by Alexandra . . . by *himself* . . . to change his mind. He was a coward, he had chided himself. But he truly believed it was best. Her face appeared in his mind. He was going to miss her intuitiveness and her faith in him; miss the sweet, open response of her body during their lovemaking.

Even now, Parker knew he couldn't tell Alex that he'd tried to reach her after he'd left, because to do so would mean having to fully explain what had happened. He wasn't at liberty to do so, and it might do more harm than good. It was much too late to wish that he'd left the handwritten letter after all.

Parker got back into his car and sat there a long time before he started the engine. When he'd left Washington years ago, he'd found what he'd been looking for: freedom, and energy, new music—and himself. He'd made musician friends in smoky little dives in towns no one had ever heard of, where local talent was raw and natural. He'd learned from a bunch of much older men and women whose music had survived by word of mouth, not because they were famous or ever likely to be. He'd met alluring, sexy women who'd satisfied his physical needs, but who could not connect with him in any other way. Parker had found his own unique voice in music, but had lost a human consideration that was pure and open and honest, like that he'd had with Alexandra. He'd sometimes felt the loss, but he'd always gone on without it.

Parker had no idea that Alexandra was to be the soloist at the wedding. Perhaps the surprise element had worked in their favor: they could only be absolutely natural with each other. He'd been forced to deal with the fact that at that first instant of seeing Alexandra, he didn't recognize her. So firmly had his earlier memory of her planted itself that Parker had been surprised, shocked, maybe even disappointed, to find not a wide-eyed, animated, lovely young teenager, but a woman who was cool and self-possessed, and who held herself very much in control.

The second thing he'd had to deal with was the unavoidable sense that Alexandra harbored a great deal of resentment toward him.

It began to feel cold and damp in the car, and Parker started the engine. He didn't want to continue to sit in front of her building, but he wasn't ready to head home, either. He'd had quite enough to drink at the reception, between the cocktails and champagne, so going to a bar would do him no good, either. Parker decided instead to just drive into D.C. and meander around the streets of the capital.

He'd always been sure he'd made the right decision

when he'd left D.C. years ago. But that had not stopped him from waffling over the wisdom of leaving Alexandra. Parker could now admit to himself he'd found no one quite like her since.

Parker tensed his jaw and sighed into the chilly silence of the car, although parts of his body were suddenly, unexpectedly, recalling the incredible warmth of having held her and kissed her, of having made love to her. She'd felt more than good beneath him. He'd felt more than satisfied loving her. And Parker knew that this time, he couldn't just walk away. The past had caught up with him.

Chapter Five

The final lyrical strains of the song ended, the last note held for a prolonged beat as the clear voice faded. The drummer rat-a-tatted dramatically, then hit his cymbals to clearly end the performance. The audience came to life then, spurred on by the momentary silence. The applause and whistles were scattered and almost halfhearted, while the spotlight on Alexandra's face grew into a small circle until she was no longer clearly visible. Finally, the dim house lights came up.

Alexandra smiled and nodded demurely. She gracefully brought her left leg back and dipped into a stage curtsy, her aqua blue strapless dress shimmering under the stage lights. She made one more bow, sweeping her arms to include the three-man combo accompanying her. Quickly, feeling chilly in her stage outfit, Alexandra headed for her cubicle-like dressing room. She struggled not to cough, her lungs affected by the air which was heavily polluted with cigarette smoke. Alexandra thought it was probably not a good idea to let her voice teacher know the conditions under which she sang, even though Signora Tonelli was delighted that she'd found a part-time singing position.

"Hey, Morrow . . ." the bartender yelled after Alexandra's retreating form. "There's some guy here to see you."

Alexandra never stopped walking, but raised her chin and waved briefly as she opened the door leading from the narrow, dark hallway to the absurdly small dressing room. Ruefully, she thought there was always "some guy" waiting to see her. She never knew any of them, of course, but they were usually more than willing to introduce themselves and change all that. Anyone else would have been flattered. Anyone else might have held out the slim hope that one of those guys might be a producer or director, or another nightclub owner or a musician, ready to offer a bigger opportunity. But Alexandra had learned quickly, after first attempting to be polite and gracious to those men, that they'd obviously had other thoughts in mind than her career. And she was not about to be part of the school of thought that said you had to sleep your way to the top of the music field. She was determined to become a good singer on merit alone—or not at all.

Alexandra sang at the club for only two reasons. Foremost, for now, was the extra money, which allowed her to afford private voice lessons in preparation for the upcoming light-opera tryout. She had finally decided to audition for it this year. The second reason was that it gave her performance experience, teaching her to cope with the jittery nerves and unexpected stagefright that happened no matter how often she sang. She was also getting a first-hand, up-close lesson in how to deal with the occasional malcontent or patron who'd had too much to drink and who often found it necessary to voice his opinions on almost any topic, but usually while she sang.

Alexandra had also found the musical range that was best for her. She could manage love ballads and light popular music. She could not manage the gospel-laced inflections and impromptu arrangements of an Aretha Franklin. And she was good at weddings. Nevertheless, she'd not been happy with her performance tonight. It went beyond the fact that the combo, permanently fixed musicians of the club, played without passion and care. Alexandra knew her concentration was off as her mind had wandered during the course of the evening to Parker Harrison. She had been thinking a lot about him, remembering their emotionally charged lovemaking, which had held little tenderness, but which had sparked within Alexandra the fires of desire and passion she'd only had for one man. She thought that that occasion had meant the permanent closing of a chapter of her life. She'd heard nothing from Parker the whole week, and Alexandra was wondering why.

With a sigh, Alexandra entered the small room and closed the door. She began stripping out of the sequined dress. The garment, which left her shoulders and neck bare, was heavy and stiff. When she wore it, or something similar, Alexandra would give her performance feeling cold and exposed. She hated having to wear the dress, but the club manager insisted that she needed something flashy to make her more noticeable on stage. It was annoying to think that, as the manager seemed to be suggesting, without the "flash," she wouldn't be noticed. She'd given in to him, now thankful that she did only one show on Friday and Saturday night, which was finished by eleven-thirty.

She hated the stale air of the club, the noise, and the often unsavory people, who seemed none too interested in her voice. She also didn't care for the feeling that her part in what the club offered its customers was really insignificant. The manager had always been clear that he made money from people who drank, not the few who might quietly sit and listen to an unknown performer. In other words, she was not much more than window dressing.

With another weary, resigned sigh, Alexandra reminded herself she was just paying her dues. Everyone had to start somewhere. But it was with a noticeable lack of enthusiasm that she came to the club each weekend evening, and the feeling only got worse. She convinced herself to keep returning by remembering the ultimate dream that kept her going, that hopefully she would soon be performing in a better place, with a more attentive audience.

Alexandra was just stepping out of the dress when her door suddenly opened. She gasped and quickly pulled the dress back into place to cover herself. She was apprehensive but not surprised to find the club manager, Joe Jefferies, standing in her doorway. Alexandra forced herself to remain calm and hoped that she appeared indifferent and in control.

"Do you mind? I'm changing," she said, trying to speak firmly. "I'll be out in a moment."

Ignoring her protest, a short, squat man closed the door and leaned back leisurely against it. "Good show," the rough male voice said.

A smiling leer spread over Joe Jefferies's blunt features, his thick moustache making him look sinister. His eyes roamed appreciatively over Alexandra's creamy brown shoulders and throat, the upper curves of her breasts visible over the top of the loosened dress. Alexandra clutched it tighter.

"We'll have to see about getting you another dress, Sugar. Something a little more . . . revealing. An audience likes to see as well as hear what they're getting for their money."

Alexandra's eyes narrowed at him. "I don't think you get the kind of audience that really cares. For the money, they don't get my body—only my voice."

Joe chuckled at her, shaking his head at her naïveté. "Well now, Sugar, it ain't enough. A pretty face helps. There's a nice crowd tonight. We always do a good first show when you're on," he crooned.

Alexandra raised a shoulder indifferently. "It's crowded because it's Friday night and everyone got paid today."

"Maybe . . ." Joe said absently, his eyes locked on the rising and falling of her chest as Alexandra clutched the dress to her. "But you sure don't hurt, either."

Three months of working with Joe Jefferies at The Outer Edge had been more than enough time to show Alexandra that she was a ready target for his male interest. It hadn't occurred to her when she'd first taken the job that he could pose a problem. She never imagined she'd spend so much time fending off his unwanted advances.

"Look, can't we talk about this later?" she said quietly. "I'd really like to . . ."

"So would I," Joe filled in, his voice low and suggestive. He came away from the door moving slowly toward her.

Alexandra caught her breath and tried not to panic. She could scream, but how embarrassing if everyone came running in while her dress hung loose around her. She could try reasoning with him as she'd done in the past, but her mind was suddenly blank as he continued to come closer. She could fight him . . .

"Ummm. You sure are fine." A wide, thick hand reached out to rub a palm over the soft round point of Alexandra's shoulder.

Goosebumps rose quickly on her skin, and she

shrugged her shoulder out of his reach with distaste, taking a quick step backward.

Joe was just Alexandra's height. He was stocky, with a thick neck and hands that were callused. She could look right into his face and hear his raspy breathing.

"Joe . . . don't," Alexandra whispered firmly.

He grabbed her arm to hold her. "When are we gonna get together, Sugar? I've been waiting weeks for you to say the word."

"We're together two nights a week," Alexandra said nervously, being deliberately obtuse. "I see you more than I see my own father."

A grin cracked his face, showing slightly crooked, slightly yellowed teeth. "I ain't your daddy, Sweetheart. I have something else in mind."

"Will you get out of here? Can't you understand I'm not interested?" Alexandra said, trying to push against his chest with one hand.

Joe now took hold of both her arms against her protests. "Yeah . . . but you know you don't really mean it. All you women love to play hard to get. But I know what you want." He pulled her toward him abruptly, making Alexandra unsteady on her feet.

Alexandra began to struggle in earnest, feeling scared now. "Let me go, Joe," she said, anger also lending strength to her words.

"I could do a lot for you, Sugar. I know a lot of people," he panted, as he tried to kiss her.

Alexandra quickly turned her head and felt his mouth on her neck. She closed her eyes in revulsion and pushed against his chest with her fist. She lost her grip on the fancy dress and it sagged heavily to the floor around her feet.

"Oh, Sugar . . ." Joe groaned, gathering Alexandra tightly in his arms.

Tears of anger and frustration welled in her eyes as she squirmed and wiggled to pull herself free from him. She couldn't move except for her legs, and she instinctively brought her knee up sharply to try and use it as leverage against the man. Her knee jutted into Joe's middle and he immediately released her, cursing as he doubled over in pain, grabbing himself. Alexandra stumbled backward.

Suddenly, there was a knock on the door and Alexandra hastily reached for her dress again. Joe was still cursing as the door opened.

Parker stood there in the doorway.

Alexandra felt rooted, her breath catching in her throat as embarrassment sent a rush of heat over her body. But just as quickly, a chill followed in its wake, leaving her shoulders and arms raised with goosebumps. She blinked at Parker, so surprised at seeing him that for a second Alexandra forgot she was standing there with almost nothing on.

A cigarette burned in Parker's mouth, and Alexandra watched while he slowly removed it. A frown gathered over his dark brows as he surveyed the scene before him, looking pointedly at Joe Jefferies before his narrowed gaze shifted slowly back to Alexandra. Alexandra's own eyes were enormous with relief as she saw instant understanding for the situation darken Parker's eyes to cool black and his jaw muscles knotted. He stepped into the already tight space and closed the door.

"Parker . . ." Alexandra managed in a combination of relief and surprise.

Joe at last tried to stand straight and he turned an angry, still contorted face to the taller man behind him.

"Who the hell are you? You're not supposed to be back here."

Parker's expression remained the same, but his study of the shorter man was hard and steady. Parker slowly drew on his cigarette, then exhaled. He swung his gaze back to Alexandra. "Do you want me to leave?" he asked her smoothly.

Joe's head swung from Parker to Alexandra, finally jerking a thumb at Parker. "Do you know this guy?" he asked rudely.

Alexandra suddenly realized the absurdity of the situation and just wanted them both to go away and leave her alone. "Yes," she answered in a tight voice. "This is Parker Harrison. Parker, this is the club manager, Joe Jeff . . ."

"Parker Harrison," Joe interrupted, impressed despite himself. He forgot his injury, forgot Alexandra standing in a stiff huddle as he turned to Parker. "Hey, man, I follow your style," he said, straightening his jacket and tie, and trying to look as cool and pulled together as Parker appeared.

Parker raised a brow at the stocky manager. "I hope not. It's not my style to come on to women who have to fight me off."

Alexandra caught her breath and looked fearfully at Joe. She was well aware of Joe's short fuse. He could be mean and cruel and unfair, and there weren't many men who would tangle with him. Alexandra could clearly see now that he was stunned for an instant, but then anger made him take a threatening move toward Parker. Alexandra quickly intervened.

"Joe was just discussing my . . . my singing," she interrupted quickly. With a dawning sense of horror, Alexandra realized that it wouldn't take much for the two men to start swinging at each other. She hoped that Parker, at least, would not let it go so far.

"Do you always discuss business in your underwear?" Parker asked sarcastically.

His tone was cutting, and Alexandra stared at him. And then her look became defiant at his unwarranted attack. Parker's jaw muscles continued to twitch angrily in the otherwise smoothly controlled features of his handsome face.

"I don't think that's any of your business, man," Joe said, but there was no threat in his tone as he took a step toward Parker and then stopped.

"Maybe you're right," Parker acknowledged, still looking at Alexandra.

Joe glanced back and forth between Parker and Alexandra. "I've got a club to run," Joe said impatiently now, but looked once more at Alexandra. "We'll finish our talk later."

There was no apology, and no show of blame or guilt for the way he'd compromised her. He brushed past Parker and out the door, leaving the small room charged with tension.

The silence was awful as Alexandra tried to read Parker's suddenly closed expression. She wondered if he thought that what he'd walked in on was her fault, or had been at her bidding. His look made her feel even more angry, as if he was judging her.

Parker, however, in that first instant as they stood silently appraising each other after Joe's departure, was suddenly seeing Alex as he'd first seen her, standing barefoot in the hallway outside her apartment. Then, as now, her pretty, youthful face had seemed impossibly guileless and open, her eyes enormous and direct with interest. And then Parker saw her sense of humiliation, a perplexed look that asked, *What should I have done?* It made him angry, too, but not at Alex. Parker was angry because her life, unlike the smooth passage of his own, had led her to this unpleasant circumstance, a circumstance she didn't deserve. He knew that Alex, here at this club, was out of her league.

Alexandra gave in first, her chin beginning to quiver as she fought tears. She turned her slender back to Parker, biting into her bottom lip.

"Alexandra," Parker said, his tone still angry.

She didn't answer. She stood silently and heard him put out his cigarette in an ashtray on the vanity. Then she could feel him moving closer to stand right behind her.

"Alex," Parker tried again, the voice now hoarse and gentle.

Alexandra felt the light, cool touch of Parker's fingers at the back of her neck. It was tentative, and so light that she felt a warmth begin to cover her. Parker's fingers splayed over her neck and shoulders and forcibly turned her around into his arms. "Come here . . ." he whispered.

Once again, Alexandra released the dress and let her hands be sandwiched in between the two of them. She crossed her arms to cover herself modestly, garnishing more warmth from Parker's arms. Alexandra rested her forehead on Parker's shoulder and closed her eyes. She felt comforted and safe against the black woolliness of his turtleneck sweater. She could smell the leather of his brown trench coat, and hear the unique stretching and caressing of it as he moved his hand up and down her back.

She was grateful he was there, for if he hadn't come, she didn't want to think about what might have happened with Joe. She was grateful that for the time being he said nothing and asked no questions.

Parker, for the moment, didn't need to. It was very obvious what had been going on the instant he'd walked into the dressing room. He'd been out on the professional circuit long enough to know and to have witnessed the sacrifices and compromises people made to get what they wanted.

Parker let his hands move along the slender, very fragile curvature of Alexandra's back. Right now, holding Alex helped him as much as it comforted her. Nothing probably would have happened, Parker knew, because Alexandra would not have let it. That realization pleased him and confirmed every impression he'd ever had of her.

She snuggled unconsciously closer as his lips pressed lightly into her hair.

"Are you all right?" he asked low.

She merely nodded into his shoulder. His arms tightened just a little, and Alexandra forgot she'd had angry, hateful words with him just a week ago. She forgot that they'd made tense, passionate love, fraught with raw, angry need, the emotions torn from both of them as if they were combatants. She suddenly felt totally safe and protected. She knew Parker wouldn't let anything happen to her. There was complete silence in the dressing room, but again, unlike last week, it was not awkward, but had a kind of familiar comfort to it. Parker must have felt it, too, for he chuckled silently.

"It's been a long time since I just held you like this," he growled in a low, throaty tone. "You feel different."

Alexandra sighed. "I'm not as skinny," she said playfully.

"Yes, I noticed last week," Parker said, a note of seduction in his voice. "But this is different. Not at all like last week," he added, and then abruptly stopped.

Alexandra could feel the stiffening in his arms, and

knew he regretted his easy words. Last week, there had been more anger than anything between them.

Parker slowly but firmly pushed Alexandra away from him, lifting her chin so he could see her face. "Jesus. Your lip is bleeding," he whispered tightly.

Alexandra drew the bottom lip inward and tasted her own warm blood. She'd fought so hard against crying that she'd bitten into her lower lip. Parker bent to examine it, using his thumb to gently pull her lip out again. Alexandra was held captive by the look of pure concern and anger in his dark eyes, his face close, and the familiar odors and scents of him assailing her.

"Did he do this?" Parker said shortly, his jaw muscles tightening again.

"No. I guess I did," she responded.

Parker raised his eyes to hers, and she had not recovered sufficiently to remember that he was still somewhat out of favor with her, or that he had recently stepped back into her life to play havoc with her uncertain emotions. She just let his thumb press to the broken skin of her mouth before he replaced his finger with his lips gently, as though to heal.

Alexandra held perfectly still because she liked his gesture, and didn't protest when he tilted his head to press closer, seeking a deeper kiss by encouraging her to answer him. It was quick and thorough, his firm male lips pulling at her until Alexandra let her mouth open slightly and Parker's mouth branded himself on her, seeking to mate his tongue with her own. He was reclaiming her, staking out a territory he wanted from her. She complied reluctantly but naturally, until she remembered her undressed state. She turned her head away, breaking the unexpected kiss, keeping her gaze lowered. Parker didn't push her, but finally pulled back to try and see into her face.

"Has this happened before?" he asked roughly.

Seconds passed before Alexandra realized he was referring to the encounter with Joe. "Not exactly," she answered softly, embarrassed, not willing to add that there had been hints of Joe's intentions in the past, but nothing overt, like tonight. Actually, Alexandra had done a very good job of innocently avoiding Joe, needing only to tolerate his leering looks and suggestive smiles.

Alex knew what Parker was leading to; that it could happen again. The very possibility made her stomach tense. She didn't want to get into a wrestling match with Joe Jefferies just to keep her job.

Parker looked deep into her eyes, his own dark and stony, although his voice was even. "Will you know what to do next time?" he asked. Alexandra's eyes widened, and she knew she wouldn't.

She hadn't considered a "next time." She knew a lot about music, a lot about what she wanted, but she clearly had no idea the price that her career goals might exact.

Parker said nothing because he also understood the drive, the need. He slowly shook his head and grinned at her ruefully. "You obviously haven't thought about that part."

She frowned. "I don't understand."

"The ways you'll be asked to pay in order to achieve what you want. Joe Jefferies is a piece of work, but he's not uncommon in this business, Alex. All along the way there are going to be people, *men*, asking for your body and your soul to help you become a performer."

"I can always say no," she countered.

"If they're not animals," Parker said darkly. "There's also coercion and compromise."

"You're not painting a very pleasant future," Alexandra said with some annoyance.

Parker's grin became an indulgent, warm smile. He ran a knuckle down the side of her face. "It may not be. It's not easy; this can be a dirty business."

"But you do it. You're successful."

"At a price. Everything comes at a price," Parker murmured sagely.

Parker knew, however, that his own successful career had meant life constantly on the go, and a loneliness he hadn't expected and never wanted. It meant leaving Alex behind so that she could grow up and he could find out what he wanted to do with his life.

"You're not sorry about how your life has gone, are you?" Alexandra asked.

Parker rubbed her arms. "For the most part, no. Even the tough times had something to teach me. I certainly don't regret the year I dropped out of sight; that's when I met you." He watched her avert her gaze with its hint of regret. "Just be careful. Nothing is worth giving up your soul for."

"Have you lost your soul?"

Parker let his thumb touch the small abrasion on her lip again. He gazed into her eyes. He shook his head. "Sometimes I think it's the one thing I haven't lost." Alexandra opened her mouth to respond, but he gave her a quick silencing kiss. "I'll wait outside for you to change," Parker said quietly, and left her alone in the tiny room.

Alexandra hung up the aqua dress and began to change into a rose-colored sweater with dolman sleeves, and a pair of black corduroy jeans. She combed her hair out from its severe pulled-back styling with the huge fake gardenia attached and twisted the medium-length strands into a soft, easy bun at the back of her head.

All the while, Alexandra knew Parker waited for her outside the door. She had a few questions about his fortuitous appearance. How had he known where to find her? What did he want? Alexandra also knew an unexpected excitement at Parker's sudden presence. She had not forgotten his parting words of the week before, and couldn't help but wonder now if he'd indeed been serious. Even she was not sure if the final realization would be love or hate. Her eyes seemed overly bright in the mirror, and her lips were moist and parted. Her freckles stood out pertly as ever, but all in all, she didn't seem any the worse from her tussle with Joe. Her annoyance with him had been replaced with the new expectation of what would now happen with Parker. Once changed, Alexandra stepped in the corridor and found Parker slowly pacing the small hallway, smoking. When she closed the door and turned to face him, he drew on his cigarette and slowly exhaled.

He eyed her carefully, noticing the feminine hairstyle which emphasized her heart-shaped face and large, dark eyes. He felt a sudden regret that his Alex of jeans and T-shirts was gone, perhaps forever.

Alexandra suddenly felt uncertain with him as she met his steady, considering gaze. She spoke first to break the sudden awkwardness.

"What are you doing here?" she asked.

Parker concentrated on the growing ash at the end of his cigarette. With his thumb he flicked the cigarette to loosen the embers and send ash drifting to the floor. "I owe you an apology for last week," he began. He stared at her, his eyes narrowed. "I should have realized you'd be angry at me. What happened at your place was my fault. I should have had more control."

Alexandra felt a rush of heat to her face at his confession, but she looked him in the eye. "It wasn't like it used to be between us," she whispered with poignant honesty.

"We couldn't just pick up where we left off. We've changed."

Parker nodded in agreement. "I know."

Alexandra waited, hoping he would voice his feelings more about the intimacy that had swept through them both last week. How was he going to explain that? Did it need to be explained? It had come quickly, but Alexandra now recognized that more than anything, their impromptu lovemaking had been an uneasy, but less destructive conclusion to the things left between them. They'd hidden behind hot embraces and erotic kisses, behind the physical euphoric release of energy and feelings that were almost a decade old.

"I caught your show," Parker said abruptly, changing subjects. "I saw an ad in this afternoon's paper that a 'bright, new singer, Miss Alexandra Morrow, is performing the seven-thirty show at The Outer Edge every Friday and Saturday night,' " Parker quoted verbatim. He lifted a brow. "Didn't the bartender tell you I was waiting?"

Alexandra shrugged. "He said there was some guy waiting, and I thought . . ."

"You thought it was some jerk with a fast come-on," Parker guessed. Alexandra only nodded. "Obviously a lot of guys try it. Even the manager," Parker observed dryly.

He was absolutely right. She took a silent moment to smooth back an errant strand of hair. When she looked at Parker once more, an appreciative smile played at the corners of his full mouth.

"You were good out there tonight."

Alexandra only lifted her shoulders diffidently. "I was okay. I could have been better." She did an admirable job of hiding the bubble of joy and appreciation his words brought.

Parker nodded once, conceding the point. "That's true, but all in all, I don't think it mattered."

Alexandra frowned at him. "What do you mean?"

"I mean, your talents were wasted. Your efforts to entertain the audience were noticed by me, but not by them. I mean that your renditions on a couple of songs were original and clever, but no one seemed to care, or could tell the difference. The backup combo was barely adequate and didn't know how to pace with you. I mean, Alex, what are you doing in a place like this? You don't belong here."

"I'm getting practice, experience, and exposure," she said, somewhat flippantly.

"You belong in a better club than this," Parker said firmly.

Alexandra smiled ruefully. "I'd *love* a better club than this, but no one wants to hear from someone like me with no experience."

"Someone like you has to be more aggressive. You want to sing and you know you're good, right?" She nodded. "Then you have to tell the other club managers flatly they'd be making a mistake by not at least hearing you sing. You have to make them give you a chance."

Alexandra grimaced. "I hate that part."

"What? Auditioning?"

"Selling myself."

"I thought you wanted a career. The first thing you have to be besides ambitious is assertive. You want people to pay attention to you. Can you do that?" Parker asked bluntly.

A frisson of doubt sliced through her. "I don't know."

"Ten years is a long time not to know. What does it mean when people listen and then applaud you afterward? What does it give you to know that all those years of work and study meant something?" Parker said, almost urgently.

Again she shrugged. "I . . . I don't know. I want to be sure. I want to be really good before I move on. It's like, I'm not really paying attention to the audience, but to how I sound. I need to know."

"You can look into a mirror, sing to yourself, and get the same results. You have to start paying attention. If you lose your audience, you have no career. That audience will grant you a career."

Alexandra couldn't help but realize that on one level, Parker was talking about himself, and the double roads of his own career.

"What if no one takes me seriously?"

"That's part of the risk of putting yourself out there on the line. Believe it or not, I've been turned down. If you believe in yourself, it won't matter. Only a handful of people make it on luck alone. If you want it, you have to show you deserve it." He was firm and hard with the truth.

Parker looked with distaste around the dim and dingy cracked walls backstage at the club, annoyed that Alex would settle for such a second-rate place.

"The Outer Edge can't do a thing for you. Come on . . ." he said, and taking her by the arm, led her back out through the smoky and crowded main room.

"Where are we going?" Alexandra asked, bewildered, nonetheless allowing him to lead her.

"I'm taking you to Blues Alley."

"Blues Alley," she gasped. "Parker, that's one of the best clubs in D.C.! Getting auditions with them is next to impossible."

Parker stopped to look into her face. "Don't you think

you're good enough? Fish or cut bait. It's that simple," he said bluntly.

It was a question that she'd honestly never been able to answer.

"Tonight we're just going to go and listen to the competition. And then you tell me."

He started heading toward the door, and Alexandra knew with a kind of panicked excitement that Parker was right. She could be months or years working up to Blues Alley just by playing it too safe.

As she followed Parker through the smoky lounge, Alexandra spotted Joe at the bar, brooding into a Scotch glass. She knew he had not forgotten her or what had happened in the dressing room. She knew Joe was thinking up new ways to compromise her. Alexandra needed this job at The Outer Edge for the time being, but she wasn't going to let someone like Joe Jefferies intimidate her.

She turned to Parker and touched him lightly on the arm. "Can you give me a minute? I have to take care of something."

Parker looked at Alexandra with a frown, and then automatically to the club manager sulking at the bar. "Are you sure you want to?" he asked.

Alexandra pursed her lips and nodded. "It's important."

Parker reluctantly gave in. "I'll wait by the door."

Alexandra paused momentarily before taking a slow breath and approaching Joe. She glanced once over her shoulder to see that Parker was carefully watching her, and it felt good that he stood ready to come to her aid again, if necessary. Alexandra knew, however, that it wouldn't be.

She touched Joe on the arm and he gave her an un-friendly, baleful look before turning back to his drink.

"I want a lock on the dressing room door," Alexandra said in a quiet, calm voice. "And I want to choose some of my own dresses for the show."

"Where do you get off being so uppity?" Joe questioned in annoyance, scowling at her.

"Yes or no?" Alexandra persisted.

"You sure give me a hard way to go, woman," Joe mumbled.

"Does that mean I'm fired?" Alexandra asked evenly.

"Hell, no," Joe said gruffly. "I'm no fool. You're a good singer. You're good for the club."

"Thank you," she said automatically, not particularly flattered. "Then I'll see you tomorrow."

He grunted into his glass as she turned to leave. "Oh, and another thing . . ." he looked warily at Parker. "That other business tonight. It never happened, okay?"

Alexandra lifted a corner of her mouth into a triumphant smile. "And it will *never* happen again."

"Yeah, yeah," Joe said, dismissing her.

Alexandra met Parker at the door, and he could tell from the bright gleam in her eyes that whatever was said between her and the manager had accomplished what she wanted. But Parker knew men like Joe Jefferies, and he was not inclined to be as trusting or forgiving. People like the burly manager were persistent, insensitive, and had short memories. Sooner or later, his interest would turn to Alexandra again.

The thought enraged Parker, because it was so obvious. He knew he'd only alienate Alexandra if he tried too hard and too often to tell her what to do. He realized that there were other ways around it.

Alexandra, who didn't own a car, followed Parker to

his, and recalling their ride together a week earlier, again sat uncomfortably next to him. But whereas before she had tried valiantly to deny the effect his male presence had on her senses, even after so much time gone between them, there was now the tangible evidence in her cold hands and nervous stomach and rampant imagination that something more *would* happen.

Their lovemaking a week ago had effectively crumpled old barriers and bridged a yawning gap in their sensual awareness of each other. It had also proved that the strong attraction they had for each other was still there, even though in other ways they might be worlds apart.

"How long have you been singing in that place?" Parker suddenly interrupted her thoughts.

"About two months."

Parker made an impatient sound. "I hope you're not planning on going back there."

"Why shouldn't I? Besides, I need the money," Alexandra said stubbornly, her previously languid thoughts giving way to defensiveness.

"What for? Are you buying your own opera company?" he teased, and she had to smile.

"No. But I need the money for private voice lessons. I don't have much time left to prepare for the auditions for the Light Opera Company."

"When is that?"

"About a month, the week before Easter."

Parker was quiet for a time. "You shouldn't go back there, Alex." And he sounded so serious.

Alexandra was a bit annoyed that he would presume to tell her that. Her earlier romantic musings shriveled.

"Look, I realize I've taken my time to achieve my goals, but that doesn't mean they're not important to me. This may well be my last chance to try out for the opera. Don't be so cavalier with my future." She refrained, however, from reminding Parker that she didn't have the resources or opportunities he'd had.

"I don't want you to go back because Joe Jefferies thinks from below his waist and he's not going to leave you alone. No matter what he promised," Parker emphasized sharply.

"You can't expect me not to, Parker," Alexandra said stiffly, her voice laced with hurt and anger. "I missed my last audition for this company because of you. I won't do that again."

Parker considered that and let out a deep sigh. "At least consider singing somewhere else. Somewhere that's not a dive, somewhere the manager has respect for you as a person and will keep his hands off you."

His voice was slowly rising, and Alexandra was surprised at the vehemence. When she didn't say anything, Parker chuckled dryly.

"I know I have a lot of nerve, and I know you think I'm meddling and I don't understand, but . . ."

"Yes?" she coaxed, turning to look at him.

He hesitated. "I care about you, Alex. I care what happens to you. I know you don't believe that, but it was always true."

"Even when you left?" she questioned softly, her heart pounding, waiting for his answer.

"More so, then," he answered in a low, hoarse voice, recalling the events at the time which had left him so little choice. Should he tell her about the phone calls he'd made to her home? It seemed pretty obvious to Parker that Alexandra knew nothing about them. He glanced briefly at her and back to the traffic.

"Where else have you been singing?"

She tilted her head thoughtfully. "Oh . . . I'm part of

the chorus at the Kennedy Center. Last year I did a Christmas special with a local TV station. You didn't see me, but you heard my voice. I sang at Howard University's commencement ceremony several years ago. And I tried auditioning for a musical that was opening here before it went up to New York."

"What happened?"

Alexandra shifted restlessly in her seat. "Well, I at least made the third round of callbacks, but I discovered I couldn't act."

"They couldn't use you in some other way?"

"Not really. It was pretty laughable. Even my own sister thought I was pretty bad and should just stick to singing."

Parker thought quickly for a moment. "Your sister . . . I almost forgot you had one. How is she doing?" When Alexandra didn't answer, he continued. "And your father?" Parker asked quietly. "Is he still dependent on you?"

"He's doing well. He's stable as long as he follows his diet and tries to get some exercise. Unfortunately, that only entails walking from one end of the house to the other."

Parker chuckled silently. "And is Christine all grown up now?"

Alexandra silently thought what an understatement that was. "I would say so," she replied quietly.

Their car finally pulled into the side lot for Blues Alley, and after parking, they proceeded into the club. As soon as they stepped inside, Alexandra sensed that there was a world of difference between this more popular and well-received club and the questionable one they'd just left. But she was already feeling intimidated by its long history of featuring distinguished performers.

Parker gave her a look that asked if she wanted to forget going in. He could see the uncertainty that made her silent, and he drew her close to his side. Alexandra lifted her chin and rose to the silent challenge.

The interior was visible under dim atmospheric lighting that made the room warm and welcoming. There were only a few vacant tables, yet the room was not overpowered by cigarette smoke or noise. The maître d' recognized Parker, but didn't carry on about it or draw unnecessary attention to his presence.

Parker led her to a table and ordered them both drinks. They sat talking about the surroundings, and except for one casual mention that he'd studied music with one of the owners of the nightclub, they studiously avoided any other mention of the past. The show started with a solo saxophone player, followed by a female singer.

The saxophonist was a virtuoso, clever and lively with his music, playing pieces that had the attentive audience tapping their feet and moving shoulders and heads to the beat. Alexandra got as much pleasure listening to the audience's response as she did listening to the extraordinary playing. Parker would occasionally whisper little comments or observations about the saxophonist's technique, or a tricky musical departure. At one point they joined the audience in spontaneous response to a particular rendition, and they caught each other's gaze for a moment.

Reflected in each one's eyes was a mutual love of hearing wonderful music. For this moment, gone were Parker's stardom and her performance at The Outer Edge; the unsettled emotions of last week, and earlier tonight; and ten years ago. For the moment, it was all about them.

The saxophonist got the warm round of applause he

deserved, and the singer came onto the stage. The first thing Alexandra noticed was that the woman was not wearing a suggestive gown. In fact, her plump body was well covered. Her ensemble was loose and without sparkles and shiny beads, and she was given a comfortable stool to sit on.

Alexandra listened and watched in total absorption, observing the woman's act, and noticing her ability. Alexandra liked her very much, and her admiration made her doubt her own ability to perform. Not to sing . . . but to *perform*. The woman's voice was good, but certainly nothing special, yet she had a presence and style that captured the audience's attention and made everyone follow her every move and note.

Between songs she had an easy repartee with the crowd, and a sense of humor that emanated naturally from her. She seemed totally at ease on the stage, and in total command. She wasn't thrown or confused when specific requests came from the patrons. Alexandra knew that her heart would have been in her throat if there had been a deviation from her own chosen set of songs.

Alexandra suddenly realized that she didn't know how to be spontaneous and to just go with the flow. With a light dawning in her mind, Alexandra recognized that there were only two ways in which she'd ever performed and been totally comfortable with herself. One was in teaching and demonstrating to her children. The second had been with Parker.

Alexandra frowned as these new thoughts took hold in her mind, as a new perspective allowed her to see and examine her heart, her dreams, the past. She cast a furtive look at Parker only to find him watching the female singer. Alexandra could see that he was entertained by her. Alexandra suddenly questioned whether she had the ability to hold Parker's attention. But not just Parker's . . . *anyone's.*

Parker hoped Alex was paying attention. He didn't want her just to hear how the singer sang, he wanted Alex to see how she performed. It took more than just having a great voice and a long repertoire of songs. There was also presence, style, ease, and even acting. The audience had to believe that she was up there performing only for them. Parker's attention roamed over her quiet profile. *Is this what you want?* he asked silently.

The songstress took several bows after her performance and promised to return for the midnight show.

"Well, what do you think?" Parker asked, as he signaled for the waiter and ordered two fresh drinks.

Alexandra gnawed on her lip, forgetting that she'd already done injury to it once tonight. "She was excellent. So lively. I enjoyed it," she said, not sounding very happy about it.

Parker took a thoughtful sip of his drink, still watching her, his eyes watching for a particular reaction. "What about you, Alex? Can you hold an audience? Make them glad they came to hear you?"

His voice was low, but the questions were pointed, going deep into her, and the heart of the matter, which she'd not considered before. After a long moment, Alexandra raised her dark eyes to Parker. "I think so."

He raised his brows. "You only *think* so?"

"I'm sure I can," she said softly.

"Then what are you going to do about it?" he asked now. "And I'm not counting your engagement at The Outer Edge."

Alexandra felt as though he was putting her on the spot. "I'm doing everything I know how."

Parker twisted his glass around on the coaster. "Blues

Alley holds open auditions every Saturday. Are you going to be here tomorrow?"

Again Alexandra detected a gentle challenge in his question. "I teach tomorrow. And I'm taking my class to the Kennedy Center to hear the children's program."

"Fine." Parker nodded. "I'll pick you up there." He lifted his drink. "We'll come together for the tryouts."

Alexandra stiffened her back and her eyes went quickly from confused to stormy. She heard the challenge again, and resented that he thought so little of her commitment. She, after all, had never had a moment's doubt about his, and look how far it had taken him.

"What's the matter. Afraid I won't show up? You don't have a lot of faith in me, do you?"

Parker hesitated in mid-air with his glass, and then put it back on the table. "If I didn't have faith in you, Alex, I wouldn't have dragged you away from The Outer Edge and brought you here. Do you have the desire and the guts to show up tomorrow?" Parker asked bluntly, no longer mincing words.

"Yes," Alexandra said through clamped teeth, angry that he was pushing, and angry that already the tension of anticipation had grabbed at her stomach.

"Then you're not afraid?" he pushed.

"Of course I am. I don't want to make a fool of myself," Alexandra said.

Parker slowly grinned at her. "Good," he nodded. "A little fear will keep you hungry and honest. That helps your music."

"Are you speaking from experience?" she asked flippantly.

"Absolutely," Parker readily admitted. Then slowly he leaned across the table, closer to her. "As you recall, you used to prod me quite a bit. You wouldn't give an inch.

You'd never let me get away with saying that there was something I couldn't do. Don't you remember what you'd tell me, Alex?"

She was fascinated by the calm in Parker, by the dark, caressing regard in his eyes, by his sultry voice, which whispered their history without rancor, but with seeming regret and fondness. "An audition will only cost you carfare there and back," she said by rote. "You'll never know if you never try."

Parker arched his brow. "Are you going to eat those words?"

Alexandra sighed. Her anger began to dissipate. "No. I know I'm good, but nothing like you."

He shook his head. "Don't use me as an excuse. We don't do the same kind of music. And you're wrong. You're *going* to be great."

Parker pulled some bills from his pocket to pay for the drinks, and they stood up to leave. He helped her put her coat on and then reached out to take her hand. Without thinking, Alexandra put hers into his firm grasp. She looked at the joined hands, loving the instant familiar feel of his long, narrow fingers. She looked up at Parker and into his handsome face, with its gentle, ironic smile. He had extended the olive branch.

"And besides," Parker murmured, as they headed for the exit, "how many people go to auditions with their own fan club?"

She smiled at him. Parker winked at her and squeezed her fingers, and Alexandra relaxed. It was amazing how much Parker's firm belief in her mattered.

The drive to her apartment was very different than the drive the night of Debby and Brian's wedding.

"What music will you sing?" he asked, as they discussed the open audition.

"I guess soul ballads, torchy love songs. I have a couple of jazz compositions I do well with."

"Just don't try to practice tonight. It's too late to do you any good. Be prepared to give it your best shot tomorrow. Another thing—get some rest. Sleep as late as you can in the morning. And don't yell at the kids, no matter what they do to drive you crazy . . ."

She began to laugh. "You sound like a coach getting his athletes ready for a major tournament."

"I am. I know you can nail this, Alex."

Parker's faith in her made Alexandra feel so terrific. "Thanks, coach," she murmured in amusement.

Alexandra realized that this evening had changed the relationship. Last week had caught them both off guard, and swept them back into an unresolved chapter in their lives. Somehow, tonight they'd gotten forever past it. Whatever the past had been, it was now over and done. It served no useful purpose to continue the resurrection of it. The hurt still lingered, but only because she had loved him so much. And even recognizing that that love might still be the same only made for a bitter sweetness of how glorious the future might have been for both of them together.

At her door, she turned to face Parker. He made the moment easier for both of them by stating it was too late for him to come in. Alexandra nodded gratefully in agreement.

"Were you ever nervous at your auditions?" she asked him, as they stood outside her apartment door.

Parker shrugged. "I was probably too busy being annoyed," he grinned sheepishly, slowly starting to light a cigarette.

"Why annoyed?" she asked. Parker grimaced, but his brows were ominous across his forehead.

"I was never all that interested in performing, Alex. I just wanted to create my music. I could have been just as happy letting someone else play it."

She'd never known that. She shook her head. "No one could have done it as well."

Parker began to smile at the compliment. "Thank you," he said quietly.

"Thank you, too," she chuckled nervously.

"Don't thank me yet," Parker said.

As they stared at one another in the silence of the hall it seemed a small moment of déjà vu to Alexandra. She suddenly recalled the first night she'd ever met Parker. She remembered his teasing, his kindness and care. She remembered thanking him, just to have him say, "Don't thank me yet." *It's happening all over again*, Alexandra thought.

His eyes searched her face, settling on the pretty curves of her wide mouth. He was charmed by the freckles on her cheeks, which only served to make her seem young and unworldly. Parker knew in a way she was. And he was grateful for it. His hand stroked her cheek tentatively, to test how much she'd actually forgiven him.

"Alex?" he questioned quietly, and when she said nothing, he slowly bent his head until their lips met.

Alexandra's lips parted of their own will, and she knew again the heady feel and taste of his lips. There was faint alcohol and tobacco, and for some reason, her senses responded to the residual stimulus. She enjoyed the gentle play of his tongue against hers. His movement was so erotic and tantalizing that Alexandra swayed toward him, wanting him to put his arms around her.

Parker made no move to hold her, only taking control of the kiss, probing deep within her warm mouth with his tongue, boldly imposing himself before slowly pulling away to separate them with a moist little sound. He could smell the sweetness of her skin, the perfume on her clothing.

When Alexandra opened her eyes, she found Parker regarding her with tenderness.

"Goodnight," he whispered against her mouth. His hand slipped from her cheek, and he backed toward the stairs. "I'll see you at ringside tomorrow."

Alexandra smiled and waved goodbye.

Chapter Six

Alexandra felt like her coat was totally useless against the cold March wind. The sunshine was deceptive, promising more warmth for the day than was truly possible, and she clamped her teeth together to stop the chattering and hunched her shoulders deeper into her wool coat. The ten children in her charge seemed totally unaffected by the weather as they laughed and squealed playfully in youthful abandon.

"Michael, please, come away from there," Alexandra shouted at one boy, who'd decided that throwing bits and pieces of his lunch into the Potomac was more fun than eating it. But he scampered away at the strident sound of her voice, and joined several other youngsters in a game of tag.

Twice a year, Alexandra brought her young music students to the Kennedy Center to hear concerts or watch films. Last September they'd seen *Fantasia* and seemed to enjoy hearing classical music used as a background to the famous Disney animation.

Today, it had been the Young People's Orchestra, playing *Peter and the Wolf*. The audience had been filled with children, some there with parents just to hear the music and the narration that went with the story. But many more in the audience were future musicians themselves.

As a child, Alexandra had never had the opportunity to hear a live performance, and so the outings were just as much a treat for her as for the children.

Alexandra had always hoped that seeing and hearing other children perform would inspire her own kids to greater efforts. At least she tried to convince herself of that as she sat almost frozen, watching their energetic play, music far from their thoughts as they waited to be picked up by parents.

She was also very much aware that for some of these children, the study of an instrument was done more to please their parents; many of them were in her class reluctantly. Still, all the children enjoyed the biannual outings because each one meant a Saturday afternoon away from practice.

Two thin bodies streaked past Alexandra, one little girl in hot pursuit of a boy who'd been teasing her. The little girl's braids and ribbons were being pulled about by the wind. Alexandra gasped at the sight of the child hatless and gloveless, with her coat hanging open.

"Marsha, button your coat, before you catch a cold."

Marsha hastened to obey, but Alexandra suspected that she herself was the only one who was cold and uncomfortable. She could feel the chill seep into her very bones, stiffening the joints. She kept recalling how cold she'd been the night before in the strapless blue dress while performing. She remembered, also, the draft which had blown from the narrow hallway leading to the dressing room, to the small stage where she sang. The fact that Alexandra had awakened this morning with a headache and slightly stuffy nose did not bode well for the state of her health. She couldn't afford to be sick right now. There was still work to be done for her audition. There were all her classes, and those of Debby's until Debby returned from her honeymoon. And now she was also wishing she hadn't agreed so readily to the tryout session this afternoon at Blues Alley.

Alexandra could still envision the ease of the female singer the night before, the woman's calm assurance and professional performance, and she began to experience quelling self-doubts. Her years of amateur singing hadn't made her *that* confident and at ease. She began to blame Parker for urging her on. Maybe she wasn't ready yet. After all, Joe Jefferies notwithstanding, what was so bad about The Outer Edge?

"Well, for one thing, it certainly isn't Blues Alley," she muttered wryly to herself, knowing full well the great reputation of the famed Washington club. But the question was, was *she* ready for the big time?

Alexandra sighed, blew her nose miserably into a tissue, and stood to call her brood together. A number of parents were already waiting in the red carpeted lobby when she hustled the children inside. There were brief conferences with some parents who wanted to know their children's progress, and gentle words to the children themselves, reminding them to practice. After thank-yous, most of the children and their parents left.

Alexandra, scanning the group hastily, caught sight of one woman just as she was leaving with her son.

"Mrs. Evans, can I speak to you for just a moment?" Alexandra called out, hurrying through the dispersing group to the woman's side.

The woman, a little shorter and plumper than Alexandra, looked over her shoulder and smiled.

"Of course. David, don't wander too far. I'll only be a

minute," she said to her son, who was already wandering off with mischievous ideas of playing on a nearby escalator. Then she turned back to Alexandra. "Yes?" she asked.

"I feel that David isn't practicing as much as he should between classes."

Mrs. Evans relaxed, the frown clearing from her round brown face. "Quite honestly, Miss Morrow, I'm not surprised. He likes music but hates the practice. I try to keep after him, but David has baseball on the brain and not much else."

"Perhaps you could talk to him. I mean, he's so talented. He's months ahead of the other children. He seems to understand the concepts so easily. I know David enjoys playing, but his attention wanders."

Mrs. Evans had already begun rolling her eyes heavenward during Alexandra's entreaty. "I know, I know," she said. "Right now, he can't decide if he wants to be on stage or on Astroturf. I have to tell you, baseball's got an edge. It's not your fault his mind is elsewhere. He likes you very much and tells his father and me about the great games you invent to make practice more fun. But with David, you almost have to sit on him to make him work hard."

Alexandra wanted to scream in her frustration; David was one of her most talented students. "Then maybe he can come to me three afternoons a week and I'll work with him."

Mrs. Evans sighed and shook her head. "We can't afford more lessons, Miss Morrow. We put off getting a new car this year so we could get David a decent piano . . ."

"I wouldn't charge you anything more. It's just that David is so promising."

Mrs. Evans sighed again, looking toward her son with both pride and exasperation. "So everyone seems to think. My husband and I were truly happy when David's teachers said he had a good ear for music, and recommended you for lessons. But what good are all the lessons if he simply doesn't care, or if he's not sure? Sometimes he'll sit at that piano and play for hours without me saying a word. Other times . . ." she merely shrugged.

Alexandra couldn't respond, and she felt defeated because Mrs. Evans was right: all the talent in the world meant nothing if one wasn't willing to put in the time or work or if there was no encouragement. Against her will, Alexandra thought fleetingly of her father's own wasted talents and lack of opportunity. She thought of Parker and his easy success. But she frowned now as she suddenly remembered his own evaluation of his career, and his training. Parker was lucky and he didn't know it, she thought. She knew that if someone had offered her music lessons at ten, she'd have been in heaven.

Mrs. Evans shrugged and shook her head helplessly at the other woman. "Maybe the lessons are a waste of time and money. I've been thinking of not making him come for a while. I could just put the money aside. Maybe he'll miss the classes."

Alexandra shook her head vigorously. "Don't worry about the money. It's not important," she said generously. "I just don't want David to lose this time."

"I appreciate that."

"I was hoping he'd try out for the Young People's Orchestra in September. He's that good. He still has a few weeks left to apply and fill out the application forms."

David's mother laughed softly. "I know he enjoyed today's outing. He just said to me, 'Ma, I can do that. I can play as good as those kids.' "

"He can," Alexandra agreed, her eyes bright with hope.

"You're very patient," Mrs. Evans sighed.

"It's easy with David. He's a very talented little boy. Look, why don't you just let him come to classes as usual? He can come to me during the week. If he needs motivation to practice, I'll work with him and we'll practice together. It doesn't have to be every week, just whenever he wants. 'Half a loaf is better than none,' " Alexandra grimaced with a smile.

The other woman chuckled, already summoning her son. "That's real nice of you, and I'll keep your offer in mind. His father doesn't want me to push him. After all, he's only ten, and naturally he's more interested in sports. He's got all of those heroes in sports. It's a little tough to beat."

"But there are many heroes in music, too. Luther Vandross hasn't done so badly."

Mrs. Evans laughed softly at the truth of Alexandra's words. "You're right, of course. All those professional musicians lead such hard lives."

"Please don't discourage him. He may only want to play for fun. But he should learn as much as he can *now*. He can always decide what he wants to do later."

Mrs. Evans smiled. "I'll try, Miss Morrow. But it's really all up to David."

The boy came back and pulled on the sleeve of his mother's coat. "Mom, could we stop for pizza before going home?"

"Didn't you eat your lunch?" his mother asked.

David shrugged. "I'm still hungry."

Mrs. Evans looked at Alexandra. "That's where the rest of our money goes—into his stomach."

Alexandra smiled and winked playfully at the young boy. "What's your favorite food, David?" she asked.

David thought for a moment. "I like hamburgers, and brownies, grilled cheese sandwiches."

"I tell you what. If you come to an extra practice next week, I'll make brownies for you, and we'll go have hamburgers afterward."

"Ms. Mrrow, that's not really . . ." Ms. Evans started.

Alexandra gave her a silent pleading look and the woman hesitated.

"Can I, Mom?" David piped up, surprising his mother.

She raised her brows. "Well . . . that's up to you. You could practice at home, you know."

"I'd rather do it with Ms. Morrow."

Alexandra laughed. "Is it the practice, or the promise of a hamburger?" she asked. "I'll give you a call on Monday and we'll pick a time, okay?"

"Okay," David said, already moving toward the exit, and the hope of pizza on the way home.

"Thank you," Mrs. Evans said sincerely.

Alexandra watched as a moment later David left with his mother.

Music had always been important to Alexandra. When she was a youngster, it offered an escape. Like reading a book, it was something she could do alone for entertainment that took her out of her ordinary world and transported her to someplace wonderful and new. It made her feel good. And all she wanted was to let children like David learn, as she had, that good music was like magic.

Alexandra sensed she was not alone and turned to look into the face of Parker Harrison. She was startled at suddenly seeing him, and had a surprising mixed reaction. She was glad to see him, and then again, she was not. Her stomach knotted apprehensively as she recalled the upcoming afternoon audition, and the thought of Parker listening to her perform.

"Hello," he said quietly, and there was gentle amusement in his watchful dark eyes. "Why do I get the feeling that you were about to bolt like a scared rabbit?"

"Because I probably was," she admitted dryly. Her voice cracked and she softly cleared her throat.

Parker raised a brow and frowned slightly.

"I think I'm coming down with a cold," Alexandra told him.

Parker studied her face alertly for a second, listened to her excuse, and shook his head. The collar of his leather coat was pulled up, framing his neck and jaw. He drew on a lit cigarette held in his hand.

"Are you saying you would rather not try out this afternoon?" he asked casually, exhaling and watching her through the gray haze.

Alexandra thought about it. She had always been waiting for another time, the right time. There was never going to be a right time unless she made it for herself. "I want to sound my best," she equivocated, but she wasn't being totally honest with herself or with Parker.

Parker's brows furrowed in further thought for a moment, and he glanced briefly at his watch. "Tell you what—let's get warmed up. Then we'll see about the tryout."

Alexandra let out a sigh of relief and lifted dark, warm eyes to his handsome face. She wondered if he guessed her inner thoughts. She sensed he was perfectly capable of it. "That would be nice," she responded.

He winked and gave her a reassuring smile. "Good. I'll leave the car parked here. Let's walk to the Georgetown Inn. It's not too far away."

Automatically Parker held out a hand to her, and Alexandra let his hand close around hers as he led her out into the cold but bright day.

Her fluffy blue turtleneck sweater was swathed protectively around her throat and chin, and a matching beret was pulled over her hair and ears. Her wool coat was buttoned up to her throat. Nonetheless Alexandra was cold. With a great deal of effort, she held back the shivers. Parker seemed right in his element. His leather coat flapped open in the wind. Alexandra was glad when they finally reached the restaurant.

Alexandra removed her coat and hat. As Parker also removed his coat and muffler, it struck her, certainly not for the first time, how good-looking he was. Even more so than she'd remembered. Parker seemed to have come to full adulthood so much in command, so unlike the younger man she'd known. There was a strength about him now that had obviously been gained over the last several years. She had been so stunned into letting down her anger at him a week ago that she'd missed the subtle differences. He might almost be an entirely different person. Now that she'd been able to spend some time with him, no matter how awkward or emotionally confusing, she could see him through different eyes, more adult and realistic ones. Alexandra liked this Parker better. And while she didn't want to change the earlier memory she had of him, of that time when they'd first met, she was at last putting the relationship in proper perspective. She had been awfully young when Parker had come into her life.

Parker was also enjoying his assessment of Alexandra, but it only confirmed what he'd seen and recognized the week before at Brian and Debby's wedding. Alex was very much a woman now, no longer the young girl he'd last seen.

The thought came to Parker that he'd never told his parents about the student he'd met who'd had more of an influence on him than he would have admitted at the time. They'd never been overly impressed with the women he'd dated or known primarily from being on the road and being so visible. But Parker wondered what they'd think of Alex and her stubborn pride, her determination, and her youthful prettiness. She ordered a pot of hot chocolate, too nervous to think of eating, but Parker ordered coffee and a club sandwich. They sat comfortably opposite each other, waiting for the order.

Unaware of Alexandra's thoughts or her melting change of heart, Parker leaned toward her, resting his elbows on the table. "So, how did the kids enjoy the outing? Are you hoping a serious interest will seep in through the pores?"

Alexandra grinned ruefully. "I think they enjoyed being away from piano lessons and my prodding. But they're a good group. Some were impressed by the show and a few felt intimidated, but I think it's important for them to see what's possible for themselves."

Parker grinned. "Remind you of anything?"

"You mean last night at Blues Alley? The thought crossed my mind. I guess the difference is I've already made up my mind what I want to be when I grow up." Parker laughed lightly with her. "The kids still need all the training they can get *before* they make their decision."

Alexandra suddenly became excited about her really exceptional students, like David Evans, and told Parker how she hoped he'd change his mind about practicing seriously and come to appreciate his unique gift.

In her glowing report, Alexandra missed Parker's quiet enjoyment of her animated features. "You obviously like teaching," he observed.

"Oh, I do. You have no idea how wonderful it is to get a talented child and watch his progress, to feel that I might have contributed to it. I want them *all* to go on to great things."

Parker watched Alexandra closely, somewhat surprised at her excitement and wholehearted enthusiasm for her work. Did she realize that she seemed to have much more faith in her children than she had in herself?

"But you know most of them will only be just competent. You realize, of course, that most of them will give up in a few years, or be discouraged in high school. A precious few will go the distance, Alex. In any case, you can follow their progress long distance—after you become rich and famous yourself, that is," Parker said casually.

Alexandra's focus became sharp, and the glow of her eyes began to burn out, to be replaced by confusion and deep thought. It was as if she'd never considered that if her own career took off the way she'd dreamt, her teaching would end. There'd be no time for it. Either or.

"Yes, of course," Alexandra mumbled, distracted.

Parker chuckled soundlessly, but shook his head as he reached for his cigarettes to light one. "Nobody gets to have it all."

"You did."

He shrugged. "You can't judge by my career. I wouldn't want anyone else to think I've had it so easy. It's relative.

"Just don't forget that they're still kids, Alex. Sometimes a movie or a house party, a softball game, or a date is more important."

Alexandra shrugged and smiled. "You're right. I think sometimes I do forget. The ones that are serious are serious about music no matter what. Some of the others take lessons because of parents or friends."

". . . And hope to just coast along and not be noticed,"
Parker added. "As I recall, the students are late a lot, or
call in sick, or just don't show. The excuse is that there's
too much homework, or relatives are visiting, or the dog
has to go to the vet again."

A smile of surprise and recognition played on Alexandra's features as Parker recounted some of the ingenious
excuses of students.

"Once or twice a grandparent has passed on, usually of
some awful, unknown disease. Do you have any idea how
many grandparents have gone to heaven to spare a kid
music classes?"

Alexandra nodded, laughing softly as their order was
served. The waitress seemed to linger over the simple
chore, her gray eyes, under a droopy mop of skewered
blond curls, taking furtive looks at Parker.

Alexandra, still amused by Parker's revelations, felt a
momentary twinge of annoyance and pride at the waitress's attention to Parker. He was totally oblivious to the
young woman's interest.

"Can I get you anything else?" the young waitress
asked, hoping to draw Parker's attention. But he merely
shook his head and gave her a vacant smile.

"This is fine, thanks," he said, returning his attention
to Alexandra.

It was in that moment that it occurred to Alexandra
that there were probably women who came on to him
constantly, who tried to capture his interest, to be drawn
into his charmed circle. But here he sat with her, telling
amusing anecdotes, and willingly giving time to encourage her goals, but also to instill reality. Parker could have
walked away last week, and seen their brief and volatile
encounter as just "for old times' sake." But he hadn't.
He'd returned not once, but twice, and it was to her that

his time was given. Parker was not playing at being a celebrity. He was being a friend, and one who certainly knew her better than anyone else, except her father.

As Parker poured himself coffee, his eyes narrowed with further memory and the storytelling continued. "Another good excuse I've heard is the one where the dog ate the music sheets, or they got thrown out in the trash by mistake. But my all-time favorite is the one where the music sheets were *accidentally* used to line the cat's litter box."

Tears of laughter filled Alexandra's eyes as Parker sipped from his cup, grinning broadly at her amusement.

"So how did you know all that?" she asked, wiping away the tears.

"I made up most of them," Parker admittedly wickedly. "And there are some others that come to mind now."

"Maybe you should tell me so I'll be warned," Alexandra urged.

He squinted at her. "I don't think so. I wouldn't want to spoil the efforts of some creative kid."

Her amusement slowly faded. "You surprise me," she whispered, watching him as he chewed his sandwich. "You're so good, I assumed you always were, that you *always* worked hard and practiced."

Parker nodded. "I did. But sometimes it wasn't by choice. Believe me, I know how your students feel sometimes," he observed.

"You sound like you approve of what they do."

Parker put his sandwich down and he began to play idly with his napkin. "You're wrong, Alex. I don't approve at all. But I do understand. When you're eight, nine, ten years old, piano lessons are not the beginning and end of the world. Only parents and teachers think so."

Alexandra shifted uncomfortably, acutely aware of the conversation just that afternoon with David Evans and his mother. "You resented it, didn't you?" Alexandra observed.

Parker didn't comment at first. His eyes were following her movements, the small, narrow hand that smoothed her hair, the bright glow of her face with the dusting of freckles which made Alexandra look so appealing. For the moment, he was seemingly more fascinated with her as he raised a hand to smooth her dark hair. The gesture was caring and personal, something he used to do often, affectionately, long ago. It was as if the talk of music and classes was merely a smokescreen to disguise the fact that they were each in turn still filled with questions about what they were to each other. The talk of music was an easy, common link, but it hardly dealt with their real feelings, whatever they were.

Parker let his hand drop just short of stroking her cheek, and turned his attention to Alexandra's last comment.

"I suppose I resented the constant reminders to practice," Parker said around a mouthful of sandwich, his brows furrowed. "Music was always easy for me. I didn't understand why I had to practice all the time if I was supposed to be so good."

Alexandra suddenly recalled Parker's ambivalence about all his earlier years of training. But until this very moment, she'd never considered the powerless frustration he must have felt as a child urged onward by doting parents and encouraging teachers. David Evans again came to mind, and Alexandra could see the beginning of similarities between the child and Parker. She understood now that David had to make the choices himself, something Parker had not been allowed to do. A whole new vista of enlightenment brightened her eyes as she regarded Parker over the rim of her steaming mug.

"Are you still sorry?" she asked.

"No, of course not," he shook his head. "My parents did what they thought best, and believe me, Alex, I'm grateful. Look how far it's taken me. I just would have liked other things in my life besides the obsession with music. I've missed a lot." As he spoke, he reached out and suddenly lifted her hand and turned it palm up. "I hope you don't make the same mistake. Don't make music the center of your life," he added softly, almost to himself, and rubbed his thumb over her soft palm. "What were you like as a little girl?" he asked with a small smile.

Alexandra pursed her lips. "I don't remember being a little girl," she replied thoughtfully. "I think I was always serious and always had responsibilities."

"And who took care of you?" Parker crooned.

His thumb made circles lightly on her skin, leaving a path of tingling sensations that radiated outward through her. Alexandra briefly closed her eyes, fighting the lovely languid feeling that was spreading through her limbs. She didn't feel so cold now. "I didn't need to be taken care of." When he didn't respond, she raised questioning eyes to his brown features. Parker was watching her intently.

"I'm not so sure about that," he murmured. Then, with an effort, his mood lightened and he looked at her mischievously. "Shall I tell the lady's fortune?"

Alexandra nodded with a smile. Parker pretended deep concentration over the delicate lines etched in her hand.

"Swami says the lady will have a bright future . . ."

"As in, under spotlights?" she grinned.

"Very possible," he hedged. He frowned over the slender limb. "I see that she is very talented. There is a great opportunity coming her way that will bring her many followers."

"That sounds intriguing," Alexandra chuckled.

"Ahhh, I also see someone with her."

"You do?" Alexandra asked, forgetting this was make-believe, and bending forward earnestly.

Parker nodded sagely, tracing the lines along her fingers. "Yes . . . yes, his image is coming in clearly now."

"*His* image?" Alexandra questioned.

"Yes. He's tall . . . dark . . ."

"And handsome," she finished the predictable description with a grin. "No doubt we're talking about you." She was going to pull her hand free, but Parker held fast.

"I didn't know you thought me tall, dark, and handsome," Parker said, with provocative intent. His brow arched.

Alexandra grimaced at him, but was embarrassed that she was so readily caught in her admission. "It could be you," she murmured.

"Could be. Is there anything wrong with that?" he questioned smoothly. "What if someone came into your life and you fell in love, Alex? Would there be room for him, too? Or are you only dedicated to your career?"

Alexandra became alert now, as Parker examined too closely the questions she hadn't asked in a long time. He had already been the someone she was in love with. And she might very well have given up her singing, her golden chance, for him. But he had made one decision, ending that possibility, and she had made another. She would not give up her goals so easily a second time.

Parker leaned across the table, his hand squeezing her fingers almost painfully as he questioned and searched, pinning Alexandra in place with his intensity. Her heart began to race, and she sat staring at him.

"I want a chance, Parker," she began softly. "You had yours. My father even had his. My sister seems to get more chances than seems fair because everyone finds it hard to tell her no. I just want to try for myself. I *need* to."

There was a long silence as Parker's brows drew together. He did see how much it meant to her. He tried to hold his feelings in check, but there was a tight, forceful plea to his whispered words to her.

"I know you do." He stared at her as though determined to make that clear. "But it's hard and lonely out there, Alex. I know, I've been there, and I just don't want to see you hurt. I don't want to . . ." He stopped suddenly, clamping down on the rest of the sentence.

Alexandra felt the chill of strong emotion crawl over her, bringing moisture to her eyes. "I've been hurt before," she whispered.

Parker's jaw tensed and twitched and he clasped her hands warmly and protectively in his own. "Will you ever forgive me, Alex?"

She blinked to clear her vision. Suddenly, the anger was all gone. There was only regret, because she could still love him, and there seemed to be no chance for them now. She swallowed hard, and was actually able to smile. "I already have," Alexandra said. So now he knew she didn't really hate him. But she would not let him know she loved him more than ever. There would be no point in that kind of confession.

They were interrupted when the waitress brought their check and began clearing the table. Then, coyly smiling with youthful feminine charm at a good-looking man, she asked if he was Parker Harrison.

"I'm afraid so," Parker said dryly.

The young woman found that amusing and laughed. Then she wanted an autograph. Then three other people made uncertain approaches to their table with the same request.

The electric intimacy they shared had been intruded upon thoughtlessly, Alexandra noted. Watching Parker sign autographs politely, she also had a glimpse into what his life must be like day after day, being well known and so visible, the demands made, the concessions granted, the compromises.

The waitress departed, as did the patrons who'd recognized him. Parker had given them his attention, as he had the guests the week before at the wedding, but the moment was gone and he quickly was, once again, the Parker she knew.

Parker stood and looked at his watch, and back to her. "Ready?" he asked, making no further reference to their unfinished exchange.

Alexandra swallowed and nodded and pulled her hat on once more against the cold. She knew grimly now that Parker meant was she ready for much more than just the audition at Blues Alley.

It occurred to Alexandra that everyone gathered around the small stage and lit piano would probably know who Parker Harrison was. But he didn't enter the club at all beyond escorting Alexandra into the dim entrance. Once there, he'd turned to her, his face shadowed and solemn.

"Remember what you used to say when I was working on a new piece of music? Even before you'd heard it?" he asked throatily.

Alexandra hesitated, then she remembered. "Yes. I'd say, 'I'm going to love it, Parker. So will everyone else.' "

He nodded. Then he stepped forward, gathering Alexandra into his arms. He was holding her close, with his cheek bent to touch her own, and their skin began to warm up as he surprised her with the sudden embrace.

"They're going to love you, Alex, but so will I," he whispered.

And before she could say anything, before she could question what he'd said or if she'd heard correctly Parker moved his head to settle his frosty lips over hers. Her response was immediate; she was melting against him and answering the serious urging of his mouth and tongue.

His kiss confused her, fogged her thinking, made her forget what she was going to ask, even made her forget her fear. His hands rode up her back to hold her head as he purposefully gentled his kiss and let his lips caress and tease at her until Alexandra wanted to press closer to him and have him send her senses reeling delightfully again.

He wanted her. She knew he did, and admitted to herself that it would mean something different, something more to her as a woman this time and not as a teenager, to have him love her. Alexandra wanted to feel, too, how they'd changed and grown.

Parker abruptly released her, and pulled open the club doors to step back into the cold before she could recover herself, or change her mind about the audition. Alexandra stood still for a shaky moment, her breath caught in her throat while she still savored the feel of his mouth. The door swished closed behind him. She pulled herself together with a sigh, and went through an inner door.

There were several men and women gathered near the piano and stage, a number of others still wearing outer coats, like herself, who were hopeful auditioners. They sat quietly, scattered in chairs through the room, which looked different and imposing with its house lights up, the magic of late night lighting and decorations gone.

Alexandra slowly approached the small group of people. Spotting her through a curling haze of stale smoke and air, the pianist snapped his fingers at her and held out his hand.

"Let's see your stuff, baby," he mouthed abruptly around a smelly cigar. There was no greeting and there were no accommodations.

For a moment, Alexandra had no idea what he meant, until she remembered the music sheets in her shoulder bag. She hastily pulled them out and gave them to the burly man. He glanced indifferently at them, and added the sheets to a small pile on the piano top.

A man and woman seated at a small, cluttered table beckoned her forward. They barely looked at Alexandra as they asked her name and where she'd last performed. She felt mildly annoyed at their offhanded attitude, and when she was asked what she was going to do, Alexandra foolishly answered, "To sing."

The man and woman looked at each other and laughed. "We kind of figured that out. We want to know *what*. What's your style, your program? Know what I'm saying?" the woman said patronizingly.

Taking a deep breath, Alexandra answered, "I guess I do ballads and some love songs. One or two slow numbers."

"Show tunes don't go over so big here. Can you give us some deep soul?"

Alexandra mutely shook her head.

"Okay, Baby. Take a seat." The woman gestured toward the open room.

Looking around at the others, Alexandra noticed two women, a musician testing out his trumpet, and a pianist reading the *Washington Post*. One of the women was doing her nails, and the other hummed quietly to herself.

What struck Alexandra as odd was the way everyone

ignored everyone else, seemingly unconcerned about the competition, or as if being here for the same reason precluded being friendly and open. Alexandra found it cold, but couldn't bring herself to break through the imposed silence to ask where they'd performed before or what their career goals were. She wanted to ask if they were nervous, too, and to ask the two attractive women how they would dress for their shows if chosen. Just simple questions that would have established a common ground of support and understanding for all of them, something Alexandra needed. But no one else there seemed to need that connection. So Alexandra sat alone, waiting her turn, feeling isolated and insignificant, and wishing Parker was holding and kissing her again. She began to daydream and lose track of her surroundings, her imagination entertaining her.

Two hours later, the trumpet player was hired, as were one of the two women and Alexandra. The managers told her she had a nice, easy presence, almost romantic. They hired her for two weekends, and she would begin in a month. She'd be paid a salary plus tips, and she had to provide her own outfits.

It was quick and professional, and once the shock wore off, Alexandra felt more bewildered than elated. The excitement that she'd expected would accompany her selection never materialized. She felt relief that the audition was over and had been a success, as Parker had said it would, but already she could sense her worry, and the anticipation of performing in front of an audience that was going to be much more discerning than the patrons at The Outer Edge. She was given a contract to look over, sign, and return sometime before the start of her show.

There were no signs of pleasure or encouragement from the management. With a curious sense of disappointment, Alexandra went to find Parker, who was waiting outside the club.

He was standing under the now-lit canopy, smoking a cigarette, deep in thought. He turned at the sound of the door opening and watched Alex exit. He scanned her smooth, calm face for a long moment. She only frowned at him.

"Were you standing out here all this time?"

"No. Too cold for that. I went to a record store a few blocks from here and got some tapes." He patted one of his pockets. "And I stopped to shop for a gift." He patted the other pocket, but didn't elaborate. "When do you start?" Parker asked confidently, tossing away the cigarette, and pulling up the collar of his coat.

"Next month . . ." Alexandra answered breathlessly.

She expected Parker to kiss her or hug her, or in some way, bring back the magic he'd created before she'd gone in to audition. She suddenly felt as if she desperately needed it, as if it was the only thing she was sure of in the last few hours. But Parker made no move toward her. He only curved a corner of his mouth and stuffed his hands into his pockets.

"Congratulations," he murmured.

Alexandra was disappointed, not hearing the pleasure she'd expected from him.

"This calls for a celebration. How about dinner and champagne?" he asked.

Alexandra shook her head. "I can't. I have a show tonight at The Outer Edge, and I always cook for my father on Sundays." She saw his even acceptance of this and thought quickly. "Would you like to come home to dinner with me tomorrow?"

Briefly, a hesitation and wariness passed over Parker's strong features, and his jaw tensed nervously. Then his face relaxed, and finally he smiled warmly. "I can't tell you the last time I had a home-cooked meal. I'd like very much to meet your father. It's time," he ended mysteriously, and Alexandra nodded in agreement.

Chapter Seven

The house where Alexandra and her sister were raised was a small, simple, two-story wood frame house in a neighborhood where all the houses looked pretty much the same. The middle-class black community was a quiet suburb in Virginia, just an hour or more outside of D.C., and accessible by Metro and bus. The colors and wood trim of the neighborhood houses changed here and there, and some residents had done more elaborate landscaping than others. Some homes were in disrepair and needed work, some looked freshly sided or painted. Alexandra's childhood home fell somewhere in the middle.

As Parker got out of his car, he slowly looked over the neighborhood. Even though it was night, he had a clear sense of order, quiet, and community. He smiled to himself wistfully. He, who had grown up in a large, attached townhouse, locked in between a long row of like structures, had always wanted to live like this, with trees and lawns and spaces between the houses, with driveways and backyards and neighbors who invited you over. The apartment he'd had in Washington the year he'd first met Alex had certainly not come close to fulfilling his fantasy of home, but then, being in D.C. served another purpose:

it placed distance between him and his family and was temporary enough not to matter.

He and Alexandra had never spoken of their childhood or of where they'd grown up. In a way, when they'd first met, perhaps they were both trying to get away from it, to live it down; both were anxious to begin a life that was different from the past. But Parker had traveled enough, had gone and come back enough to realize he'd always wanted to return home to something like this.

Alexandra had always been less sure. As she stepped out of the car, she unconsciously scanned her old neighborhood, as if deciding whether it was good enough, wondering what Parker thought of it. Even now, as they slowly approached the porch of her family home, Alexandra wondered nervously why Parker was smiling. Was he amused or surprised?

Alexandra herself was more than a little surprised at the meeting between her father and Parker. There was an almost imperceptible moment when the two men shook hands and silently measured one another before Mr. Morrow stated with an odd pensiveness, "Well, well. It's a real pleasure to finally meet you."

Parker was impressed with the firm grip of George Morrow, whose hands were thin, long-fingered, and sinewy, the hands of a piano player. He also had the dark, intense eyes of his daughter, observant and filled with feeling. He was hardly taller than Alex.

"Same here," Parker responded to Mr. Morrow's quietly cordial welcome. "I told Alex it was time."

Alexandra smiled at the way they greeted each other, as if they'd always known one another and hadn't been in touch for years. Of course, her father knew who Parker Harrison was. It was just interesting to have him treat Parker comfortably and easily as he would any longtime friend visiting the family. Mr. Morrow showed no surprise or curiosity about how his eldest daughter had come to know someone of Parker's standing and reputation. Alexandra wondered why he didn't.

Alexandra was further surprised to see the two men hit it off right away, as if they already knew and understood a lot about each other, but they were an incongruous pair. Parker, neatly and expensively attired, towered over her shorter, slightly built father in his loose, limp trousers, a favorite worn plaid shirt with too-short sleeves, and bedroom slippers. Neither of the two men was the least interested in putting on airs or in impressing the other. Once introduced, it was as though they'd always known each other. Parker barely had a chance to remove his leather topcoat before her father was engaging him in a comfortable conversation about how he enjoyed having company. This led, in some mysterious way Alexandra couldn't follow, into sports and spring training of the ball teams.

Her presence was suddenly ignored, and with a rueful chuckle, she slipped away to the kitchen at the back of the split-level house, where she made a weekly inventory of what was needed from the market. As she wrote out her shopping list, she listened to the low murmuring and occasional laughter from the living room and smiled at the sense of warmth and family she felt with the two men together.

It was surprising that her father was being more than just polite with Parker. Her father had never spoken kindly of professional performers. He was honest in admitting that most of them were very talented and real nice, too, but he didn't feel any of them lived in the real world. Alexandra knew that this attitude accounted for her father's less than enthusiastic acknowledgment of her own desire for a music career.

Alexandra peeked into the living room at one point and found her father and Parker deep in what seemed to be a serious conversation. She retreated back to the kitchen, but hoped her father wasn't doing something totally embarrassing, like asking Parker what his intentions were.

Alexandra began preparing Sunday dinner, which consisted of mashed potatoes, sauteed chicken in a lemon sauce, kernel corn, and a salad. She then set the dining table in the small alcove off the kitchen. These simple chores of making dinner for her father always managed to bring her back to earth, the "real world," as her father reminded her. And there was certainly a sense that her father's welfare and needs had more importance than music. In this, Alexandra also believed she could do both. After all, other people managed.

As she laid out placemats, her movements were stilled when she heard the strains of the old family piano. It was Parker playing, and although his touch and selection of keys were idle, it was easily recognizable, even on the ill-tuned and ancient keyboard. He finally settled into a melody he'd composed several years ago that had firmly established his own special style in the music world. As she continued her preparations, Alexandra experienced almost personal pride because perhaps she, better than anyone else, knew how far Parker had come.

In the living room, Parker was impressed by the pride Alexandra's father showed in his piano. It was a good, serviceable instrument, and when Parker ran his fingers absently over the keys, the sound was still clear. He smiled to himself. This was where Alex had learned to play! She had watched her father and followed his example.

Now that he'd finally met George Morrow, Parker

realized he liked him. George seemed to be a simple man who was happy with his life, one who didn't moan or regret that it could have been something more. His credo was simply to live honestly and try not to hurt anyone. As a father raising children alone, he was as protective of his daughters as Parker knew he would be. It was good that they had this chance to meet and to dispel any possible misconceptions.

"Never could afford a better piano," George Morrow said with a wry shake of his head. "But this old baby, it's held up pretty good. I used to sit in the middle with a daughter on each end, and Lord, the sounds that would fill this house." He rasped out a chuckle at his own memory, as he watched the wistful playing of the younger man. "I wish I could have given my girls the training you had."

Parker raised his brows, his wide mouth slanted into a slight smile. "I'd say your daughters had the best kind of training—it came straight from your heart. I envy them that."

From the kitchen, Alex heard the music stop for a while, and then begin again, but now with her father seated at the bench. His style was untrained and chaotic but lively and definitely musical. He was bold and inventive at the keyboard, unmindful of techniques which he didn't know while bringing into play his own. Parker's playing was smooth and neat. But only now that she was able to hear a comparison did Alexandra gain an awareness of her father's individual and unique style. Absently considering the differences in ability, Alexandra went to inform the two men that dinner was ready.

Her father watched her approach from over his left shoulder, beaming from a thin, excited face. Her father brought his music to a flourished, noisy end.

"Did you hear that?" Mr. Morrow laughed. "There's

life in the old joints yet." He wiggled his thin, knobby fingers in the air.

"Yeah, you sound real good. Carnegie Hall next?" Alexandra teased.

Her father merely grunted out a derisive laugh of doubt as he rubbed his aching fingers. "Maybe not Carnegie Hall, but I can certainly start some feet tapping in church."

She turned smiling eyes to Parker, grateful because her father was having such a good time. "I'm glad that there's no rivalry between you."

The two men exchanged quick glances and her father's expression was guileless.

"Why should there be?"

Parker pursed his lips and said quietly, "We've just had a chance to talk and get to know one another." He smiled at George Morrow. "Your father is a wise man."

Alexandra was slightly astounded by Parker's confession. Her father waved the comment away, and Parker began to read the music sheet on the piano stand.

"Your father told me he wrote that piece," Parker began, but was interrupted by Mr. Morrow.

"Oh, that was years ago. It wasn't anything," George Morrow said, embarrassed, as he half turned toward his daughter.

Alexandra's gaze swung back sharply to her father. "I didn't know you wrote that." Not only was Alexandra surprised, she was fleetingly disappointed that she never knew of her father's input into the work.

Mr. Morrow was looking very uncomfortable now, not used to being the topic of conversation. He shrugged and plunged his hands into his trouser pockets. "What's to know? I was just fooling around a bit. I didn't think it would come to much, and it didn't."

"Perhaps the timing was all wrong," Parker said introspectively. "Sometimes those who care least about the recognition will find themselves pushed into the limelight. And those who want it most never find it."

Mr. Morrow was shaking his head vigorously. "I never wanted all that. I just enjoyed the music. I played just for myself."

"All the same, your music is good. I'd like to hear more," Parker said to the older man.

"We'll see, we'll see," Mr. Morrow responded demurely, but he was still pleased.

As her father slowly got up from the piano and Parker moved out of his way, Alexandra caught sight of two glasses on the piano top. She glanced quickly at her father. She indicated the glasses with a tilt of her head.

"You know this isn't a good idea, Daddy."

"Aw, come on, girl. That's the only drink I've had in days."

Alexandra ignored her father's mild protest, not wanting to debate the point right then. She headed back to the kitchen, taking the glasses with her and leaving the two men to follow.

Alexandra poured the contents of the glasses into the sink and began digging for serving utensils from a drawer. When she turned, Parker was standing in the doorway, watching her. Alexandra leaned a hip against a counter, and stared down at the utensils in her hand.

"My father has a heart condition and high blood pressure. He's not supposed to drink."

"I'm sorry. I'd forgotten, and he never said anything," Parker replied apologetically.

Alexandra sighed heavily. "I'm not surprised. I can't begin to tell you the time I've spent trying to convince that man to take better care of himself. If I'm not around, he doesn't."

Parker chuckled at the picture she drew of her father. "He sounds stubborn. Just like someone else I know."

Alexandra shrugged at the comparison and chose to ignore it. "Anyway, there are so few things he enjoys anymore—like fooling around on the piano, or a drink now and then. And he's often alone, now that Christine and I are on our own."

"Do you see your sister often?"

Only when she wants something, Alexandra thought to herself ruefully. "No, not often." Alexandra answered vaguely. She turned around to the cabinets again and reached for glasses on an overhead shelf.

"You never talk about her. Is she musical, like you and your father?" Parker asked, moving closer to stand behind her.

"No," Alexandra chuckled dryly. "Christine has other talents."

"Like what?"

Alexandra hesitated in her motions, acutely aware of Parker's nearness. She was aware that suddenly it seemed only to set her on edge, as if she expected it to lead to something more complex between them.

"If you ever meet her, you'll know," she responded absently, nearly losing track of the conversation. He was standing so close now that she could feel his subtle body heat.

"And does she have freckles like you?" His voice had gotten curiously low and seductive, and frantically Alexandra wondered why he was doing this to her now. He was deliberately attacking her senses. Slowly she turned to face him, giving him a chance to see the dots sprinkled across her face.

"No. No, I'm the only one."

"You see?" Parker murmured, his eyes ignoring the freckles, and seeming to search everywhere else, particularly her mouth. "I always said you were different and special."

Parker only smiled at the expression in Alexandra's eyes. He didn't know how to say she was also different to be around in the home where she grew up, with her father, who was a lively, funny, very talented man of extraordinary good sense. He particularly didn't know how to tell Alexandra how much softer and more feminine and more comfortable she seemed here.

Here, in her childhood home, Parker could forget about their mutual involvement in music, which seemed all-consuming. Here, the music was for pure pleasure, adding to the quality of their lives, which was normal, real, grounded. Parker saw clearly in Alexandra, as she stood here in her family kitchen looking both pretty and unusually domestic, what he wished he could come home to, what he knew he could never leave.

There was a quickening of Alexandra's heartbeat as she felt the virile magnetism of Parker standing so near. His presence made her feel softly vulnerable, and she, too, was seeing him differently. She wondered what he was thinking. What was it that was causing Parker to seem so intimate?

"Alex . . ." he began, and then stopped as she watched curiously the play of emotions over his strong, dark features. He raised a hand and with a bent index finger ran his knuckle down the side of her neck just below her ear. He could see Alexandra let out a shaky breath, her skin reacting, quivering. "I'll bet no one knows how sensitive you are right there," he teased in a low, hoarse voice.

"I haven't just been sitting around for ten years, Parker," Alexandra said, with a touch of coyness.

"Has there been someone else?" he asked, suddenly curious.

Alexandra's chin lifted, the stubborn pride clear in her eyes and mouth. "I hope you don't expect me to answer that."

Parker tilted his head for a moment to study her further, his eyes once again more interested in her pouting mouth. "You just did," he replied, his mouth twisting in sad irony. He slowly took the silverware and glasses from her hands and put them on the counter behind her. Then he placed his hands on her narrow waist and in the same movement pulled her closer to him until he could rub his hard chin against her temple.

The action was slow, but still happened too fast for Alexandra to do anything beyond bracing her hands on his upper arms and letting her thighs rest intimately against his.

He sighed. "I'm not surprised there may have been other men in your life. But I don't want to know about it. Pretty arrogant of me, isn't it?" he said tightly. "I remember everything about you."

His voice grew husky, the utterance of words warm on her skin, creating a tingling that began to drift down and throughout her. Parker closed his arms gently around her until her breasts were pressed into his chest. Alexandra clutched his upper arms, her heart beginning to race.

"I can remember holding you just like this against me, knowing you trusted me."

"Parker . . ." she began, only to have him squeeze her silent. She sensed that he needed to talk and say these things. She needed to hear them. But not now.

"But the best part was making love to you. I remember

making love to you most of all. I have all the memories of those moments."

It was an incredible admission to make just then, and Alexandra could only stand stunned, quiet, and enormously excited as she listened. The intimacy of their bodies together sent a curl of warm passion coursing through her. She could sense that Parker was trying to say something important and personal to her, without actually saying it. Alexandra's stomach twisted into little knots of desire and tension. Her fingers dug gently into his arms.

Parker pulled back so he could see her face again. "No one else has what you gave to me. I know that now," he said, in a voice that was somewhat poignant and wistful. "And no one else will."

The silence that followed was suddenly like a deep, empty pit that Alexandra felt herself falling into. She blinked away a sort of slumberous desire. She opened her mouth, and not a single word came out.

She never thought of a relationship anymore, because Parker had been the only man she'd ever wanted, and that hadn't worked out. He'd left her. He'd never said he loved her. But did he want her back now?

Alexandra pushed slowly but firmly out of his arms and took a step back. It was by pure chance that Parker Harrison had walked back into her life. His leaving had allowed her to see that she didn't have to rely anymore on someone else to make her happy. And his sudden arrival into her life meant she could stand the risk of letting him go this time in order to fulfill herself.

Alexandra suddenly realized that Parker had probably made the best decision years ago. She could do him a favor and not let him continue to feel guilty for it. She would not let him pretend to love her, either.

Alexandra smiled sadly at him, shaking her head. "I've learned to be careful who I give my affections to."

"You should be," Parker remarked smoothly. "I want you to be very selective."

For a moment longer, they stared in silence. And just as Parker bent his head to kiss her, the kitchen door swung open and George Morrow's head popped through.

"Are we eating tonight, or what?" he asked, apparently not fazed at finding his daughter in Parker's arms.

"My fault," Parker apologized, his eyes still thoughtfully on Alexandra. "I had to find out something important."

"I'm serving now," Alexandra said, squeezing past Parker, and reaching for pot holders and the oven door.

"Good," Mr. Morrow boomed. "You two can . . . er . . . finish your private affairs later." And with that, he left.

Parker and Alexandra managed to grin sheepishly at each other before Parker picked up the glasses and followed behind her father.

Dinner started out a little awkwardly, but with Mr. Morrow's unconcerned air of what he might have heard or witnessed in the kitchen, there was soon lots of laughter and funny little stories. Mr. Morrow told Parker all about what his eldest daughter was like as a child. Parker, in turn, told of his upbringing as an only child. Alexandra assiduously avoided mentioning how they'd met, but then Parker, in recounting another anecdote, made it obvious that he and Alex had known each other before. George Morrow silently nodded, but clearly did not seem surprised.

There was, of course, talk of music. Parker was particularly interested in George Morrow's compositions and his lack of attempts to do anything with his work. He asked a lot of questions, and Alexandra was stunned to learn that her fathe apparently had dozens of pieces he'd "tooled" with. George Morrow said he wrote them for the simple love of doing it, and that had always been enough. As far as he was concerned, he *had* done more. He'd passed his talent on to Alexandra, and there was pride and quiet joy in his words.

His admission surprised his daughter, who suddenly realized her father thought far more of her abilities than he'd ever let her know. With a slight tinge of anger, she wondered why he hadn't thought to encourage her more.

"That was good," Mr. Morrow declared with a satisfied sigh and a pat to his flat stomach.

"It sure was. Thanks for sharing it with me," Parker added sincerely, watching Alexandra.

"Oh, anytime," her father offered magnanimously.

Alexandra grimaced at her father's generous sharing of her time.

"Unfortunately, I only get such good cooking on the weekends, myself. For years, she had some grand ideas about becoming a singer, and most of the time she's busy living, breathing, and thinking music."

Quickly Alexandra looked at Parker, who pursed his lips and raised a brow as if in complete understanding.

"My singing is important to me," Alexandra defended stiffly, as she began clearing the table.

"It should be," Mr. Morrow nodded. "But I think you go overboard, Baby. Just because you want it bad doesn't mean it's going to happen. It hasn't happened yet. I don't want to see you count on it so much and be disappointed."

"I won't be," Alexandra argued, but there was a lack of conviction and strength behind the words, as well as an apprehensive tightening of her insides—almost like a warning, or a prediction.

"Besides, I thought you really loved teaching. I would think that would keep you busy enough," Mr. Morrow said.

Parker merely sat there as an interested observer, listening and watching how Alexandra responded to her father. Parker wasn't surprised that she was just as stubborn with him.

"I don't want to just be busy. I want to find out if I'm any good as a singer," Alexandra said, her rising annoyance manifesting itself in the way she rattled the silverware and noisily stacked the dinner plates.

"You are," the two male voices said at once, and Parker and her father looked quickly at each other. Mr. Morrow nodded sharply, glad to have someone in his corner.

"That's fine for you both to say," Alexandra argued heatedly, putting the stacked plates down so hard they clattered dangerously together. She rested a small fist on one saucily elevated hip and looked at her father. "You decided you didn't want a career. Maybe you were worried you weren't good enough, or that others wouldn't think so. Maybe you thought there were too many sacrifices to make." She swung bright, sharp eyes to Parker. "And you're past the years of practice and struggling and can enjoy your talent and success. You *both* decided what you wanted to do and you went for it. That's all I want to do. Why won't you let me try it my way in peace?"

The two men exchanged looks again and Alexandra was suddenly suspicious of some kind of conspiracy against her. She sighed in exasperation. "All I need is a chance and my voice will do the rest."

Mr. Morrow sighed in equal exasperation and threw up his hands in surrender.

"Look at what almost happened last night," Parker reminded her softly.

Mr. Morrow frowned. "At the club? What happened last night?"

"Nothing," Alexandra ground out shortly, coldly eyeing Parker and angry that he had to remind her of that embarrassing moment as well. Parker met her stare with one of his own. "I know what I want," she added firmly.

"Alex, what you want is freedom," Parker said softly.

His words hit so clearly on the truth that Alexandra felt as though the wind had been knocked out of her.

"And something else," he whispered mysteriously. "But what you'll get are managers, agents, hotel rooms, and propositions. You'll spend more of your time on the business of singing than on singing. You'll eat lots of horrible food, not get enough sleep or exercise, not do anything. Everyone you meet will want something from you. And let's say you finally make it. There's your name on the billboard, or the marquee, you've gotten your first record contract, and now come the tours. Forty concerts in three and a half months, until you forget what city you're in, or don't care. When do you see family? Will you have any friends? Not other musicians, but friends who tell you about their perfectly ordinary, unfamous lives, but who make you feel real and at home and don't treat you differently than they ever did. When do you meet a man, fall in love? You believe in love, don't you? How do you squeeze in having a marriage, a family?"

Alexandra was breathless with Parker's observations. "Are we talking about my life, or yours?" she asked astutely.

Parker acknowledged her counterattack with a rueful tilt of his head and a sad smile.

"You're not being fair. I'm capable of compromise,"

Alexandra added. "You've been able to manage, and you look none the worse for a life of being in the spotlight. Would you have me believe that you wouldn't love to go all the way and someday receive a Grammy?"

Parker shook his head and stared at her. "My happiness doesn't depend on a Grammy. I won't let it."

"But I'll also get recognition, appreciation, and a sense of accomplishment," Alexandra reasoned.

"You already have it," Parker declared, "if only you'd let yourself see that."

"What are you two talking about?" Mr. Morrow asked, dazed. He sensed that the conversation had changed to something far more personal between the two young people. His head swiveled back and forth between them.

"Well, from the sound of it, they're *not* talking about music."

All heads at the table turned simultaneously to the entrance, where a young woman stood.

"Hello, Baby," Mr. Morrow beamed.

While Parker sat staring, Alexandra glanced at him quickly to test his immediate reaction to her younger sister, feeling a sinking in her stomach as Parker seemed riveted in place. All conversation about music careers came to an abrupt halt, and for the moment Alexandra was no longer the central topic.

Christine Morrow moved slowly into the room. She acknowledged her father with a brief touch of her red glossed lips to his sunken cheek. She gave her sister a quick smile and passing glance, and then turned the full force of her considerable female charms on Parker.

Alexandra watched the male response to her sister with her usual sense of the inevitable. As she watched the intent brightening of Parker's gaze, she felt a quickening of annoyance. She listlessly brushed table crumbs onto a napkin, and shook it out over a plate. She didn't have to actually watch the unfolding scenario to know what was happening. Her sister was laying claim to the kingdom.

Alexandra had always been assured that she was a very attractive young woman, with appealing youthful features that made her likable. She was not always aware of her own assets, but she'd guessed correctly when she'd decided long ago that she and Christine could not be compared.

At five feet nine inches, Christine Morrow was beautifully proportioned. Her body was slim and curved in total femininity in all the right places. Her skin was more amber than Alexandra's, flawlessly smooth and clear. Christine's hair was cut very short, no more than two inches in length all over, but curly and glossy over her well-shaped head, making her look almost ethereal. She had thick, dark, lovely long lashes that she'd learned to use well since adolescence, keeping her lids demurely lowered until just the moment she wanted to achieve a complete coup and reveal stunning, pale gray-green eyes. The results were always predictable, and Parker was no less a victim now than anyone else who'd never met Christine.

Alexandra was also willing to admit that at twenty-one, Christine knew some things about the world in general, and men in particular, and how to make the best use of both, which made her seem years older than Alexandra. Christine was supremely aware of herself and her effect on others. There was no question that she basked in the attention and admiration, earned or not. Commanding so much attention had also given her undue power over most circumstances in which more than two people were present. She had an instant audience on whom to practice her charms.

"I didn't know you were coming tonight. We would have waited on dinner," Mr. Morrow said.

Christine charmingly wrinkled her pert nose, briefly lifting her sultry gaze from Parker to look with disinterest over the dinner plates.

"Probably something fattening. Besides, I can't stay." Her eyes returned openly to Parker, who was still watching her with a curious intensity that made Alexandra's spirits plummet. "I'm Christine. Should we know each other?"

Despite her turmoil, Alexandra had to raise her brows at her sister's imperial attitude. Not *"Do* we know each other", but *"Should* we." Already she was making her interest known. Alexandra watched as Parker merely smiled, tilted his head in consideration, and showed silent amusement at her question.

"This is Parker Harrison," Mr. Morrow made the introductions.

"Hello," Christine said with delight, smiling at him. She put out a slender, beautifully manicured hand, forcing Parker to stand formally and take it. "I didn't realize you were a friend of the family."

"Well, this is his first visit," Mr. Morrow confessed carefully.

"I'm a friend of Alex's," Parker said smoothly.

"Alex?" Christine questioned, looking to her sister in blank surprise. "He calls you Alex. You never even mentioned you knew Parker Harrison. I *love* his music."

Alexandra pursed her mouth against a retort, and merely smiled. "How thoughtless of me."

"Well, that's okay," Christine cooed. "Now that we've met, we can get to know one another."

She gave Parker a smile that had been known to make more than one man foolish. Alexandra stood up and began to carry the dirty dishes from the table. "I'm sure Parker will like that," she said evenly to Christine. Then Parker stood up as well.

"I would, but in a moment." He lifted a stack of plates. "I'll help with this," he said agreeably to Alex.

She was surprised by the offer. She glanced at her sister and found Christine somewhat nonplussed, as though the dishes could wait, but she shouldn't have to. Alexandra smiled at Parker, but shook her head.

"Thanks, but I can do this. Let Christine entertain you," she said, with a hint of dry humor in her tone. She headed for the kitchen alone. In her wake she could hear Christine's exuberance over meeting Parker, her father's laughter, and Parker's deep-voiced response to Christine's questions.

As she rinsed the utensils and scraped the plates, Alexandra recalled how, when she and Christine were small children, strangers or even friends would fawn over the gorgeous child Christine had been, forgetting the other, older girl standing quietly on the sidelines. In a funny way, she felt a certain pride that Christine was her sister, and she could even admit to a vicarious pleasure at seeing her predictable effect on people, men in particular. But Alexandra also wondered if her sister would ever outgrow her ego-centered need to conquer the entire male population of the civilized world.

She was almost finished with her cleanup when Christine came into the kitchen. Alexandra had half hoped it was Parker, coming to keep her company after all and maybe to secretly hold, caress, and kiss her as he had before. Christine was dressed in a white angora sweater that complimented her brown complexion, a slim black mid-calf skirt, and high-heeled patent leather boots. It was a simple, understated outfit, but Christine had always shown a talent for making simple clothing look very expensive and haute couture. Christine had always wanted to work with fashion, either as a stylist or as a designer. Since finishing school eight months ago, she was still looking for an opportunity to move to New York. Alexandra had no doubt her sister would succeed. She could get anything she wanted.

Christine stood and watched as Alexandra put away dishes. "How did you ever meet someone like Parker Harrison?" she asked innocently.

"Parker and I met when I was in school. I haven't seen him in ten years. He was best man at Brian and Debby's wedding," Alexandra admitted, as she turned to put leftovers in containers or wrap them in foil.

Christine leaned a hip against the edge of the sink and smiled. "I suppose that was better than finding out he was the groom," she commented dryly. "So . . . Parker's the one, huh?"

Alexandra dropped a spoon and quickly stooped to pick it up. "What do you mean by that?" she asked softly, not meeting Christine's sure gaze.

"I mean, dear sister, that he's probably the one who sent you home from school that year looking like you'd lost your best friend. You moped and dragged yourself around all that spring before finally going back the next fall. Was it all because of Parker?"

"No," Alexandra admitted honestly. "I was just scared and confused and inexperienced. Parker had his own set of troubles that had nothing to do with me."

"What about now? Is he strictly hands-off?" Christine asked, with smooth casualness.

Alexandra was thrown by the question. She already wondered if Parker's presence in her life now could lead to anything, but she couldn't assume it would.

"Parker doesn't *belong* to me, Christine. He's a grown man. He can make his own decisions."

Christine pursed her lips and flexed a foot, absently examining the shiny surface of her boot. "Does that mean you're not going to fight for him?"

Alexandra's brows shot up and she laughed at her sister's unexpected question. "How? In a vat of mud, or should we just pull hair? Don't be foolish."

Christine shrugged a shoulder. "I bet he's rich and knows just about everyone. And he's very good-looking," she added with a sly smile.

Alexandra thought with irony at the order of her sister's priorities. "He's quite a bit older than you, too."

Christine made an impatient sound. "That doesn't matter. I like a man who's mature. And the way he looked at me says he doesn't think I'm too young," she said with assurance.

Alexandra saw no reason to point out other differences, such as her sister's short attention span and her lack of interest in music. She smiled benignly at her. "If Parker's interested, then you have nothing to worry about," she said with false levity, and then forced her mind away from the thought of Parker and her sister together. "We didn't expect you tonight. I thought you and your roommate were going to Baltimore."

"No wheels. I came to see if Daddy would lend me the car for a few days." She dangled the car keys from thumb and index finger and smiled triumphantly.

"If you take the car, I won't be able to food shop for Dad for next week," Alexandra reminded her.

"Have the market deliver," Christine shrugged.

"And what about his doctor's appointment on Wednesday?"

"I'll have it back by then."

"Then you'll drive him."

"I can't," Christine moaned contritely. "I have an interview at I. Magnin that I can't miss."

"What's the interview for?"

"Well, not much. One of the perfume houses wants a half-dozen models to walk around squirting customers with their product . . ."

Alexandra chuckled. "And we get to wear some great clothes from one of the boutiques. Maybe we'll even get to keep them."

"Will this lead to anything?"

"I hope. The marketing rep is dating my roommate."

Alexandra sighed and gave up. "Please return the car with gas this time," she said smoothly to Christine, who only waved airily and left the kitchen.

Alexandra stood silently and alone for several moments, listening absently to the laughter coming from the next room. She felt her slow burn begin to roil dangerously inside her. It annoyed her no end that Christine operated on the premise that what she wanted, she got. While Alexandra didn't deny that her sister was genuinely talented, it still frustrated her that so many opportunities came Christine's way simply by virtue of her beautiful face.

For a moment Alexandra, reviewed the recent communication and levels of intimacy that she and Parker had been able to establish after such a long time. She was not indifferent to him, and she wondered now if she really stood in jeopardy of losing what they'd gained together to her sister's interest in Parker.

Alexandra finished the last of the cleaning up in the kitchen. She was reluctant to go back to the living room and sit as an observer while Christine, with her bright personality, controlled the rest of the evening. And Alexandra did not want to see if Parker was going to succumb before her very eyes.

When Alexandra ventured forth at last, Parker was shrugging into his heavy leather coat. He swung around at her approach. She tried not to show her disappointment that he was already leaving.

"Your father told me you'd be staying over tonight."

"Yes, I try to at least one night a week to give him a hand with some household chores."

Parker picked up a couple of composition-type notebooks and tucked them under his arm.

"What's that?" Alexandra questioned, nodding at the books.

Parker looked sheepish. "Your father has agreed to let me see some of his original work. I promised to guard them with my life."

Alexandra had to smile. "That's quite an honor." She looked around. "Where is he?"

Parker gestured toward the door. "He stepped outside to say goodbye to your sister."

"Without a coat on, no doubt," Alexandra commented dryly.

Parker laughed at her worry. "You're a good daughter."

"I hope that's not something to make fun of," she mumbled with a pout.

"No, Alex," Parker said gently, putting a hand on her shoulder and massaging the joint with his fingertips. "It's something to admire." Then he sighed deeply, looking briefly over his shoulder toward the front door, which stood ajar. "So . . . that was Christine." It was a kind of statement that had finality to it, as a fact of irrefutable certainty.

Alexandra crossed her arms over her chest to stop the

start of nervous tremors. "What do you think of her?" she asked lightly, her eyes searching Parker's expression.

He chuckled with a short shake of his head, and arched a brow. "She's one of the most beautiful women I've ever seen. I bet she was deadly at sixteen."

"Long before that," Alexandra admitted without rancor.

"And I bet she always gets her own way."

Alexandra smiled again. "Some find it hard to say no to her."

"What she needs is a very firm hand from someone who can see beyond that gorgeous exterior."

"You seem to read her pretty well," Alexandra commented tightly. Could Parker possibly be interested?

"Believe me, I know the type," Parker said.

He stared at Alexandra, seeing the vulnerable lift to her brows and the soft drooping of her mouth. He would guess that Alex had made more than her share of concessions to someone people found easy to adore. And where had that left Alex? Wanting something that was purely her own that people could admire or find enviable. Her music. Her magnificent voice. For a moment Parker had a realization of what it must have been like, growing up with a sister like Christine. Alexandra had always spoken of her goals and dreams with such iron-clad conviction. Now he understood why.

Parker slowly pulled her closer, releasing her shoulder to slide his fingers around the slender column of her neck, to gently tug until Alexandra's face tilted up to his. Quickly and gently, Parker nibbled and pulled a kiss from her mouth. He kissed her again.

Alexandra felt like he was releasing a tightness that had gripped at her insides ever since Christine's arrival. It frightened and surprised her how much she needed

Parker to touch her. Parker's kiss was as personal and private and every bit as intense as it had been before Christine's arrival. She sighed with relief.

"Thanks for dinner. And the chance to meet your family," Parker whispered softly to her.

"You're welcome," Alexandra croaked out, more formal than she wanted to sound. Parker suddenly bent his head toward her until his forehead touched hers. She could feel the warmth of his breath.

"Do you still hate me, Alexandra Morrow?" he asked in his deep voice.

"I've never really hated you," Alexandra answered honestly. He relaxed his fingers as he let go of her neck and let out his breath. He kissed her briefly again, his lips firm, but so warm and mobile.

"Then that only leaves one other question to be answered, doesn't it? Think carefully what it will be, Alex," Parker suggested quietly.

They stared at one another and then there was a short, impatient tooting of a car horn. Alexandra blinked in a startled expression as she realized he intended to follow Christine, in his own car, back to town.

Parker didn't say any more. Instead, with a pat to her cheek, he turned and went out the door, and shortly the cars motored off into the night.

Alexandra beckoned her father back inside and closed the door. For a moment she felt a shot of jealousy grip her as her sister and Parker drove away. She knew perfectly well what Christine was capable of, and Alexandra's own past inexperience made her feel insecure. Yet she had only to recall that Parker had come to hear her sing on Friday, had encouraged the audition the afternoon before, had kissed her goodnight just moments ago. She smiled thoughtfully as she followed her father back into the living room. She was by no means ready or willing, yet, to concede the evening to Christine.

George Morrow was again seated at the piano where, as Alexandra finished reading the Sunday papers, he'd provided a kind of melancholy background of slow, moody music. It was random and the melodies couldn't be placed to any one composer or musician. Alexandra had wondered idly, though, how much of it was his own. She put the papers aside, approached the piano bench, and sat down unobtrusively next to her father so as not to disturb this rare recital. The musical play continued for another ten minutes before Mr. Morrow let his arms drop away from the keys and he turned his thin, tired face to his elder daughter.

"It's been a long time since I've felt so much like playing. A long time since music brought back so many memories," he smiled wistfully.

"Oh, Daddy, I didn't realize. I'm sorry if bringing Parker home made you uncomfortable or . . ."

Mr. Morrow chuckled softly, shaking his head and raising a hand to hush her. "No, no, Baby. You don't understand. I wasn't uncomfortable at all. It was a *good* time. *Real* good. I like Parker. He reminds me of my younger days . . . my passion."

Alexandra had to smile silently to herself. It was hard to imagine her father having a passion of any kind. Her father again played chords upon the keys with just one hand. The music sounded vaguely familiar to Alexandra, and as he played she could almost anticipate the unfolding notes as the soft, sweet melody touched the quiet air of the room.

"I wrote that for you the day you were born," he said, and smiled fondly at her.

She was surprised, and her widened eyes expressed it. "I didn't know that. I've always loved that piece."

"Yep. Wrote one for Chrissy, too, when she came along. Only she'd never sit still long enough to hear it through. But when you were just a little thing, you'd make me play your piece over and over again. You were four years old when I first realized you were interested in music. Your mother and I head you banging away on the piano one day. You'd pulled yourself up on the stool, and knelt there with your tiny fingers poking at the keys—and singing! You *know* what it must have sounded like." They both laughed over the image.

"Your mother used to say you came by your talent honestly." He sighed again and stopped his playing. "She was always sorry we couldn't afford to give you real music lessons."

Alexandra leaned forward and touched her father's cheek with her lips. "I *did* have real music lessons, Daddy. I had *you* to teach me."

"I did my best. But you know what I mean. My postal salary wasn't bad, but it didn't allow for a lot of luxuries. Then your mother got sick, and I got sick, and . . ."

"You don't have to apologize. I have no complaints," Alexandra said emphatically, but feeling an uneasiness in her heart of hearts, wishing now that she'd been more sensitive, more understanding of how her parents had both worked so hard to give her and Christine the best they could.

Her father nodded in contradiction. "I do have to apologize. You were too young when you suddenly had to take over for your mother when she passed. Too young to have to be a second mother to your sister and a helpmate to me. I knew that your music meant escape in a way and having something of your own. But lots of things happen that you never count on, and I really believe that things usually turn out for the best." He sighed and, shaking his head in some private reminiscence, stood up and stretched his body. Alexandra stood up, too.

"You're tired. Let's just forget this for a while and get you to bed. Tomorrow I'll do some marketing and maybe we'll have lunch somewhere."

As she spoke, Alexandra looped her arm through her father's and walked him to the den behind the stairwell, which had been converted into a small bedroom so he would not constantly have to climb the stairs. Her head was filled with the music played by Parker and her father that evening; but also, she couldn't help but notice the different paths each man's life had taken.

"Daddy?"

"Yeah, Baby?"

"Why didn't you follow through with your music?"

Mr. Morrow looked at his daughter and smiled sadly. "I did. I just didn't have any plans to build a career with it. I just wanted to play a piano. Well, I did, and I was pretty damned good even without training, like Count Basie. I had some good times jammin' with my friends, but that's all it was.

"Then I met your mother, and what with getting married and starting a family, why, music wasn't all that important. I still have it, you understand. The music is still in me, and that's enough for me. I guess the bottom line was, I loved you girls and your mother more than a life on the road all the time."

Mr. Morrow stopped one more time and he looked at his daughter. "Your friend Parker is a sight more talented than I ever could be. His music has taken him straight to the top. Now, that's a dream come true. But he's not happy, and I don't envy him."

Mr. Morrow yawned expansively as Alexandra stared blankly at him. "Do you know why? What did he say to you?"

Her father moved into the room and turned to face her with his hands on the doorknob. "He didn't have to say anything, but I could see what it was. The minute I met him, I knew." He made to close the door. "I see that same thing in you, sometimes. I also see that you're in love with that young man," he chuckled, shaking his head. "Lord, don't I remember what it's like."

"Daddy," she began, with as much calm as she could manage. "It's only been a week or so since Parker and I met again."

He cackled mischievously. "I know, I know. But you've loved him long before now. I *know.*"

Alexandra only stared at her father, absolutely speechless at his observation, and helpless to deny it.

"Don't look so surprised," Mr. Morrow said.

"But what has any of this to do with Parker not being happy? Why shouldn't he be?"

Her father sighed and rubbed his chin with its stubbs of black and grey hair. "You're a smart girl, Alexandra. You'll figure it out," he said, as he gently closed the door.

Chapter Eight

Parker had trouble following the aged Toyota. Christine Morrow drove by her own reckless rules. At first, Parker thought she was just an erratic driver, until it occurred to him that Christine was deliberately leading him a merry, unsafe chase.

The lady liked to be in control.

Once Parker realized what Christine was up to, he had no trouble following her unpredictability. It was her idea that he follow her back into the city, and Parker had agreed. He was familiar enough with D.C. that he didn't believe he could get lost if Christine outmaneuvered him, but he wasn't going to let her do it. Parker had a very clear impression that Christine Morrow liked to test people and push the envelope.

Parker admitted to himself, however, an ulterior motive for agreeing to Christine's idea: he was intrigued by her because she was, as he'd been able to realize in an hour, a total contrast to her sister.

Alexandra had never talked about her younger sister in any detail. Christine had always been mentioned in an offhanded way without been assigned characteristics, personality, looks, or opinions. Now Parker knew why: Christine was a phenomenon that had to be experienced. Although he was not drawn to her as he imagined most males over twelve would be, there was no denying that Christine didn't need to throw out any lures.

Her car turned into a street of restaurants and cafes and she pulled up in front of Emerson's. Parker pulled in behind her, lifting a corner of his mouth in a knowing smile and put his car into neutral. Then he waited.

After thirty seconds, Christine got out of her father's car and walked back to Parker. He rolled down his window.

"Is there a problem?" he asked.

Christine smiled demurely and tilted her head. "I don't know. Is there?"

Parker looked through the windshield. "This isn't the block you told me you lived on."

"That's right. This is a block that happens to have a really nice cafe. I thought maybe we could have a night-cap before . . ." Her lashes lowered. "Before going on home."

"It's not a good idea to drink and drive, especially given your driving skills," Parker said wryly.

Christine shrugged. "Coffee, then."

Parker considered that it might be interesting to watch Christine in action. It might even be entertaining. He inclined his head. "After you . . ."

Christine gave him a triumphant smile and got back into her car to pull it into the lot. Parker followed right behind her.

It was a little after ten, and the dinner crowd had thinned out considerably. Christine's height and regal carriage, her outfit, so understated and so obviously more fashionable than anything else in sight, announced her arrival. She didn't wait to be seated, but found the table she wanted and proceeded in graceful feminine strides. Parker held her chair as she sat, and a waiter left them with menus. Christine draped her coat back over her shoulders and smoothly slid her arms free of the sleeves.

Parker reached for his cigarettes. "Mind if I smoke?"

"Please," she gave permission with a negligent wave of her slender hand.

Parker took his time, openly watching her as she wiggled in her chair to get comfortable. She propped her chin on her hand and quickly looked over the menu. Parker only had to glance briefly about him to see that interested eyes struggled not to stare at the beautiful woman seated across from him.

"So, what is this all about?"

Christine raised a beguilingly innocent face to Parker. "What's *what* all about?"

Parker slowly smiled and exhaled his smoke. "What is it you want to know?"

"I thought it would be nice to get better acquainted, but not in Daddy's living room while he listened. It's obvious you and Alexandra know each other—well, I take it?"

Parker gave nothing away in his expression and didn't respond. How well he and Alexandra knew each other was not Christine's business, and he hoped his silence conveyed that to her. He saw a fleeting doubt in Christine's exotic eyes. "We're good friends."

"I felt left out when I got to the house," she complained.

Parker tapped his cigarette into the ashtray. "We could have gotten better acquainted back there. You didn't stay to visit, and you left rather quickly."

She shrugged. "Don't you think it's nicer this way? One to one?"

Parker chuckled silently. "Christine, with you I honestly don't think it matters."

Christine stared, not understanding his point. She closed her menu. "What were you fighting about when I came in?"

Parker arched a brow and needlessly shifted the ashtray. "It wasn't a fight. We were having a discussion."

"About what?" she asked persistently.

"Music," he said vaguely.

"You're very good at it," she complimented.

"So is Alex."

Christine shrugged lightly. "Did . . . *Alex* talk about me?"

"Actually, no."

"I'm not surprised."

"Why?"

She wiggled in her chair again, her expression charming and thoughtful. "Alexandra and I are different. She's too dreamy."

"And you're full of life, a go-getter, and if you're not famous someday, you're certainly going to be rich."

Christine smiled. "How did you guess?"

"You and your sister *are* different, but you're more alike than you realize."

Christine looked disappointed at the comparison. "Let's not talk about Alexandra."

"What would you like to talk about?"

"You and me," she said softly.

Parker narrowed his eyes against the cigarette smoke and inhaled. He suddenly thought of the concert halls and arenas, the stages and clubs where he'd performed worldwide. He thought of the hundreds of women he'd met, some beautiful, some exotic, some incredibly sexy, and all with an interest in him that always had a hidden agenda.

He thought of the gushing compliments, the sometimes painfully obvious ploys of trying to gain his attention and affections. He thought of all the lonely times when he wished he could just relax and not be *on*, when he wished not everyone was expecting him to be, when everyone didn't want *something* from him.

Parker thought of all the people, but especially the women, who tried to link themselves to him. Not *for* him, but *because* of him. He could only think of one person who'd always treated him like a normal person: Alexandra.

"We've only just met, Christine. There is no 'you and me.' "

"But that's why I thought it was a good idea to stop. We can get a chance to know each other."

"What do you think of your sister's talent, her ambitions?" Parker asked quietly.

Christine became impatient. "Why are you so interested in Alexandra?"

Parker waited.

She shrugged. "Her voice is nice. It's pretty, but nothing special. All this fuss and bother over her. She's been singing for years. She doesn't even know how to go about getting well known."

"How would you do it?" Parker asked.

"I'd meet people. I'd always be where things were happening, and believe me, I wouldn't let anything stop me."

Parker nodded, putting out his cigarette. "That's how you have to do it sometimes," he agreed.

Christine beamed. "See? We're two of a kind."

"What would you do if you didn't become famous?"

She leaned across the table. "Marry someone who was. Alexandra would never do that. She's the kind who would marry for love. She believes in it." Christine tilted her head. "I don't know what went on with her when she was in school that first semester, but she suddenly gave up and came home. She moped and cried and was depressed because I think she was in love. Who needs that?" She tilted her head. "Was it with you? You didn't let love get in your way."

Parker frowned and burned under the painful truth of Christine's cold observation. It struck him as doubly ironic and sad that Christine, whom he wouldn't have credited an hour ago with having much depth, was showing a remarkable degree of intuitiveness. Parker was less reluctant to admit how her insights were causing him to freshly evaluate the year he and Alex had first been lovers. For one thing, it wasn't that he hadn't let love get in the way. It was only that he hadn't realized that what he was feeling was love. He had never known it before. Not like what Alex had given him: faith, hope, and herself.

"What if I told you I believe in love, too?" Parker asked.

"Then maybe you can change *my* mind," Christine laughed lightly.

"That's an interesting challenge," Parker murmured with a smile. "How would you like to come with me to hear Alex perform next weekend?"

"What has that got to do with you and me?"

"I'm trying to change your mind about love, remember? You might learn something," Parker said with a wink.

"Welcome back, Mrs. Geison-Lerner," Alexandra exclaimed over the phone, and was answered with a laugh.

"Thank you, thank you. I'm still not used to being called 'Mrs.,' but it sounds just lovely."

"How was the honeymoon? Did you guys ever leave your hotel room for air, or to eat?"

Debby giggled. "Eventually. When we started getting weak and noticed dark circles under our eyes. Then we made up for the lost time by sitting in the sun for days. When my sunburn fades, I think I'm going to have a great tan."

"I'm happy to say I don't have such problems," Alexandra teased.

"Lucky you."

"In any case, welcome home."

"I'm not so sure," Debby murmured dryly. "It's rather disappointing to leave Barbados in sandals and arrive in Washington to four inches of snow."

"Well, spring is coming. April showers should be next, followed closely by the cherry blossoms."

Debby groaned. "Can't wait that long. I want to go back to Barbados." Alexandra's laugh was muffled in a tissue as she blew her nose. "Oh, I'm sorry, Alexandra. Here I am complaining and moaning, and you're fighting a nasty cold."

"The battle is over; I lost," Alexandra corrected on a sniffle.

"Has the weather been so bad?"

"No more than can be expected for this time of year. My resistance was low. I think I've been overdoing it," Alexandra confessed, tucking her feet further under her robe. She pulled it closed around her throat and reached for more tissues from the box next to her.

"Did any of my classes give you a hard time?" Debby asked contritely.

"Oh, no. They were fine, no trouble at all."

"I had my first class yesterday since getting back, and all I heard was how much fun Ms. Morrow's classes are, and how come *we* don't play games."

"I'm glad they enjoyed the sessions."

"I think you've spoiled them forever," Debby lamented.

"But I also made them work very hard."

"How's prep coming for your audition? It's just a few more weeks, isn't it?"

Alexandra snuggled more into the corner of her sofa, and took a tiny sip of the orange juice she'd poured over ice. In all honesty, the audition had not been paramount in her thoughts, and because it wasn't, she didn't know if she should be concerned or relieved.

"Well, I haven't had one voice lesson in the whole time you were gone. There were the classes to teach. I'm doing extra tutoring to prepare some of my kids for the Kennedy Center auditions in August, and my father has his ups and downs, and then I switched clubs after Parker took me to Blues Alley . . ."

"Parker," Debby interrupted sharply. "Wait a minute. Did you say Parker?"

Too late, Alexandra realized that Parker's name had slipped out, and of course Debby had noticed. There was no way to retract her innocent comment, but Alexandra also knew that having said this much, she'd have to explain more. She didn't want to explain a relationship which she still didn't understand.

Alexandra hesitated. "He came to hear me at The Outer Edge and persuaded me to try out for Blues Alley. I was accepted, and I start in another week. If I ever get rid of my cold . . ."

"Boy, you *have* been busy the last two weeks," Debby remarked. "And I thought you weren't interested in

Parker. At the wedding, you gave the impression you found him annoying."

"I know, I know," Alexandra said hastily. "But the fact is, Parker and I had met before. When you and I were in school."

Debby was very silent for a moment, and then she sighed deeply. "Oh, I get it. A love affair gone sour?"

"Not sour, just gone. It's a long story," Alexandra said lamely. She really wasn't inclined to go into details over the phone.

Debby groaned. "Oh, Lord. When I think about how Brian and I plotted to get you two together! You must have wanted to kill us."

Alexandra shrugged. "It was awkward. But Parker and I thought it best just to play along. I didn't want to spoil your day." Alexandra chuckled soundlessly. "He didn't even remember me right away."

Debby sighed again. "Well, it sounds like he got over *that* quickly enough. Can I ask what you two have been doing the last two weeks? On second thought, maybe I'd better not."

Alexandra thought instantly of Debby's wedding night and the sparking of passion between herself and Parker. She certainly couldn't tell Debby about their having made love when it had been born of both anger and regret. She couldn't even tell Debby of her ambivalent feelings because so much was predicated on a past that now seemed so unreal, and so long ago. Whatever she and Parker were to each other now probably had little to do with the past.

"Mostly we've been getting to know each other all over again," Alexandra said. "I took him to meet my father, and he had dinner with us." She paused significantly. "He met Christine."

Debby chuckled softly. "That must have been worth

the price of admission. Did he lose his cool altogether and go ga-ga? Or is he still interested in you?"

"All it is *is* interest. Maybe no more than morbid curiosity because we knew each other before," Alexandra sighed. And no, Parker had not lost his cool over her sister. At least, not so she could tell.

That night, after Parker had left with Christine, Alexandra was angry with her sister for smartly manipulating the rest of the evening, and at Parker and herself for allowing it to happen. If she'd wanted to, Alexandra knew she could have made it impossible for Christine to have her father's car. She could have changed her mind about staying the night with her father and had Parker drive her home. But Alexandra had *never* allowed herself to be drawn into her sister's plotting, and she wasn't about to start now.

In any case, it had become a mute issue. Parker had called her later that night to thank her again for dinner and for the chance to meet her father. And Christine had not talked about what had happened after she'd left the house with Parker, a very clear indication that absolutely nothing had happened.

"Well, how about you? How deep is your interest in Parker these days?" Debby hazarded cautiously, sensing the conflict in her friend.

For a quick second, Alexandra thought of denying her feelings, but she couldn't see the point, and knew that perhaps saying it out loud would ease the tightness in her chest, the holding in of real feelings. She took a deep breath and plunged into the truth.

"I've always been in love with Parker Harrison, Debby. That's never changed. But I don't know how he feels about me. I've never really known. I never expected to see Parker again, and I'm confused. And if you repeat any of this to *anyone*, Brian is going to be a widower," she added tightly.

"I don't understand. You love him, but . . . you're resisting?"

"Yes," Alexandra said vehemently. "Parker once made a choice between me and his music, and I lost. Yes, I'll resist, if this is just another phase in his life, like last time. Yes, if he doesn't understand how important a music career is to me, just as his music is to him."

Debby laughed at that. "Given my choice, I'd rather have Parker."

"Why can't I have both?" Alexandra asked quickly.

"Oh," Debby said softly. "So you *do* want him."

Alexandra bit her lip and wiped the raw skin under her nose with the tissue. "It sometimes doesn't matter very much what we want, Debby. Things have a way of not always working out."

Debby sighed. "Maybe it's because we sometimes want the wrong things. Things we only think we want. Sometimes we go after things that aren't good for us."

Alexandra shifted restlessly. "I wish someone would write a user's manual so a person would know," she said with a sarcastic chuckle.

Debby laughed. "You wouldn't believe it anyway. So, tell me about Blues Alley."

Even the mention of it caused Alexandra's stomach to churn. She knew that in all honesty, she was nervous. But somewhere, there was another fear. Alexandra pretended that the nebulous feeling churning within her had no significance and wasn't real at all.

"There's nothing to tell, except that I have a show Friday and Saturday for two weeks. If they like me, perhaps I'll get invited back."

"I don't hear a lot of enthusiasm," Debby chided lightly. "You're about to make your debut."

The uncomfortable gnawing kept at Alexandra's insides. "I . . . I think it's my cold. It's made me a little tired, and I'm trying to get over it before my first weekend at the club," Alexandra improvised. "Besides, I don't want to get too excited. I can still flop, you know."

"I don't believe that, but I understand how you feel. Brian's going to be thrilled when he hears. Would it bother you if we came and acted as your official fan club? We'll bring lots of applause."

"Only if I deserve it," Alexandra advised, with a small shrug of her shoulder.

"How about your Dad, and Christine? Will they be there?"

"My father said he'd come on Saturday. He says he's giving me one night's grace to get over the jitters. I have no idea about Christine. She's not impressed with my singing anyway."

"And Parker? Since it was his idea, I suppose he'll be there, too?"

Alexandra shredded the tissue in her slender hand. She tried to infuse offhanded indifference into her tone. "I don't know. He didn't say he would."

"You could have asked him," Debby said in a soft voice.

Yes, she could have. But Alexandra was silent because it had never occurred to her to do something that straightforward. And she wasn't giving herself or Parker enough credit that it was important that he be there. She was not at all sure of what Parker expected of her. In any case Alexandra believed Parker had to make the next move.

"I never got a chance to." Alexandra stretched the facts

a bit. "As I said, Christine made a timely grand entrance and everyone's attention was diverted."

Debby groaned. "Yes, that would do it. I can guess what happened next. Parker was dazzled right before your very eyes."

"Something like that," Alexandra admitted with wry humor in her voice.

"Well, I wouldn't worry about it. Parker has been around the track once or twice. He'll know that batting-eyelash routine when he sees it."

Alexandra laughed in sad amusement. "You underestimate Christine when she decides she wants something."

"No . . ." Debby corrected smoothly. "You're probably underestimating Parker."

Alexandra hugged herself to stop the shivers, but it didn't help much. It seemed that every part of her body was being attacked by nerves. Suddenly she was overly warm and perspiration pricked at her scalp until she was afraid the moisture would cause her careful sidesweep of curls to go limp. Her stomach was a mass of knotted tension that seemed to have movement of its own as she pressed her fingertips against the churning and wondered in a panic if she was going to be sick.

She'd heard of this kind of reaction in famous people just before they were to perform, but she'd never before understood it. She'd always felt that if you were good and knew what you were doing, the positive energy would naturally transmit itself to the audience. She couldn't believe that Parker ever went through such trauma. She never thought that *she* would. But as Alexandra stood in the wings, she knew that she was about to eat her words.

A peek through the silver lame curtains showed a full

house. The three-piece band that she'd rehearsed with only twice during the week were taking their places and idly warming up on their instruments. The people nearest the platform were shifting their chairs around for the best vantage point. And everyone was waiting on her.

As quickly as the panic seized her, it melted away. It was replaced with the dawning realization that she was about to give her first professional performance. In her mind, she didn't count the few awful weeks spent at the Outer Edge because she was sure that no one there even remembered her. Certainly the clientele there was not as appreciative of her talents. This was different; this was a true testing ground.

Alexandra rubbed her palms together. They were no longer damp and clammy.

She could do this.

She was ready.

It was what she'd always wanted, she reminded herself as she straightened her shoulders and took a deep breath.

"Are you ready, Baby?" a technical assistant asked Alexandra in passing, but he didn't wait for an answer. He was checking the position of the overhead lights and the microphone, and the amplifiers.

A piano chord cracked the air and Alexandra came alert with a start. She thought instantly of Parker. She'd missed not hearing from him all week, but she herself had been working on reserve energy while battling a cold, teaching, and seeing after her father. She didn't want to consider if he was now preoccupied with Christine. She did believe, however, that Parker would be there to hear her sing.

As Alexandra waited to be introduced to the world, she couldn't help but realize the irony of her circumstances. It was *she* who had declared over and over how much she wanted to be a professional singer. Yet after all those long years of her steady pace, it was Parker who'd made tonight possible. It was Parker who'd eased her out of the past. She also had to recognize that she was not just willing to step aside so that Christine could have a clear shot at Parker. If she wasn't willing to put herself on the line for her music and for Parker, then she was going to lose them both.

The lights suddenly dimmed in the club room, drawing Alexandra's anxious thoughts back to the situation at hand. The introduction for her happened so quickly that any lingering thoughts about Parker were suddenly pushed to the back of her mind. She was on.

"Ladies and gentlemen, Blues Alley is proud and pleased to present a hot new singer from right here in D.C. How about a warm welcome for *Miss Alexandra Morrow.*"

To the sound of encouraging applause and the curtains magically parting before her, Alexandra placed a confident smile on her glistening rouged lips and stepped through the curtains and stood before the microphone. She moved carefully, her walk unwittingly seductive. She heard a half dozen or so wolf whistles from the invisible depths of the room. Her cobalt blue chiffon dress, shirred and gathered over one shoulder, exposed the other and fell in soft folds to her ankle. It flattered her slender form and lent an air of regality to her. Her controlled movements successfully disguised the quaking inside her, the suddenly hammering heart, and the irrational fear that she'd forgotten how to sing. A slender hand reached for the microphone to pull it a fraction of an inch closer as she felt the need to hold on to something solid.

The musicians continued the notes of the introduction to the first number until the applause had died down, and then the guitarist signaled for her entry. Alexandra took a deep breath, opened her mouth, and sang.

The first number was fast and snappy, grabbing the audience's attention at once and holding it as they waited to hear in those first bars and lyrics whether or not she'd been worth the cover charge. For the first half of the song, Alexandra was gripped with a fear that she was performing badly, and it took the rest of the song for her to calm down and realize she was in command of her song and the audience. Alexandra did not go in for theatrics on stage. Her performance was her voice, although unbeknownst to her, her slight feminine gestures added to the image, and set that image with the audience. They knew after the first few numbers that she definitely came across as a lady with her own soft, romantic style.

Alexandra sang numbers best suited to her abilities. She concentrated on the emotion in each piece, drawing all she could from it, and gave it back to the audience. She reached out to touch their hearts with her voice. And the audience, in turn, showed its appreciation for her efforts with genuine applause.

At the end of her fifth number, Alexandra began to feel a shift from her audience. It was almost tangible, as if she knew they were trying to be polite, trying to give her their full attention. Then someone shouted a request. Alexandra's stomach muscles twisted into knots again. She hadn't thought of that happening, and she wasn't sure how to respond. In the mere second or so she took to consider, two more requests came. Her hands grew damp again and her throat dry. She stole a quick glance at her band and found them waiting, watching for her decision. This was, after all, her show.

For a moment, Alexandra felt as though everyone was sitting in judgment; when they issued an opinion she'd be found wanting. They were not going to be happy with what she gave of herself, and they weren't going to let her get away with just being good.

She swallowed hard and held the mike tighter. "I have a song I think you'll like better," she said smoothly into the audience, and tempered it with a slow smile that earned her some applause and a few shouts of approval.

The number was "Delta Dawn," a popular ballad about a woman wearing a faded yellow rose as she waited day after day at a train station for her lover to return. The song started out slow, a story being told. Then the sadness and hopelessness of the forsaken woman became a refrain repeated over and over and increasing in tempo and pitch until the music and words were almost like a cry of pain from her heart.

Alexandra had not been sure she should include this song, knowing that it called for a kind of bluesiness of tone and voice that was not her style. But she worked hard with it, maybe because the audience expected so much. Maybe because she related in some way to the anguish in the song.

She ended the song on an unexpected drawn out "Oh, noooo . . . ," the woman realizing the futility of waiting for the man who was never to return.

The response this time was enthusiastic and vocal. Alexandra nodded her thanks. But she knew in her heart that she had just squeaked by, and she doubted if she could do it again. Rather than exhilaration, she felt relief.

She sang two more songs, but at the end of her performance the response was polite again. It said she had done a very nice job—no more and no less.

"A rising young star, ladies and gentlemen. Let's hear it for Alexandra."

Alexandra took one more demure bow and gratefully

left the stage. Almost in a daze, and feeling as though the last hour had never happened, she made her way to the dressing room, and nearly collided with the young woman who was to perform next. The young woman was stunningly dressed in an outfit that was revealing and suggestive.

"You did real nice, honey. You have a pretty voice," the woman said, with a sympathetic smile.

"Thank you," Alexandra murmured, a little surprised.

"But you gotta give them more on stage than a pretty voice," the performer said with a small movement of her shoulders.

"What do you mean?" Alexandra asked, but she knew.

"The audience wants an 'act.' You know; they want you to move around and speak to them. They want to see you work. And you need a little more . . . 'hot sauce' in your numbers. More 'Delta Dawn,' " the woman explained like an expert. She put her hands on her hips and took a posture.

Alexandra took a deep breath and plucked absently at the fabric draped over one shoulder.

"I don't think 'hot sauce' is really my style," Alexandra confessed simply.

The woman shrugged and touched her hair to make sure it was in place. "Honey, you give them what they pay for. That's what this business is all about. Don't worry, you'll get the hang of it." She smiled again and walked past Alexandra.

Alexandra felt an immediate stiffening in her spine, felt indignation rise. Not at the woman's words, for she sensed the truth in them, but in the implication that just because she performed for people, she somehow belonged to them. The idea was unsettling, and she wondered at what

Parker had repeatedly said to her about being a performer. Understanding was just dawning on her.

Parker had always said that what he loved most was *creating* music. Anyone could *play* it. It had just worked out that he played it better than most. Parker had told her from the very start, all those years ago when he'd given up concert hall recitals to do what he truly wanted to do, that he would have loved to have been more normal, *not* so well known, *not* so public. It seemed incredible to Alexandra that when you were willing to give so much of yourself for someone's enjoyment, they could possibly think of asking for more. Could she tolerate giving up so much?

Something clicked inside.

A puzzle piece, long missing, fell into place while scenarios and conversations Alexandra had had with her father, with Parker, even with Christine, came flashing like neon in her head. Blindly she began to walk toward the dressing room, feeling as though a key had been used inside her to open a door. Alexandra knew that she had a gifted voice. She knew how to sing. But only this moment did she suddenly truly wonder why she wanted to sing, and for whom.

The door was partially open when Alexandra entered the bright room the female performers used. It was empty, except for Parker, whom she saw half-sitting on the edge of the Formica vanity. He was dressed in black slacks and a black turtleneck sweater worn with a stylish wool sports jacket of a subtle black-and-white tweed. Alexandra had only a second to register his appearance before she unthinkingly rushed forward into Parker's arms. Her realization had twisted the very center of the dream she'd maintained her whole life, now asking her point blank, *are you sure this is what you want?*

Parker stood to take the gentle impact of her body, his

arms closing tightly around her. Alexandra tunneled into his coat and wound her arms around his waist. She was so glad to see him, even as she was surprised at her need to have him there now. Parker was a haven from the unpredictability of the evening and the audience. But she also knew he would recognize some of her feeling.

"Alex?" Parker whispered, caught off guard by her sudden action. "Are you okay?"

Alexandra raised her eyes to look into his curious gaze, his mobile mouth lifting at a corner, his brows furrowed in question. What they both needed and wanted in that instant came together and communicated between them.

A look of sudden understanding softened Parker's eyes. He immediately saw the dawning in her bright eyes that recognized what being a performer was all about. One needed a spark, a drive, determination to play for the audience, to make them love you. And the strength to continue against all odds.

He kissed Alex, claiming her and calming her with his control and care. He gave her back a sense of reality after the taut strangeness of performing.

Alexandra melted willingly into him, feeling him stiffen the hard muscles of his thighs to take her weight against him. She welcomed the warm, rough texture of his tongue, and Parker held her captive until the emotions within her changed slowly from confusion to calm, from chilled tension to warmed flesh.

Parker sensuously rode her lips with his until their shortened breaths demanded air and he released her. Alexandra let out a deep sigh and allowed her eyes to drift closed. She leaned against him, her cheek on Parker's chest. She wanted to stay there forever. She didn't have one thought at the moment for the performance she'd just given, or the one that remained. She was just feeling overwhelmingly lonely. She felt Parker's lips in her hair, felt a large hand stroke her back and shoulders, sliding over the soft fabric of her gown.

"Now, that's a welcome to warm a man's soul. What did I do to deserve it?" Parker teased in a low drawl. "And how can I get it more often?"

I needed you. Alexandra heard the anguished reply in her head but bit her lip from actually saying it. She pulled back a little out of his embrace so she could see up into his face. "I'm sorry. I shouldn't have come running at you like that."

"Don't be sorry," he said, tilting her chin up so he could see her features, running his gaze over her face, making note of a warm sort of glow in her creamy skin. "I'd much rather have you rush into my arms than into someone else's."

"Even Christine?" Alexandra heard herself ask pertly, unable to stop herself.

Parker tilted his head down and narrowed his eyes. "Even Christine," he answered softly.

Alexandra averted her eyes against a sudden light of determination in Parker's. That's when she noticed the clear glass vase filled with fresh water and a dozen deep red roses. She smiled gently and reached out to touch a velvet petal with her finger tip.

"They're beautiful," she said softly, in surprised awe.

"They're for you," Parker said, setting his arms comfortably on her lower back and smiling at the joy on her face. He was not unaware that the flowers had brightened her eyes far more than her first show. "They're to mark the debut of your singing career, and to wish you luck." He lifted a hand to cup it against the side of her face. "I'm happy for you, Alex. I know this is what you've always wanted."

"Parker," she interrupted, in a soft, anxious voice, but he went on.

"Let me finish. Many years ago you gave me something that even I didn't know I needed: belief in what I wanted to do, and belief that I could do it. You gave me understanding and love," Parker said sincerely.

Alexandra felt a rush of blood warm her face, and her hands inadvertently tightened on his forearms.

His thumb rubbed gently over her rounded chin, and his voice dropped. "I took all you had to give me, Alex, and gave almost nothing in return," Parker said reflectively, almost to himself. He carefully examined her features to gauge her response to his words. He wondered, was it now too late to admit how much he still needed her? If he told her he loved her, what would happen to her dreams, all of which were about to come true?

"That's not so," Alexandra demurred, surprised by Parker's unexpected confession and filled with an unexpected, swirling feeling of dread.

"I want you to know it never meant I didn't want to give as much to you. I always wanted you. Always," Parker said firmly, his eyes serious and searching, his words tender and sincere. He clenched his jaw muscles, but his hand was still gentle against her face. "I'm proud of you, even if I give you a hard time about it. I realize now how much singing really means to you." Parker dropped his hands to his side and released her. He could see the slight frown in her eyes as his arms slipped away, but he didn't want to hold onto her as he said his next words. He knew if he wanted another chance with Alexandra, he'd have to let her go . . . the same way she'd let him go so long ago, when she'd had no say in his leaving. The decision he'd made was suddenly haunting him. He hadn't given Alex a choice then. Was it fair that he ask for one now?

In all the years since he'd known Alex, Parker had frequently found himself making a comparison between her and the packaged and polished facade of other women. Now he realized that the comparison was too simple, because the image he'd carried of Alexandra had been of her at nineteen, sweet and unpretentious. It had been a jolt to meet her again and find that not only had she grown up and matured and blossomed into beautiful womanhood, but that she had rekindled all the feelings for her he'd set aside. Now, Parker wasn't even sure he could admit them to her. He didn't want to win her over from her dreams; he wanted to join her in them.

He let out a small sigh. "I have another surprise for you. I persuaded my manager to consider letting you open my concert in New York next month. I talked to him long distance a few days ago."

Alexandra's mouth opened in surprise as she just stared at him. Parker was being too helpful, too accommodating.

"That's kind of you," she said, disappointed in a way she couldn't explain. "But I'm not ready for that."

"Why not? You have as much talent and experience as anyone I'd find to open my show. Remember that the whole idea is to give you exposure. Let people see and hear you and remember who you are," Parker reasoned.

Alexandra swung away from him, clasping her hands together. "Why are you pushing me?" she asked angrily. "First it was Blues Alley; now it's your concert in New York." She swung back to him. "I don't know if I can do that. I'm not even sure it's what I want."

The words were suddenly out. The silence that followed seemed to stretch on forever.

Parker was watching her, a look of surprising calm on

his face, even after her outburst. "Then what *do* you want?" he asked softly.

Alexandra slowly unclenched her hands and let them fall to her side. She was wondering nonsensically why he couldn't read her mind. She wanted *him*. It was the only thought that was absolutely clear to her. But she couldn't say so. The reasons she couldn't had nothing to do with a fear that Parker wouldn't understand. She *knew* he wanted her. But that wasn't the same as love. That wasn't the same as commitment. It wasn't the same as a future that they could build together.

Alexandra knew she need not fear Christine staking a claim to Parker and then pursuing him relentlessly, or even of Parker being enthralled with Christine's beauty; Parker had never been that shallow. No . . . Alexandra knew all the answers and decisions lay within herself, and as she stood facing Parker, she was afraid of making the wrong one.

"Parker . . ." she began softly, taking a hesitant step closer to him.

Suddenly the door burst open and Debby and Brian came tumbling in, their words running together and not making much sense, beyond the pair's obvious excitement and congratulations. Parker's question went unanswered.

"Hey, you were terrific," Brian said, gathering Alexandra into a crushing bear hug and swinging her in a half-circle off her feet.

Alexandra came out of her trance. "Brian, be careful. I have another show to give in this dress," she said, laughing softly.

Brian obligingly set her down, and Debby hugged her next. "Oh, Alexandra, I can't believe you actually did it. I'd be scared to death in front of all those people."

Alexandra stood back, straightening her gown, and

forced herself to smile at the exuberance of her friends. "What makes you think I wasn't scared to death? I kept expecting someone in the audience to boo me off the stage."

"You were very good," Parker said smoothly.

Alexandra gave him a wan smile as a slight frown gathered between her brows. "I'm not sure 'very good' was good enough. I'm not sure I had the audience with me all the way."

There was silence as Parker studied her intently, his eyes half closed. "Sometimes you don't. Sometimes you're not with them all the way, either. Audiences can be very fickle—loving you one performance, hating you the next."

Brian and Debby shook their heads. "They *loved* you out there. 'Delta Dawn' stood the place on its ear. Even Christine 'yeahed' you through the number." Debby looked behind her. "Where is she? I thought she was right behind us."

"Is Christine here?" Alexandra asked, looking at Parker.

"She came with me." He looked right into her eyes. "I thought she should hear her sister perform. I wanted her to appreciate how talented and special you are."

Alexandra clenched her hands together, trying to decide if the warmth she and Parker had just shared was real or not. Suddenly, she had a vivid image of Christine being held by Parker. "I'm surprised. She's always told me I'm wasting my time."

"Well, *she* was surprised. She heard the audience's reaction as well as we did. She even liked your dress," Debby said in dry humor.

"Although she admitted she likes other singers more," Brian added.

Alexandra chuckled. "All of whom have more 'hot sauce' in their act," she said, a private joke, but Parker understood.

The door opened yet again, and all heads turned as Christine entered, looking bright-eyed and excited. She was wearing a magenta knit dress, the electric color of the outfit bringing Christine's beautiful brown coloring into exquisite clarity. The dress, with its fashionable dolman sleeves and cowl neckline, was a perfect foil to anyone around her who was more likely to be dressed in simpler fare. Even Alexandra had to admit that her sister had a wonderful dramatic flair with clothes and colors. But now, Christine's eyes danced quickly over the four people gathered until she spotted Parker, and she reached for him beseechingly.

"What are you doing here?" she asked, and grabbed Parker's arm, trying to guide him toward the door. "The manager is going to announce you to the audience, Parker. They want you to play something."

Parker easily lifted his arm free, not moving. "Whoa . . . wait a minute. I came to hear Alex sing tonight. I have no intention of getting up in front of an audience."

Christine smiled charmingly. "But you can't let everyone down. They're your fans, and they want to hear you."

"No," Parker said unequivocally. Brian and Debby exchanged anxious glances. "You should have asked first."

"I didn't think you'd mind," Christine reassured innocently, with a shrug of her shoulder.

"I don't mean me. You should have asked Alex."

"She won't mind," Christine said. "She was very good tonight, but *you're* famous. Everyone knows who you are."

"Alexandra is going to be famous," Debby suddenly said in defense.

While Alexandra realized that Christine meant no deliberate malice, her maneuvering stung.

"I don't mind," Alexandra intervened, struggling to keep her feelings hidden. "If I was any good out there tonight, they'll remember. Maybe you should go out. Everyone is expecting you now," she said to Parker.

Parker seemed about to protest further. For a long moment he seemed to weigh the decision in his mind. Then his brow cleared.

"All right," Parker said finally. To Christine, he said dryly, "You're not going to understand why, but I thank you."

"Brian and I are going back to our table," Debby said, giving Alexandra a quick peck on the cheek before she left.

Christine, with Parker's arm in her grasp, headed for the door. "Hurry. Everyone's waiting."

Parker gave Alexandra a private look. "The evening isn't over yet," he said, and winked at her before disappearing with Christine.

Alexandra let out a sigh in the silence that followed, feeling as though she'd just witnessed a badly written comedy routine where the joke was on her. She felt tired and just wanted to go home. She had no idea where she was going to get the energy or enthusiasm for her second show. She would have been just as happy not to have to.

Through the still open doorway, Alexandra could hear the manager giving a glowing and flowery introduction to Parker, and listened to the applause and enthusiasm building even before he'd finished. She wasn't angry or jealous that Parker could command such instant consideration at an impromptu set at a club where he hadn't been scheduled to play. She stood alone in the doorway of the dressing room, distinctly aware of the difference in the reception Parker was receiving and that which had welcomed her. Alexandra slowly began to smile. She had opened for Parker, anyway.

Alexandra tilted her head, listening to the excitement building in the audience and quickly became infected by it. Three years ago she'd attended one of Parker's concerts in Baltimore. As much as she loved Parker's music and understood his creative motivation, as much as she loved Parker, it was the only time she had ever seen him perform. On stage he had been cool, gracious, phenomenally talented and versatile. He had an aloof style with the audience. And the audience loved him.

Alexandra walked back to the stage, under the double spotlight from the side of the performing platform, in time to see Parker take a seat at the piano. He shook hands with the musician who'd stepped aside for him. He'd removed his sports jacket and looked like magic, dressed in black, as he nodded politely to the audience, which had come to its feet, the room filled with the sound of applause.

Alexandra joined in the adoration, a smile of pure pride curving her mouth as she watched him. He had a presence that was very unique. She felt so much love for him in that moment that her heart began to race.

"Thank you. Thank you very much," Parker said, as he repositioned the microphone near the piano. "Hey, I'm supposed to be on vacation and incognito," he said easily to the audience, and received warm laughter. "I came this evening for the same reason you did. To hear a beautiful lady sing some beautiful songs . . ." There was more generous applause. "I'm honored that you want to hear me. But I'm going to need some help.

"As you know, I do a fair job of writing music." There were whistles and shouts of agreement. "And I can hold my own on the keys. But I guarantee that you *don't* want to hear me sing. So, I'd like to call upon a very special friend of mine to give me a hand. This is someone I admire and respect tremendously, who many years ago was there to listen to some of my music being composed. Sometimes even wrote a lyric or two."

Parker turned his head, finding Alexandra, knowing she was there waiting. "Alex . . ." he whispered to her. Surprise swept through the audience, and the applause began anew.

"Go on, Baby. Don't just stand there," the manager hissed behind her.

Alexandra was taken unawares, and her eyes widened as she saw Parker look pointedly at her. His eyes held a mixture of emotion. There was tenderness and a sort of all-knowing look because he had managed to surprise her yet again.

Once more Alexandra found herself before a microphone. But this time there was a confidence and giddiness to being there that was attributed to Parker and to having him seated at the piano. She felt safe with him and not at all nervous. He immediately took his seat again and started to play. Alexandra needed no coaxing, no cues or intros to his music or style. She knew it by heart. She knew what to expect and how to work with it. When she sang the words to his music, some of which she had indeed written, the love of the music and the man lent power and emotion that was second nature. Their performance together was spellbinding.

Alexandra was not singing to the audience, nor was Parker playing for them. This was private. It was a long overdue duet that was just between them. It brought them together on every level that was important to either of them in their music.

Parker cross-faded one song into the start of another, and Alex followed his every beat perfectly. She felt the charisma that had been between them years ago born anew. A special aura was warming her, lighting her eyes, enveloping them both. Everything around her faded away except for Parker. It was just the two of them, surrounded by her voice and his playing. They were each other's private audience. When the music finally ended, Alexandra caught her breath in the momentary silence. She felt like it would never be so perfect again as it was right then. She let her breath out slowly, and blinked back to the reality of where she was.

At the end of the second number, Parker stopped and stood up. The audience exploded in an electrifying response.

Parker took Alexandra's hand and gave it a hard squeeze, communicating volumes through the touch. Together they faced the audience and bowed. They faced each other. Alexandra, who was preparing to curtsy to Parker, was pulled into his arms instead and given a brief, sweet, gentle kiss. Parker chuckled softly at her embarrassment as Alex released his hand and left him alone with the final tribute. She hurried back to the dressing room feeling breathless and exhilarated.

There was a second convergence upon the dressing room, but there was no more opportunity for Alex to be alone with Parker. She could tell that Christine was a little put out by all the attention everyone was giving to Parker and Alexandra, yet she had only herself to blame.

"How much time before your second show?" Brian asked.

"Only forty minutes," Alexandra responded. "Are you planning on staying for that one as well? You don't have to. The songs will be different, but . . ." she spread her hands almost shyly, "you've seen my act. I can't be any different."

"Oh, I'd like to stay," Debby argued.

Parker said nothing, knowing that at that moment Alex probably would have liked nothing more than some time to herself.

"I don't. Besides, I'm hungry," Christine said bluntly. "Can't we go have dinner somewhere?"

"That's a good idea," Brian seconded, taking hold of his wife's hand and kissing Alexandra on the cheek. "I think Alexandra has had enough of us standing on top of her all evening."

She laughed. "I'm so glad you all could make it," Alexandra said.

"You were *so* good," Debby breathed, kissing her friend. "I'll call you tomorrow."

Somehow, Parker managed to be the last one to leave, and Alexandra felt her heart begin to flutter in her chest. There was still a kind of heated, sensual warmth between them that would not be explored tonight, and Alexandra wondered anxiously when it ever would. She wanted him to say something to her, something that would keep the hope alive within her and tell her how he felt. Her communication to him was silent, and private, and she hoped Parker understood. But beyond smiling warmly at her, he conveyed no other message to her.

"Are you happy, Alex?" Parker asked her softly, watching for her reaction.

At the moment, standing there with him so close, she'd hoped he'd know. "I think so," she hesitated with a whisper, and was surprised when his eyes clouded over.

"Then that's all that matters." Parker kissed her tenderly, chastely, and left without another word, giving no hint if or when they'd see each other again.

Disappointed, Alexandra slowly made her way to the makeup counter, and again spotted the bouquet of roses. She cupped her hand around one, and saw the edge of a small white card stuck between two stems. She hastily pulled it out, thankful that there was this last contact from Parker, hoping it would say something more to her.

"Congratulations on a dream come true," the card said simply.

Alexandra sighed in disappointment. She thought in some irony that poor "Delta Dawn" had nothing on her in that moment.

Chapter Nine

Alexandra closed her apartment door and carefully leaned herself against it for support. She tilted her head back and a deep sigh escaped through the slight parting of her dry lips.

Water dripped from her raincoat and umbrella to the bare floor, its light "pat-pat" sound in harmony with the throbbing in her head. With an effort she forced herself from the door, and after placing the umbrella in a stand, proceeded to the kitchen, where she carelessly dropped the wet coat over a chair. The apartment was well heated, but nonetheless Alexandra felt chilled clear through to the bone. She felt she'd never be warm again.

She put on a kettle of water to boil and stood staring blankly into space, her mind drained of thoughts, her body drained of energy. Her insides, however, the core of her being, was a whirlwind of confused emotions. She felt as though she no longer had control, or any idea of what she was doing with her life.

After making herself a cup of hot tea, Alexandra made her way slowly to the living room to curl up in a corner of the sofa. Every joint in her body was sore and she was afraid to move too fast. She tried to ignore the persistent and steady pounding in her head, but there had been no sign all afternoon that it would let up, and miserably she endured it.

She could still feel the damp chill of the strong spring winds, from having been out and around D.C. that morning, and that, too, seemed to have settled into her bones. A quiver of discomfort rippled through her huddled body and she closed her eyes on a shudder.

Alexandra reflected, through the foggy cluster of thoughts already on her mind, that if she could just get through tonight, everything would get back to normal. Her life seemed to have gotten so complicated, and unreasonably, she blamed it all on Parker. Everything had been fine until he'd come back into her life. Since that first few weeks after they'd met again, when they'd both reacted with foolish intensity, followed by slow caution, he'd assiduously become part of her life again.

He'd gone rather quietly from unannounced appearances to being a fixture in her life in one way or another from day to day. It had gotten so that she expected to see him, and that both angered and frightened her. Alexandra knew her anger was rooted in the belief that Parker could walk out of her life again as unexpectedly as he'd walked in. It had happened before, and seemed to be something he was capable of doing easily. But Alexandra knew also the wreckage that would be left behind of her emotions and love. She didn't want to give in to it, afraid she wouldn't survive a second time. Yet she felt compelled to follow the inclinations of her heart to love Parker and to trust him as he'd asked, while he developed a friendship with her sister.

There seemed to be a certain familiarity between them, and Christine could, more often than not, be found at their father's home. In a way, Alexandra didn't mind that;

she actually preferred it, because it suggested that Parker was not spending time at Christine's place. Alexandra had no intention of getting into a cat fight with her sister over Parker Harrison, or *any* man. He'd have to decide whom he wanted without an ounce of coaxing from her. Yet to be fair, there was no indication that Parker found Christine more than fascinating and amusing. It infuriated Alexandra that she felt like she was waiting with baited breath.

Parker hadn't ignored her, either. He had been to every one of her performances at Blues Alley, falling into the easy habit of taking her there, sitting through the shows, and bringing her home. He'd make casual suggestions about how to do a song, or perhaps replace one tune with another. He gave her hints on how to work an audience, and while Alexandra was getting better at it, it never became easy or comfortable. She just wanted to sing, but she was fast realizing that performing involved much more than just the ability to do it. Sometimes she and Parker would have a late supper together, talking music, of course. Or, after he drove her home, they'd sit on the sofa with coffee and talk about her audition, or of his upcoming concert in New York.

Parker was still insistent on her being the opening act for the concert, and toward that end he had his management office mail a contract for her to read and sign. She still had not done so. And the longer she delayed, the more difficult her decision became. It wasn't so much that she didn't want to do it. It was just that she was unsure.

Alexandra knew it was a terrible admission to make, given her ranting and raving about wanting a professional career. The dream was much more appealing than the reality. Was Parker trying to prove that point, or did he sincerely want her to start his show, to give her the golden opportunity she'd always wanted? Alexandra had to admit that when she and Parker performed together, whether professionally, or just when they were fooling around, she was never nervous. It was always natural, always perfect.

Parker had further surprised Alexandra by showing up during one of the piano lessons for three of her advanced students on Wednesday of the previous week. He'd quietly sat and watched her for an hour as she'd taken her three charges through a series of advanced exercises. Although it had thrown her off guard to see him there unexpectedly, she was soon able to put him out of her thoughts as she gave her full attention to her kids.

She imagined Parker had come out of curiosity. Her teaching was just another facet of her life he really didn't know much about. He had only known the driven person she was, with a dream and ambition she fervently believed in. The Alex who had talked so passionately as well about her music students was a direct contradiction.

Sometimes Alexandra thought she was at her best when she was encouraging small children. She was sincere and attentive and showed enormous patience while being firm, creative, and tireless. This was her real forte, her real challenge—teaching the *love* of music.

She joked with the children and knew how to tease them, make them laugh, and keep them interested. She never connected so well with her adult audiences.

On that Wednesday, Parker had chatted easily with the kids for a while. Afterward, when one of the girls, giggling, asked if he was Miss Morrow's boyfriend, he'd laughed lightly and responded, "I think you'll have to ask Miss Morrow," and he'd given Alexandra a sly, playful hug.

Alexandra quickly reminded the kids that their parents were probably all waiting outside in the cold for them to appear. The children had made a noisy exit, waving to Alexandra, still smirking and laughing over the presence of Parker. To Alexandra's dismay, he didn't let the matter rest.

"So, what's the answer?" Parker had asked seriously, when they were alone. "Am I your boyfriend?"

Alexandra instantly became busy gathering sheet music, closing exercise books, and shifting piano benches in the conservatory studio. She was thinking that Christine would call Parker a boyfriend, implying he was hers. But Alexandra had never seen Parker as someone who was hers, but someone with whom she belonged. At least, she'd thought so years ago.

"Am I your girlfriend?" Alexandra flippantly answered his question with a question. But when she'd turned her clear, challenging gaze to his, she was stunned to find Parker's eyes gentle, his mouth in a sensual smile. He was shaking his head very slowly.

"You are much, much more than that to me."

Alexandra stopped her nervous movements around the music room to stare at Parker. There was so much confidence in what he'd said and in the way he'd said it. What was he saying? What was he *admitting*?

Alexandra lowered her puzzled gaze to the music in her hands. "What about Christine?" she asked smoothly.

Parker pursed his lips and put his hands into his pockets. "I like your sister very much," he began, and watched Alex's head snap up, her eyes wide and their expression briefly surprised and troubled. "I think she's beautiful. I also think she's stubborn, headstrong, immature, and manipulative. All of which will hopefully change when she finishes growing up. The way I see it, Christine uses it all as a defense because she's jealous of you."

It was a moment before his last remark registered, and

for a while Alexandra just stared blankly at him. Then she arched a brow, rolled her eyes, and struck an attitude. "Give me a break. Are we talking about the same Christine?"

Parker nodded. Then he walked slowly toward Alexandra and took the music sheets from her hand. He glanced through the titles one by one. When Alexandra made to quickly take them back, Parker smoothly turned away. Two of the sheets were music he'd composed when he was not even twenty. They were harmless little pop rock numbers.

Parker looked at Alexandra, his expression unreadable; but his dark eyes were intense and probing. He smiled slowly.

"Think about it, Alex. You share your father's talent with music and the sheer joy of playing it. There was something you both could discover together. I'm not saying he ignored Christine. It's pretty obvious he loves her dearly. But in Christine's eyes, you were probably always just a bit more special."

Alexandra shook her head, surprised at the observation. It had never occurred to her that she had any attributes Christine would envy. Alexandra was still very uncertain that what Parker was saying held any validity.

"It's not true."

"Sure it is. You took music lessons. And then, not only do you get to study at one of the top conservatories in the country, you get to perform at the Kennedy Center, you perform in a chorale at Rockefeller Center, you perform on public television.

"You teach children. Imagine, people come to *you*, Alex, to teach their children, because you have something special to offer. Christine can knock 'em dead on first sight, but you have staying power. You have a talent."

"Christine has lots of talent," Alexandra defended, with such sudden temper that Parker held up his hands in surrender.

He did not want to seem like he was attacking Alex's younger sister. "I know. She's very persuasive. She's very good at talking people *into* things. She's going to do very well for herself, with the right guidance and advice."

"From you, I suppose," Alexandra said archly, crossing her arms over her chest.

Parker was highly amused, but he dared not laugh again. It was clear to him that Alexandra, while loyal and loving of her sister, was still stubbornly taking a "wait and see" attitude with him.

"Alexandra . . ." he began gently.

She could instantly detect his seriousness in how he said her name.

He slowly shook his head. "I'm not in love with Christine. And I'm not going to be."

Alexandra stood still, appropriately tongue-tied. Parker had effectively answered one of her most persistent questions, but he had not addressed all her concerns.

He allowed no time to let the comment sink in, or for her to respond. He declared a moratorium on work and decided it was time to play. He immediately swept her away for the rest of the afternoon. They rambled in and out of music stores, went to a movie that was so bad they sat and laughed all through it.

They were having a date.

It struck Alexandra that she and Parker had never really dated, or had a true opportunity to know one another. They'd really just come together out of circumstances. Alexandra had to admit that starting over definitely had its advantages. On one level they knew each other very well, and there was a comfortable melding of minds and attitudes. On another level, it was a discovery. They were finding out about each other as adults.

Later, at her apartment, Alexandra had made them both a light dinner of a pasta and chicken salad. And after talking in a desultory manner, easy and languid and familiar, for several more hours, Parker had left for his own temporary lodgings. Alexandra didn't want him to go, but she also didn't ask him to stay. Everything had been perfect so far, and she didn't want to risk it changing. Her day with Parker was exactly as she'd always imagined it. Comfortable, invigorating, and fun.

She'd walked Parker to the door and allowed him to put his hands on her narrow waist. He drew her closer so that he could kiss her. Even the kiss was comfortable. It was filled with easy warmth and affection. It had liking and simple pleasure that wasn't in any way demanding or too casual.

Alexandra had had a wonderful time with Parker, knowing a companionship and comfort that was far more natural than their first relationship. He'd shown caring, support, understanding in the last few weeks. She could talk freely with him now about her music. He listened to her sing, let her air her doubts over the choice of arias that were good or not good for her voice during an audition. He calmed her unspoken fears about the competition for the Light Opera, the judging, the outcome. It was all she'd wanted and needed from a friend, boyfriend or not, but not *all* she needed or wanted from Parker . . .

The rain continued to fall outside, and Alexandra continued to feel chilly. A frown furrowed the otherwise smooth skin of her forehead as her musings played further havoc in her mind. She was on her way to getting somewhere with her music. It was what she'd worked toward single-mindedly for six or more years, wasn't it? She had resolutely intended for nothing and no one to interfere. But there was a persistent nagging sense that everything was not going according to plan.

Alexandra put her teacup on the table at the end of the sofa, and slid her body down further into the plush cushions. Her body ached with each movement. She thought she'd just rest for a little while before getting ready for the evening's performance at Blues Alley. *One more,* Alexandra thought, with an unconscious rush of relief. But then, there'd be no reason for Parker to be there at the beginning and end of her evenings. In any case, he'd have to leave soon for New York and preparations for his own concert. She would go on to her audition, on with her music, on with her life. And she'd be alone.

The frown deepened and Alexandra twisted her aching body into a more settled position. With a small mew of protest wrung reluctantly from her by her weakened condition, by her sudden vulnerability, Alexandra let her truth out.

She wanted Parker.

She was in love with him.

At nineteen, perhaps she had known him prematurely as a lover, but nonetheless, brief lovers they had been. Now, after an explosive reunion which had turned into gentle, affectionate caring, Alexandra found herself wanting him more than ever. This time she would know fully what she was giving, and what she wanted in return. She was prepared to reconsider her priorities without giving anything up. Somehow, before Parker left for New York, she had to know where their relationship was headed.

With a wrenching of her heart, Alexandra further recalled the evening she'd gone for a voice lesson with Signora Tonelli. The former Italian diva had been relentless in her pushing, forceful in her prodding, and stingy with her praise. The signora, not mincing words, had told Alexandra that the key to doing well in the competitions was to remember that she was very good in what she sang and performed, and to simply concentrate on singing well what she knew.

"However . . ." the diva had said airily, as she'd ended one two-hour session with Alexandra, "tonight you had the concentration of a turnip. I suggest you forget everything else in your life, at least for the next month. Forget your love life, paying bills, and the laundry. Nothing else must exist but your singing. And I've never known a turnip to win the competition yet."

Alexandra had left the cramped little apartment of her instructor feeling a wave of panic, a crush of self-doubt so strong that she couldn't swallow around the lump in her throat. She needed reassurance and encouragement.

Parker had been waiting to take her to dinner as he'd been doing for weeks, and this time when she saw him, Alexandra let the tears of frustration slip down her cheeks. Parker approached her with strong concern reflected in his eyes. He'd instantly discarded the lit cigarette to comfort her. He put an arm around her shoulder and squeezed gently.

"I was godawful." She'd tried laughing only to have it come out as a wretched little sob.

"What happened?" Parker had asked, folding her into his arms, while standing outside in the cold.

Alexandra shook her head forlornly and turned watery, dark eyes upward to gaze at him. "She says I'm not concentrating enough."

Parker had watched her curiously for a long moment, his hands rubbing up and down her arms.

"Why aren't you concentrating?" he'd asked softly,

carefully. It was the first sign that Alexandra's whole mind and heart were not into what she was doing.

Alexandra pressed her hand against her temple as if trying to evoke an answer. "I don't know. I . . . ."

And then, unexpectedly, Parker had closed his mouth over her falterings, forcing the words and thoughts back down her throat. His arms had held her closer to him, until it seemed his heat seeped right into her chilled body. The persuasive pressure of his firm masculine lips and the sensual possessive stroking of his warm, rough tongue were like a balm to her senses and rippled along her spine, causing Alexandra to press closer to him, to open her mouth willingly to further exploration. Certainly right then she wasn't thinking about the competition, or Signora Tonelli or her music.

The kiss was meant to calm and comfort her, but Parker didn't intend for Alexandra to forget that she had a serious concern that needed immediate attention.

Just when Alexandra was about to sink into Parker's comforting caress, he slowly released her. His eyes were blazing and dark with intense emotion, and his hands had tightened on her arms.

"Why aren't you concentrating?" he asked again.

Alexandra blinked at his tone of voice, the fire in her blood, quickly aroused, now quickly fading.

"Well, I certainly can't think when you kiss me like that," she said, feeling lightheaded. Her heart was racing, and she missed the warm security of his arms.

"Then I won't kiss you like that," Parker said evenly. "I won't even touch you like that, but I want to hear what's on your mind."

In that instant, Alexandra was on the verge of confessing everything. But it dawned on her that just because she loved Parker and wanted a life with him didn't mean she couldn't have a career as well; it was just that she was ambivalent about how badly she wanted that career.

If she changed her mind again about the audition or about doing another club engagement, it had to be her decision and her responsibility. Parker had not suggested it, but if she'd really wanted that audition ten years ago, she'd have done it, no matter what. she'd have taken her chances, risen or fallen on her own efforts, and not because he'd suddenly left.

Alexandra stopped crying. She stopped waffling because her life and future had never depended on fate, timing, connections, or love, but in knowing what was best for her. So as Parker stood waiting for her answer, she gave the only one possible.

"Nothing that I can't work out."

"Good. Remember, this is your show, Alex. It's all up to you," Parker had said firmly.

The truth of his words had not sat well with her. But it had served as an appropriate reminder of her priorities. The signora had no complaints about her lessons the rest of the week. Alex performed as if her very life depended on them.

But if Parker's treatment of Alexandra had seemed more tutorial than romantic, Alexandra was even more hard pressed to explain the affinity that had developed so strongly between him and her father.

Very soon after the two men had first met, Alexandra had returned one Saturday afternoon from her weekly shopping expedition to find the two men comfortably seated at the dining table in the alcove, laughing, talking, and finishing off a lunch that consisted of tuna salad sandwiches, some leftover spice cake, and apple juice.

Alexandra had stopped in the doorway between the

kitchen and the alcove to view this unexpected sight, her arms burdened with bags and packages.

"Hi, Baby." Mr. Morrow greeted his daughter with cheerful complacency.

Alexandra looked curiously at Parker. He wore a pair of well-worn denims and a blue sweatshirt with the word "Mellow" written jazzily across the chest in red. He looked appealingly handsome and casual, and very much at home.

"What are you doing here?" Alexandra asked, as Parker quickly got up to help her with the groceries and headed for the kitchen counter.

"I came to visit," he said easily. He began unpacking as she stood staring at him. There was something rather warm and familiar about Parker pressing himself into her life this way, into her entire family.

"How did you know I'd be here?"

Parker put down a package of frozen vegetables and grinned at Alexandra. "I remembered that you did his marketing every week about this time. But I didn't come to see you, Alex. I came to visit with your dad," he said.

The surprise effectively silenced Alexandra and she stared blankly at him. "Oh . . ." she responded softly, then turned slowly and thoughtfully away to finish the unpacking. "You seem to have developed a fascination with my family. First Christine, now my father."

That was because her family was so much more normal, more ordinary than his had been, Parker considered silently. Even in the few hours he'd shared with Alex and her father earlier, Parker could see that.

His own parents were not any less loving or caring than the Morrow family. But he'd been born to a lawyer and a private school administrator, parents who could afford to indulge him in not only their whims, but his own. Except where the whims diverged from music.

Parker's parents had been attentive to all his needs, except the one to just cut loose and be like everyone else. They had always made him feel more than special, way above average, destined for greatness. He hadn't disappointed them, and he was happy that he hadn't. But he had missed something basic and simple and easy.

He found it here, with Alex and her family.

"It began first with you," Parker interrupted quietly. "I'm sort of making up for lost time." He came to stand behind her, close enough to make her nervous, and close enough for her to be aware of his warm aura, something she found herself susceptible to. "I'm finding out there are lots of things I didn't know about you, Alex. I want to," he said, in a strangely hoarse voice, "because so far, I like everything I've seen."

Parker raised his hands to rest on her shoulder, reaching further around her for the opening of her coat. For a moment, Alexandra was cocooned loosely in the shelter of his arms. The tips of his fingers brushed innocently over the roundness of her breasts.

"Why don't you take off your coat and stay awhile," he teased into her ear. Absently, Alexandra obeyed, letting him help her with the leather jacket.

"So . . . what have you two been talking about?" Alexandra asked lightly, continuing to put away the food, feigning casual indifference. She turned her head to gaze at Parker as he laughed softly.

He took the cans and jars out of her hand and put them back on the table. Then he half sat on the edge of the table, sweeping an arm around Alexandra's waist and drawing her to him.

"Well, we talked about his music. Did you know your

father once played backup for one of Pearl Bailey's night-club acts?"

Alexandra felt Parker's hands as he pulled her to rest her hips against his. The intimacy of it left her speechless. She merely shook her head.

"Well, he did. I've persuaded him to finish some of the music he began writing years ago. There's a lot of good stuff there. I'd like to see some of it performed one day."

Alexandra let her hands rest on his chest, slowly relaxing her body against his. "You two do have that in common."

Parker wiggled a brow at her, pulling her even closer. "We have more in common than you realize," he drawled softly.

Alexandra looked into his eyes. "Maybe I should let you go back in to him. He might begin to wonder . . ."

"He might," Parker whispered. "Don't you want to know what else we talked about?"

Alexandra lowered her gaze to his chest. She used a finger to lightly trace out the word "Mellow." "Let me guess. Christine." She gave him a coy glance.

Parker sighed. He lifted Alexandra's chin and gently forced her to look at him, his expression serious. "I knew everything I needed to know about Christine the moment I met her. But you are a different story. I didn't know nearly enough about you." He paused for a moment to scan her face. "I didn't know that strawberry is your favorite flavor ice cream or that you love old Gary Cooper movies. I never knew you always wanted to fly a plane or learn to speak French. All those things make you *you*."

He released her chin and let out an impatient sigh, but still he kept his possessive hold on her. "Do you realize how little we knew of each other back when we first met?

We never talked about each other, only about music," he said, with both amazement and exasperation.

She nodded.

"You were finally getting started with your life. Your voice was going to be the magic carpet to the rest of the world. But I had already been on the magic carpet, and I wanted to get off. You couldn't keep me from that, any more than I can keep you from your dreams now."

"So you left," Alexandra said with finality, though without anger. "You're right. We knew little about each other. Maybe you did the right thing by leaving. A clean break, so we could each go on with our lives, and grow up."

"I still should have said something to you. I was a young boy myself." Parker's hand stroked her face, following the contour from cheek to jaw. His thumb rubbed along her bottom lip. "You were completely unexpected, Alex. You weren't part of the program I had planned for that year." He bent forward, his lips a hairsbreadth away from her own. "I knew I was your first love. I thought it was a little crush you'd get over. I never counted on becoming involved myself and needing you so much."

His lips opened to gently stroke a soft kiss across her mouth, and then again. Her eyes stayed open to see his face. She wanted desperately to understand what she never had before. Parker pulled back a little and let out a small sigh. "I thought it would hurt less and you'd forget if I disappeared. I can see now you didn't. Neither have I. But at the time, I didn't have a choice. If I'd stayed, or brought you with me, neither of us would have done what we needed to do."

Alexandra looped her arms gently around Parker's neck, his hands gliding up her back. She felt no anger anymore, only regret that time and circumstances had played against them, had not given them both a fair chance to see where the feelings might have taken them.

"I admit I was pretty hurt and angry with you for a long time. You have a choice now, Parker. Why are you staying?"

He shook his head silently, slowly standing up so that Alexandra was pressed against the entire length of him. "In a way, it's to say I'm sorry. And I want to be here to cheer you through your audition. I want to give to you what you gave to me when I needed it. I want to *be* there."

Alexandra searched his face, looking for the one thing she wanted from him and had yet to really receive.

"Will you leave again?" she asked quietly.

Parker's jaw tensed suddenly and his eyes were pensive. "That's up to you this time around, Alex. When I go, *if* I go, you'll be the very first person to know." Once again, he reached out to grab her chin and turned her face up to his. "But let me be very clear about this, I won't just disappear this time. Do you understand?"

Alexandra was about to kiss him when the kitchen door opened and her father came in carrying the luncheon dishes.

"Can't you two find anyplace else to make out besides my kitchen?" he lamented, shaking his head, walking past them.

Unlike last time, neither Parker nor Alexandra was embarrassed to be caught. Perhaps, Alexandra thought, it was more a statement than they realized of how far they'd come in their feelings for one another.

"We were just taking care of some old business," Parker said smoothly, finally releasing Alexandra.

Mr. Morrow chuckled wickedly. "Things sure have changed. Now, when I was a young blood, we had very different ways of taking care of business."

Alexandra was incredulous. "That's not what Parker meant, Daddy."

Parker laughed at her. "Oh, yes, it was. But we'll finish later. Right now, your father and I have other things to finish talking about, and you are definitely in the way."

The rain hadn't stopped.

And she felt worse.

Alexandra slowly got up from her prone position on the sofa. If she stayed there any longer, lulled into a stupor by her aching body, she'd never get up at all. Her head felt like it could roll off her shoulders, but with an effort she stood up to walk with heavy weariness to her bedroom. She had a show to do tonight, and the show must always go on. The audience was not going to understand that she'd stood in the rain for twenty minutes this afternoon, for the distinct privilege of meeting Christine to lend her a hundred dollars. They were not going to be impressed that one of her students was going to give his first recital, or that another had mastered a difficult piece during class. The audience would simply want to be entertained.

Alexandra laid out the gown for the evening and twisted her hair into some semblance of order and headed for the bathroom. She stripped off slacks and sweater and stared at her naked body in the mirror. Slender and lithe, she had nothing to be dissatisfied with. Except it ached. But the ache that Alexandra was feeling in that moment was not the physical exhaustion her mind refused to recognize, but the ache from wanting to be held and loved.

It had begun the night she and Parker had so precipitously made love. And although they had not done so since, the ache—the need and gnawing—had gotten worse. The touching and teasing, the gentle caresses and strokes that began as a sensory stimulus, had been growing in intensity until she didn't know what to do. But Parker had kept her at arm's length, in total control, despite the fact that Alexandra sensed he wanted her, too.

She turned on the shower water, until the hot steam began to cloud and fog the small room, engulfing her. But it couldn't keep from her the truth that what she wanted most in the world was to love Parker and have him love her. To have a life with him that was of their own music and making. To share love songs sung only for each other. But Parker had also been right when he'd said it was up to her now. The trick was that Alexandra truly enjoyed singing. She also loved teaching. And she loved Parker. She wanted to be greedy and have it all. She knew she couldn't.

She stepped into the shower, thinking that she'd spent what seemed the whole day getting wet. But the shower was soothing, the water massaging away her tension, sloughing off the concern and questions. For one more night she belonged to Blues Alley. For one more night she'd give herself up to the audience and their pleasure, before she stepped back and considered how to go about winning her own.

With a determination that was admirable, even if totally foolish, Alexandra dressed and prepared for Blues Alley. Her actions were automatic, no thought really necessary to slip on high-heeled sandals, or to adjust the wide gold belt at the waist of the black crêpe dress. But if her head had been clearer she might have considered the absurdity of it all and gone to bed instead.

She listlessly applied eye shadow, mascara, and blusher, looking suddenly, in her own eyes, like a garishly painted wind-up doll who moved and performed on command. The thought was distasteful, but not so wrong.

When the doorbell rang, Alexandra knew it was Parker. Lamenting the need, somewhat giddily, for further unnecessary movement, she walked lethargically to the door, every joint in her body, every muscle and nerve, screaming in protest.

When she opened the door, she couldn't even focus on him properly. The swaying, blurred image of a neatly dressed Parker made her stomach churn, and a sudden heated wave of nausea and light-headedness made her knees weak. It wasn't like the weakness she got when he kissed her with passion, and the thought made Alexandra suddenly grin drunkenly at Parker.

Parker's lazy, seductive smile slowly changed as he viewed Alex in considerably more detail. He was all set to say hello, but couldn't help but notice that she looked ill. He stepped past her into the apartment, and a frown deepened the grooves of his face. His expression turned into quick concern and question.

"Are you all right?" he asked sharply.

Alexandra shrugged and immediately regretted the careless move. Her grin faded. "Of course, I'm all right. I'm almost ready." She turned to walk away, but had to stop to think where she was headed. Thinking seemed to accentuate her headache, which was already accelerating with alarming intensity. Alexandra gingerly touched a finger to her forehead.

"I'll just get my coat and things and . . ."

"Wait a minute. *Wait* a minute," Parker commanded, quickly catching up to her. He was totally alarmed by the blank look in her eyes. She was not at all steady on her feet. He took hold of Alexandra's slender forearm and, halting her unsteady steps, faced her anxiously. "You look terrible," he muttered.

Alexandra made a sound of annoyance between her teeth. "Parker, there's no need to scream at me. I can hear you."

Parker's eyes quickly looked over Alexandra's face, making note of the too-bright eyes and the slow, careful way she spoke. He looked down at her arm, which his hand held lightly, and rubbed his thumb over the unusually cool surface.

"Parker," Alexandra began, trying to pull free. "We have to go. I'm late."

As Alexandra made to continue in search of her coat, Parker, now with a firmer grip on her arm, purposefully steered her to the sofa. "We're going nowhere. You're sick."

Alexandra pulled her arm free and swayed in front of him. Again her hand pressed to her temple. "Don't tell me I'm sick. I'm *not* sick. Please, can't you stand still and stop moving back and forth?"

Parker's eyes narrowed as he looked at her, and he began to remove his overcoat. "I think we'd better sit this one out. You're not going anywhere tonight but into bed."

"I can't do that. I have a show to do," Alexandra tried to reason, managing to look both helpless and confused. But she no longer resisted Parker's hold on her.

He got her seated and her head dropped heavily back against the sofa.

Her eyes closed, Alexandra felt like she was falling slowly into a spinning black abyss. It was like being on a merry-go-round with nothing moving past you but more blackness. She sighed.

It was so peaceful . . .

Parker, reaching for the telephone, looked hard at her. "Forget the show. If you go tonight, you'll probably pass out on stage. That's all the audience will remember, Alex. Not that you're having an off night because you're sick. They'll only remember the show was bad." He began dialing a number, and turned his back to her.

Inside, Alexandra knew instant and pure relief. The very fact that someone else had said she was truly sick somehow made it okay to feel perfectly terrible. Slowly, she felt her body begin to give in to the weakness, and she felt entirely too heavy even to stand.

To the drone of Parker's deep voice making explanations and apologies to the club manager, Alexandra got up from the sofa with painful, excruciating slowness and walked with increasing unsteadiness to her bedroom. She sat down heavily on the bed, her body moving in a different direction than her insides. She could hear Parker's smooth conversation as he carefully manipulated a possible new engagement at Blues Alley for her in a few months.

Alexandra lowered her body to the cotton coverlet, thinking that she didn't want ever to sing at the club again. She'd have to buy another skimpy dress. She'd have to take requests. She'd have to sing songs that pleased *them*, and not her. She'd have to pretend it was just what she'd always wanted.

It was not. She must remember to tell Parker later.

She had no idea how long she lay there, but she was more than half asleep when her arm was touched and her name softly echoed in her head. She felt her body being gently pulled into a sitting position, and forward until her head rested on Parker's chest.

"Were they angry?" she mumbled in a hoarse croak.

"Only disappointed," Parker answered, his fingers feeling for the zipper to the long gown. "People had heard about you and were coming to hear you sing. Did you hear me, Alex? The word is out about you and people are coming to hear you. They'll come next time."

The zipper was opened and the dress slipped from her shoulders. Alexandra's arms were pulled free and the room air was a momentary shock to her sensitized skin, and she shivered.

Parker murmured something soothing, and Alexandra gave herself up to his care. The belt was removed and the black dress tugged over her hips and legs. Her slip followed, and shoes thudded to the floor.

Alexandra continued to lie against him, left in only bra and panties, loving the feel of his hands and the gentleness. She wanted to become a part of him, let him take care of her. She wanted to let go of herself, let go of the past, change the present, and rethink the future. She didn't want to be strong. She didn't want to be lonely. She just wanted to be happy and to be with Parker forever.

Parker was a little alarmed at how hot her skin was. She was running a fever. It felt strange, having Alex so pliant against him and unaware of what was happening to her. He had never known her to be anything but alert, quick, bright, and animated.

Alex was not a forceful person, but she had always been in control. Except for the moments when he'd inadvertently stripped her of that power, like years ago. Except when nature stepped in to pull back the reins, like now.

But Parker felt a certain odd excitement, surely not because Alex was sick, but because he'd have an opportunity to take care of her, give back a little of the enormous care she'd given him; just love her.

Parker's hands were sure and direct. He released the clasp on her bra and removed the wispy fabric. Alexandra lifted feverish eyes to his face. Her skin was all at once hot with an odd mix of exhaustion and anticipation.

"Parker?" she whispered, watching as his eyes thoroughly examined her breasts and their erect, agitated peaks, moving with her deep, erratic breathing. She saw the interest, the hard desire in his eyes.

"Lie down, Alex," Parker said, pulling back the covers and sliding her between the sheets. The cover was pulled to her chest.

"Parker?" Alexandra tried again, not sure what it was she was trying to say, but hoping Parker would understand. Her eyes drifted closed.

He brushed a soothing hand over her cheek, letting the fingers trail down until they rested on her throat and upper breast.

"When you're feeling better," was all he said, because he *did* understand.

For Alexandra, it was enough. It answered at least one question.

With a sigh of relief, she closed her eyes, drawing comfort in knowing that Parker was there with her. All sense of time was lost, and eventually, even whether it was night or day. Alexandra had only the sensation of falling down a deep black well, spinning round and round into an abyss. Someone held her hand tightly, and whispered loving words, and the fall became a floating sensation. She didn't care where she was, or what she was supposed to be doing, as long as Parker was there to catch her free-fall into space and keep her safe. There were moments in which she could hear the continuing fall of early spring rain outside her window, and she'd imagine herself still wet and miserable. She shivered and sought comfort and warmth deep in the coverings on her bed.

Parker appeared in and out of her dark world with shirt

sleeves rolled up. He sat next to her, his image warm and welcome, but unsteady. He carefully spooned some taste-less liquid into her, and an equally tasteless and dry sub-stance that crumbled in her mouth and felt like bits of broken sponge and rubber. But Alexandra ate it all and went wearily back to sleep. Later still, he was back again with pills and juice, and a warm washcloth to wipe her face. But the world, her room, Parker, still seemed very dim and unreal.

Throughout it all, something rang incessantly in the background. It clanged in her head, forcing her under the covers for quiet. But in Alexandra's confused dreams, the sound was an alarm clock, making her twist and fret anxiously that she was going to be late for lessons. It was a kitchen timer; had she burned her father's dinner? Or was it a bicycle bell? There was a brief image of one of her less-than-enthusiastic students riding a bike and chasing her, shouting, "I don't want piano lessons. I want to play."

It was an elevator alarm. She was stuck between floors at the audition hall and was going to miss her tryout for the Light Opera Company . . . again.

There was, for a while, a need to cry and scream helplessly. But no sound came from Alexandra's dry parched throat, only moans.

She thought she heard Christine, argumentative and fussing, but there was an equally strong and determined male voice. When the apparition of her sister seemed to appear towering over her, Alexandra just wanted to shout, "Go away." Alexandra had no idea what Christine wanted of her now, but she couldn't help her. She couldn't help herself.

Yet there was also an uncharacteristic look of worry and regret on Christine's pretty face, her image moving too quickly. Alexandra felt Christine straighten the tumbled bed linens over her feverish body.

"Everything's under control. We're taking care of it all," Christine seemed to be saying.

Alexandra believed her. Her fretting quieted down. Rolling onto her stomach, she at last fell into a deep sleep, content to let others take charge.

Parker let Alexandra's hot, damp cheek rest in his hand. He watched her face closely, concerned that she might suddenly clamp down with her teeth on the thermometer he'd placed in her mouth. He took a quick glance at his watch and, finding that adequate time had passed, removed the instrument to read Alex's temperature.

One hundred and two.

Parker frowned, absently shaking out the thermometer and putting it into a glass of water on Alex's nightstand. Her pulse had been a bit fast for more than an hour, but he still didn't think there was cause for alarm.

He wiped Alex's face with a slightly cool, wet cloth, watching her as she moaned softly, turning her head restlessly on the pillow. She looked so young and vulnerable under her coverlets, with just her head sticking out, and Parker was suddenly reminded again of how young she'd been when they'd first met. He stood watching her for a while longer and then quietly got up.

Of course, she couldn't be left alone, and he never even gave it a thought. But he'd have to call her family and let them know what was going on. Parker took off his suit jacket and pulled his tie loose, reaching for the phone. It was after nine because, of course, club acts always started late in the evening. But Parker knew that George Morrow was no longer up to long days and late nights. If he was awakened, he'd know at once something was wrong. Even as he dialed the number, Parker was already wondering how to tell a father that his daughter was sick, but that he shouldn't worry.

The phone was picked up and there was a moment of coughing before Alexandra's father rasped out in a sleepy and slightly peeved voice, "I was asleep . . . If this is Christine, the answer is no."

"George, this is Parker Harrison."

The surprise was evident in the long seconds of delay. Parker could imagine from the sounds on the other end that he now had Mr. Morrow's attention, and if he was only half awake a moment ago, he was most definitely alert now. The older man cleared his throat.

"What is it, Parker?" he asked, his tone serious but firm.

"I'm with Alexandra at her apartment. She couldn't make it to the club tonight."

"Why? What's wrong?"

"I think she's caught some sort of chill, maybe a flu virus."

"Is she okay?"

"I don't think it's serious. Her temperature is over 100, and she's a little out of it. She's not going anywhere for a few days."

"Well, I'll come over and . . ."

"I'll stay with her. That's why I'm calling. I knew you'd be concerned about her being here alone."

"You'll stay?" George asked quietly.

"I'll bunk on her sofa, but someone should be giving her liquids, and using cool cloths to bring her fever down. Where's Christine?"

"Christine? Lord knows. She was going to come over

'cause she wanted to borrow some money, but I didn't have it for her. She was going to call Alexandra."

"Then if you haven't heard from her, she must have seen Alex sometime this afternoon."

"Ummm . . ." Mr. Morrow uttered. "In all that rain. What do you want with Christine?"

"I want her to bring some antibiotics. I want her to bring some juices, and I want her to help with Alex."

Mr. Morrow sighed. "Well, then . . . I'll certainly call her first thing in the morning."

Parker waited. "But?"

Mr. Morrow sighed again. "You know, Christine is a good girl . . ."

"I know that, George," Parker agreed. "I also know she's not as indifferent to things and people as she lets on. All that attitude," Parker chuckled softly, "a lot of it is insecurity."

After a moment, George Morrow gave an answering throaty laugh. "You know my girls pretty well."

Parker shrugged. "I have a vested interest," he said.

"Well, assuming I reach Christine and give her your message."

"She'll come," Parker said confidently.

"What's the payoff for her," George asked, certainly understanding his own daughter. "She's going to want one, you know."

"She's not going to miss a chance to be able to tell her older sister what to do."

Parker didn't get much sleep that night. Despite his soothing words to George Morrow, he *was* concerned about Alex. Not because he believed her to be in any danger, but because he cared and didn't want anything to happen to her. Because he missed her feistiness and quick spirit. He missed the companionship that let them laugh together, be angry together, be honest together.

It was called love.

Parker checked on Alexandra several times in the next few hours. There was little change in her temperature. Although her sleep was fitful, she didn't seem to be too uncomfortable. He finally set up a makeshift bed on the sofa, but wasn't inclined to get any sleep himself. Instead, Parker lay in the dark of the living room, wondering how he was going to convince Alex that what they both wanted and needed was each other.

The doorbell woke Parker on Sunday morning. He quickly pulled on his trousers and shirt from the night before and went to answer the persistent buzzing. Christine was at the door.

It was obvious that it was still raining outside from Christine's dripping umbrella and the beaded wet surface of her black patent leather raincoat. It was also obvious that no matter what the circumstances, weather or conditions, Christine managed to look bright, fresh, and unscathed.

"Good morning, Christine," Parker said, and stepped aside so she could enter.

"What's wrong with Alexandra?" she asked coolly, removing her outerwear to reveal black leather slacks and a bright red angora sweater. She also wore a red beret pulled down at a saucy angle over her dark short curls.

"Alexandra's sick. She's caught some kind a bug," Parker said, yawning, buttoning his slacks and rolling up the sleeves of his wrinkled shirt.

Christine pulled off the hat and expertly used one hand to fluff up her springy curls. "Alexandra is never sick."

Parker shook his head and went into the small kitchen to put on coffee.. "Did you bring the medicine?"

"Yes, I did," Christine sighed.

"Good. You can take it in to her. Here's a glass of juice. And she'll probably want help to the bathroom."

"Me?" Christine complained.

"Yes, you," Parker said firmly.

Christine took the proffered glass, and with a long-suffering sigh, turned away.

Parker watched her go, with a frown.

Christine entered her sister's room without knocking. She was impatient, and she was disagreeable. It was not so much that she didn't want to help her sister, it was just that she'd only ever seen or known Alexandra as someone who could always manage on her own. It was Alexandra who'd taken care of both her and her father after their mother had died. It was Alexandra who'd set the rules, kept things going, gotten things done. And it had always seemed that she didn't need anyone's help herself. Except for that time she'd come home from school in the middle of the semester. In all the years since then, even though she'd dated, Alexandra had never shown much interest in other men. Now Christine understood why.

It was a blow to her ego that Parker hadn't come running after her like most men did. She hadn't ever imagined that Alexandra could be in love, or that anyone would get close enough to love her. But life was full of surprises.

To Christine, Alexandra hadn't been so much an older sister as she'd been a very young surrogate mother. But as Christine stood over her sister, she had a strange reaction. Alexandra looked so small in her bed. In fact, she looked like a little girl curled on her side with her hand sand-wiched in between the pillow and her cheek. She looked sort of helpless and sad and lost in the bed, and not so strong and self-sufficient at all.

Christine had always resented her sister, telling her what to do, and even how and when. On the other hand, Alexandra had always been there for her. Christine knew she'd always taken that for granted. It felt very odd suddenly to feel that Alexandra needed her, and she might never had known if Parker hadn't sent for her.

Alexandra dragged her eyes open and they closed again against her will. She frowned and moaned, "No." Christine sat on the edge of the bed and began opening the newly bought package of flu medication.

"Don't you worry," she said in a low voice that hid sudden realization and concern. "I'll take care of everything."

Which is exactly what Christine tried to do, resulting in an argument between her and Parker over who was going to take care of Alexandra. It was after Christine had returned to the living room to find Parker on the phone with her father. She'd declared in a suddenly commanding tone that her sister needed her, to which Parker had told her not to get carried away. Alexandra needed *both* of them.

"Well, I'm her sister," Christine countered.

"And I'm in love with her," Parker was prompted into responding impatiently.

Christine struck a pose and crossed her arms over her chest. "I figured that out," she said sarcastically. "When are you going to tell Alexandra?"

It was a good question, but now was not the time to consider the answer.

Parker won the argument. He told Christine that her instant sisterly devotion was admirable, but that more than anything, Alexandra needed rest, peace and quiet.

So he dispatched Christine instead to his manager's house to get a change of clothing.

By six that evening, much of Christine's enthusiasm as a savior had cooled, but the image of a wan and weak Alexandra who hadn't been able to do much without her help had left her thoughtful. Christine had always been able to do what she wanted because Alexandra had always been right there when things went wrong. And Christine had always been able to criticize and find fault, because she'd never had to be responsible for anything or anyone. Where did that leave her sister? Who was there for her when Alexandra needed it?

Debby came late in the afternoon, bringing with her some chicken soup and one of her grandmother's cold remedies. Brian sent flowers. Mr. Morrow called. And Alexandra had no idea of what went on in her behalf.

On Monday, the fever stabilized, and Alexandra slept soundly. And Parker found the albums she'd kept of him.

At first, he thought they held photographs, perhaps of her family, of her and Christine growing up. But to Parker's amazement, they were meticulously kept, chronologized memorabilia of his career.

He was surprised, then amused. And then he realized what he was looking at: the collection of someone who cared. It was the treasure of someone who had a hero who was respected, admired, and loved. Parker looked through the albums once, and then he started all over again, slowly seeing how his career had grown and developed, made possible in no small way by the belief and encouragement of Alexandra.

When he returned the albums to the bookshelf, he was humming. His mind had suddenly turned to melodies and new music. He sat down with pen and paper and composed a love song.

He was interrupted at three-thirty by a knock on the door. He opened it to find a young boy of about ten or eleven with a Batman knapsack over one shoulder, tossing a baseball back and forth. The ball dropped to the floor and the boy stared bug-eyed at Parker.

Parker grinned, caught the ball on the bounce, and gave it back to the youngster, who was still confused and speechless.

"Don't worry. You have the right apartment," Parker grinned.

"Where's Miss Morrow?" the boy asked.

"Miss Morrow is here, but she's not feeling very well. Did you come for a lesson?"

"Yeah, but that's okay," the boy said, snatching the ball and trying to make a quick retreat. "I can come next week."

Parker smoothly reached for the dangling strap on the sack and easily pulled the youngster up short. "You must be David."

David went bug-eyed again and looked suspiciously at the tall man. "How'd you know?"

"Alex . . . Miss Morrow told me all about you. She said you could someday play like me, but you probably want to be another Claudell Washington."

"That's right. He's bad. He's a real good fielder." He frowned. "Who are you?"

"Parker. I'm a friend of Miss Morrow's."

David began tossing the ball again. "You play the piano?"

Parker grinned. "A little. Why don't you come in. I'd like to hear about Claudell Washington. And your music."

"Well . . ." David hesitated.

Parker pushed the door open. "Just a few minutes. You

won't even have to practice on the piano today because we have to be very quiet."

David thought a moment and then shrugged. "Okay."

He was there the rest of the afternoon.

They did mostly talk, because Parker was charmed by the ten-year-old. They also talked a lot of sports, and Parker was relieved that, unlike him, David was given reign to just be a kid.

David wanted to know where Parker played. Parker told him about the tour he'd just finished, and the concert coming up in New York. The boy's eyes grew round at the mention of Stevie Wonder, Elton John, and Anita Baker on the program.

"I guess you're real good," David said in wonder, and it made Parker laugh.

"It all came with practice," he hinted.

"Yeah, I know," David sighed, and then looked shyly at Parker. "Can you show me something? Maybe you can play real soft so Miss Morrow won't hear."

Parker grabbed at the youngster's sudden interest, and bought into carefully selecting some pieces to play that could hold David's attention. At the end of the day they were practically best friends.

When David's mother called to check up on her son, Parker introduced himself and explained, listening patiently to her gasp of surprise. She came to get David half an hour later, with Parker at least extracting a promise from David to keep in touch.

He was exhausted.

He recalled all the phone calls that had come in for Alex, about commitments and classes and another wedding and rehearsals. He had a whole support team, courtesy of his manager, to take care of details. In some ways, Alex's life seemed so much more complicated . . . and so much more fulfilling. Parker crawled onto the sofa for another night of thinking it was too bad Alex wanted the life he had; he would much rather have had hers.

She'd slept around all the funny noises and people in the other room, around Parker and Christine's arguments and their careful entry into her dream world to whisper to her or touch her. There had been other voices, and the phone had rung incessantly. And only when it became perfectly quiet did Alexandra come fully, alertly awake.

She sat up slowly in bed, listening to the silence, convinced that she had dreamt everything else. She got cautiously out of bed, a little light-headed and unsteady, and walked out into the living room, not bothering even to don a robe.

There was a lamp near a window, but otherwise the room was dark, and it was late evening. It was dry and very clear out, and she wondered when the rain had finally stopped. As a matter of fact, she wondered what day and what time it was.. She frowned, and peered around the room, nearly jumping out of her skin when she saw the body stretched out on her sofa. It was Parker, asleep.

He was bare chested, and his feet were raised on the sofa arm, sans socks and shoes. He'd located an extra blanket, and although it was spread over his thighs and stomach, mostly it trailed on the floor. The rest of his clothes, the black trousers and white shirt, and other articles of clothing obviously belonging to him, were folded on the coffee table.

Moving quietly, Alexandra stood looking down at him. He had stayed. How long had it been? One day? Two? It had been longer. He had never left.

Sacrifices are made because of love, compromises arranged and carried out for it, hurts and misunderstandings endured, dreams given up . . . or started anew.

Having Parker here, when she most needed someone . . . when she most needed *him* . . . made her see that he did care. She *was* important to him, and he had not been mouthing empty words.

Carefully, Alexandra relaid the blanket over Parker's prone form, and stepped back quietly when he half turned in his sleep. Feeling the room air on her naked limbs, Alexandra wrapped her arms around, hugging herself, a very satisfied sigh of peace escaping from her. She glanced with amusement at the disarray of her living room, with evidence that Parker had kept the world at bay so that she could rest and overcome exhaustion. Sheets of music lay on the floor, accumulated mail and messages on tables and chairs. A child's worn wool glove and a baseball. Overflowing ashtrays, a half-filled cup of coffee, cold for God only knew how long. She smiled at how comfortable he'd made himself.

Parker had once said, "Be careful what you wish for, because you're likely to get it." Well, Alexandra had just learned that it was true only when it was something she really hadn't wanted in the first place. But now she knew what she truly wanted, and she also knew why.

Parker had also said he meant to stay until he found out whether she hated him or loved him. Alexandra's smile broadened as she left him to go and draw a hot bath for herself, needing to wash off days of being in bed. When she was done, she had every intention of giving Parker the answer he'd been waiting for.

Chapter Ten

The hot water felt wonderful steaming around her, scenting the air with the floral essence of bath oil. The room was warm and the bath was soothing and rejuvenating, giving Alexandra a lazy, peaceful sense of well-being. It was in direct contrast to the way she'd been feeling recently, pulled and torn in so many directions. Confused and indecisive, and longing for some order to her harried, not completely satisfying life.

Alexandra smiled dreamily as she thought of Parker taking care of her while she'd been sick. She wondered how his manager and agent and lawyer would respond to the information that the world-renowned musician had fed her aspirin and antibiotics, spooned soup and juice into her parched mouth, gotten her into the bathroom and back, all with the most endearing tenderness and love a man could show.

She finally heaved herself from the tub, finding that languishing in the bath had left her a little weak, hungry, and sleepy.

She wrapped a large yellow towel around her body, absently patting herself dry as she recalled the gentleness of Parker wiping her damp brow, moistening her dry lips with a cool cloth, smoothing back her tangled hair, all the while whispering endearments which had made her feel so safe and cared for.

Clutching the towel around her slender body, Alexandra opened the bathroom door and stopped abruptly.

"What the hell are you doing out of bed?" Parker's voice boomed, causing her to start violently and gasp at the sudden appearance of him.

He was standing with nothing on but an intriguing pair of jocky briefs, white and distinct against his dark skin. His lean, muscular legs were akimbo and his hands were planted on his narrow hips. The thunderous expression on his weary, handsome face slowly transformed into one of concern and relief. Parker surveyed Alexandra carefully as she stood before him.

Her hair was twisted into a knot at the top of her head, and her face looked delicate and drawn. Her skin was still moist and shiny from the bath oil, making the smooth skin of her bare shoulders and arms look silky and soft. All in all, Parker had to admit she looked rather enticing, and much more rested than the forlorn person she had been several days earlier.

"Are you all right?" he asked, his tone soft with concern.

"I'm fine," Alexandra smiled, twisting the bright towel higher over her breast while exposing more of her long legs. I just had to get up. I felt like I was becoming fused to the bed."

Parker arched a brow, letting his gaze roam up and down the length of her, unaware of the sexy figure he himself made to her eyes. He smiled slowly. "The rest didn't hurt you any. You should go back to bed."

"Not yet," Alexandra protested. "I want to know

what's been going on. How long was I asleep? I don't even know what day it is. Did I see Christine here, too? The phone rang a lot." She pressed a hand to her stomach. "And I'm hungry."

Parker listened to this recital before suddenly starting to laugh. He moved slowly toward her. "Well I guess there's no doubt that you're feeling better." He came closer and began to briskly run his hands up her toweled back and sides to dry her thoroughly.

Alexandra felt a tightening in her chest. She was acutely aware and highly sensitized to the fact that very little separated their flesh. Parker had his arms around her. Her own were half imprisoned in the folds of the terrycloth. The brisk rubbing grew slower, but not before the movements of Parker's hands had succeeded in making Alexandra feel warm. She'd fought long and hard to deny what was so obvious in this moment—that she longed to have Parker touch her, longed to be in his arms. She just wanted to surrender to the overwhelming knowledge that she loved and wanted this man.

Alexandra stood relaxed and limp under Parker's massaging hands, mesmerized by the sensual, repetitive stroking until she felt a flow of desire quivering throughout her body. It was all the need she had held inside and kept secret from Parker, and she wasn't going to ignore it any longer.

The growing heat, the building wave of sensuality, made Alexandra's heart race. She felt a sudden urge to lean forward and kiss Parker's smooth, firm chest. She realized that Parker's stroking had become less functional and more caressing. He seemed to be slowly pulling her forward until their bodies were a mere inch apart. His breath was warm on her cheek, and every movement from him only melted and softened her more.

Parker, too, seemed entranced by the slender feel of
Alex under his hand. He was glad to see her up, relieved
to hear strength in her voice. But his body was struggling
not to react to the alluring and erotic picture she made
standing before him nearly naked.

They stared at one another for an intense silent moment. Alexandra made the first move, because she didn't
want to happen now what had happened too fast so many
weeks ago. It was truly up to her now; she was center
stage, with the spotlight marking her every motion and
gesture.

"Is there anything to eat?" she asked in a wispy
voice.

Parker slanted a wry smile at her. "I think we can put
together something. I'm a little hungry myself," he said,
but something in the gravelly texture of his voice made
her doubt he was speaking of food.

It really didn't matter to her what they ate. It was the
time together that was important, the wonderful sense of
well-being that she'd never known before. After a dinner
of spaghetti with a light butter sauce, they sat on the sofa,
catching up to three days of activity that had gone on
while she had been ill. She listened to the details: that the
great Parker Harrison had acted as wet nurse and baby
sitter for her. It was so domestic, so personal, that Alexandra found herself studying Parker for any sign that he'd
felt inconvenienced. There was none.

Alexandra sipped her tea, shaking her head in bewilderment. "I can't believe it's Tuesday. I can't believe I've
lost four whole days."

Her feet were curled under her and Parker had
wrapped her in the blanket he'd been using at night. He'd
pulled on a pair of jeans, but remained without shirt or
socks as he sat next to her.

He tilted his head back to expel his cigarette smoke toward the ceiling. His legs were stretched out on top of the coffee table and his other arm stretched along the back of the sofa, absently fingering the blanket which had loosened around Alex's shoulder.

"You didn't lose four days. You just used them differently than you otherwise might have." Parker looked at her as he tapped his ashes onto a paper napkin. "You were completely out of it. You needed the rest, Alex."

Alexandra looked at him thoughtfully over the rim of her cup. "Was I that bad?" she asked softly.

"Worse," Parker said with a soundless chuckle. "You'd gotten yourself on a treadmill and something was bound to give, with the kind of crazy pace you set for yourself. What gave out finally was you."

Alexandra silently nodded, willing to admit to herself that she'd been using music to fill a void in her life that she didn't know how else to fill. Alex gulped the last of her tea and put down her cup. The most important revelation was still to be made.

"Have you been here all the time I was sick?" she asked quietly.

Parker turned his head to study her. "Yes."

"You must have been very uncomfortable, sleeping on the sofa." She looked into his eyes.

"I was. A chiropractor could make a lot of money off me right now," he said with a straight face, but his eyes were sparkling and he made Alexandra smile.

"I'm sorry. You should have just left me to sleep," she suggested.

Parker's expression changed, becoming tight and serious. "I only made that mistake once, Alex." The past no longer concerned him; it was the future that needed clarification. As he watched the light in Alexandra's eyes, the way her body was poised stiffly in her corner of the sofa, he knew that something had to be settled with Alex here and now, or it wouldn't happen at all.

"Besides," he began, "I had a lot of help. Christine, for one."

"So, I *didn't* imagine her."

"No. I had her bring me a change of clothes, and some juice and stuff for you. She made some meals, and then I sent her off to see about your father. I didn't want him to start worrying about you."

Alexandra grimaced. "That's why I heard the fussing. She couldn't have been very happy about being a nurse-maid."

Parker frowned. "You're wrong. She wanted to stay. She wanted to take care of you."

Alexandra's eyes widened in disbelief. "Really?"

Parker smiled. "Yes, really. We fought over it, because I was afraid in her enthusiasm she'd do you more harm than good. But she was right there. Christine is not as good at taking care of people as you are, but she's capable enough."

Alexandra looked skeptical, but Parker nodded to contradict her. "You may not have given your sister enough credit for being able to think about more than herself. Yeah, she's beautiful and she knows it, but she's never sure if people see anything else. She's not sure there *is* anything else. So what does she do? She plays the vamp to get attention." Parker's fingers rubbed her shoulder through the material of the blanket until it dislodged, exposing the soft joint. "She wanted to take complete charge here, but I vetoed that."

"Did you? Why?" Alexandra asked quizzically.

"She hides her concern by being overcritical, overfussy.

Something like the way you hide behind your music because you think that's all *you* have."

Alexandra began to fidget at Parker's words, realizing he was right.

"Christine is jealous of you and has been all her life. Pretty girls are a dime a dozen, but she can't do what you do."

Alexandra stared at him and shook her head. "She's always teased me about my music. She's always said I'd never be a world-class singer because I let my feelings distract me and get in my way."

Parker hesitated as he considered Christine's observation and his response. "To some degree, she's right. You know, it takes a lot of determination and work. It's difficult to concentrate on this kind of career and anything else. You give up a lot because, more often than not, it's one or the other," he said with some knowledge.

"Is that how you did it? Not caring about anything else?"

Parker sighed impatiently. "It's not that I didn't care. But what I did was not for fame, fortune, or friendships. My music was for *me*. Recognition is fine and I appreciate it, but my music would still have been for my own satisfaction, with or without all the other stuff."

"That's easy for you to say now, but what if no one ever said you were good?" Alexandra queried bluntly.

Parker shrugged. "I can't answer that, Alex. You seem to feel the trappings will make you somebody. Don't you know you *are* somebody? And you *are* important. To your father, your students, and your friends; even Christine admires you more than you know, and more than she'll admit.

"Now other people *are* telling you that you're very

good." He gave her a wry, ironic look. "Whether you realize it or not, Alex, with Blues Alley, you have arrived."

Alexandra stared at him and gnawed on her lower lip. She wanted to tell Parker that she was now sure of what she really wanted. But inside, she felt the fear of letting go of so many dreams, and all the plans which had sustained her for so long. The other truth was that even if her feelings for Parker were not returned and she hit a dead end, the other considerations would still not be any different.

Alexandra took a deep breath and felt a somersaulting of her insides as she looked at Parker. Now, finally, she had nothing to lose.

"I don't want to sing at Blues Alley anymore. Even if they ask, I don't want to go back."

Parker looked intently at her, and he sat very still. He'd tried very hard to be honest and fair with Alex this time, but he wasn't going to deny that her answer was very important to hm. She was very important to him. His fingers stopped their caressing movement on her shoulder. "Why?" he asked softly.

Alexandra laced her fingers together and the truth lay like a hard lump in her throat. "Because it doesn't make me happy," she answered simply.

She didn't meet Parker's intent gaze and she missed the imperceptible pursing of his wide mouth and the gentle lift of a brow.

"When I'm on stage at the club I only think about doing the numbers to finish my act, and then getting off. I don't always feel what I'm singing. I sometimes feel . . . empty," Alexandra finished, somewhat surprised by her own revelation.

Parker drew his legs down from the coffee table and

turned to face her more fully. "I know," he said, apparently not surprised by her confession.

Alexandra looked curiously at him. "How do you know?"

"Because that's how I'd gotten to feel about my music when I met you years ago. You described what I went though every time I gave a concert. My music *is* important to me, just like your singing is important to you. But I had to do it *my* way."

She shook her head. "The question is, what is *my* own?"

"Only you can answer that, Alex. But it may not be performing at all. Maybe that's not where you should be heading."

Alexandra frowned at him. "But then, why did you insist that I try out for Blues Alley?"

"So that you could find out for yourself by simply trying," Parker said, and rubbed his hand along a bristled jaw that needed shaving. "When I first turned up again, you were piddling by, here and there, never putting the energy into performing. I made the mistake of trying to convince you of how difficult a stage life is. Experience is still the best teacher. That's why I backed off. It was how *I* found out. I had to *do* it first." He paused for a moment. "So you know. Now what?"

Alexandra glanced quickly at him. Her heart was beginning to beat faster as she realized that a reckoning was about to take place between her and Parker. "I don't know. I'm not sure. There's still my audition next week." Her voice dropped to a mere whisper; it was now or never. "And there's still you."

Parker lifted his hand slowly to stroke her hair. "Is there?" he asked, in a thick, low voice.

The very sound sent a spiraling of feelings cascading

through Alexandra. It was very personal and touched the sensitive core of her. It made her feel that in this moment they were closer than they'd ever been before.

"Parker, why did you stay?" Alexandra asked earnestly of him. "You didn't even remember me when we met at Debby and Brian's wedding."

"It wasn't that I didn't remember you, but you'd changed. I left a young girl, Alex, just on the verge of womanhood. I stumbled back into your life to find you'd grown up beautiful and strong, but," he paused and smiled, "confused. I stayed because I couldn't just leave. Not again; not like last time. I never had a chance before to know the things I've learned about you now. I wanted to know *all* about you, all about your family."

"Is that why you spent so much time with my father, and with Christine?"

He nodded, reaching to grasp both her hands. "I like your father. He's much more down to earth than mine, and a lot easier to talk to. As for Christine, I also learned that for someone so beautiful, she's also insecure. You're right—she's very talented in her own way. I've told her she should be in New York studying design, and I know that's what she wants to do. So I've arranged for her to stay in Philadelphia with my folks until she gets started and knows what she wants to do. With your father's permission, of course. My folks can keep an eye on her."

Alexandra looked at him in awe. "Why are you doing all of this? First me and Blues Alley, then my father with his music, and now Christine."

Parker smiled at the naive bewilderment in her voice.

"Haven't you figured it out yet?" His voice was soft, his eyes gentle and understanding.

Alexandra stood up very suddenly, dropping the blanket but holding tightly to the yellow towel. She walked over to lean against the piano.

"No. Tell me," she said in a strangled voice. A sudden apprehension was building inside. She heard Parker get up behind her, knew he was approaching. She gripped the edge of the piano as an astounding truth quickly came to her. Parker had said everything, and really nothing at all, to make her see the truth. Her mind rifled through years of memory rapidly to try and figure out why she'd missed the obvious key to what had happened when Parker had gone away.

"Alex, your father . . ." he began, and then gently put his hand around the column of her neck, his fingers soothing over the skin. She finally understood, and Parker knew that the information, the instant realization, hurt.

Alexandra turned around quickly to face him, and Parker was stunned to find tears in her eyes. She didn't give him a chance to say anything further. She was swallowing to keep control, but a tear slid down her cheek.

"My father? What did he have to do with it?" Her voice filled with shock and surprise. Alexandra stared at him. His expression was one of concern and deep regret.

"I wanted your father to know. I spoke to him a day after I left and told him my reasons. He reluctantly agreed with me that it was the best decision at the time. He asked me not to contact you for a while. A while turned into years, unfortunately.

"I called you once, several months after I'd left. Your dad said he didn't think you were ready to leave home yet. He asked me to give you more time; to give yourself more time."

Alexandra was openly crying now. "Oh, Parker." She moaned and covered her face.

Parker gathered her into his arms and held and stroked

her, while the shock of truth shook her from head to toe.

"Alex, you can't blame him. He was doing what a father is supposed to do. Don't even be angry with him. Not saying goodbye was still my fault."

"He never said . . . he never even hinted," she sobbed.

There was a part of her that wanted to be furious at her father and at Parker for deciding the direction of her life. She wanted to rage that they'd had no right to exclude her. But after nearly ten years, what was the point? She'd been angry nonetheless, and Parker had taken the full brunt of it.

Her father had been so understanding when she'd been forced to return home from school, so comforting when she'd missed her auditions. It was her father who'd reminded Alexandra that the world had not come to an end and she would survive, finish school, and go on with her life. But it had been odd that he'd also never asked any questions, never probed into those magic months which had soured for her. He'd known all about them.

Alexandra had believed all those years that Parker had really just walked away without caring. And now, of course, so many things said and done recently and in the past made it all clear to her that it hadn't been so cut and dried.

All Parker could do for the moment was hold her and let her cry. It was a release of tension. It was the realization of the truth. It was the relief of doubts proved wrong and the surprise of knowing that ultimately all that had gone before and recently had been to love and protect her.

"I'm sorry, Alex. I thought that after a while your father would tell you. I thought all these years you knew. When I ran into you at Brian and Debby's wedding, I couldn't figure out why you were still so angry with me.

That night when I brought you home, I knew you believed I'd just walked away." Parker squeezed her to him, murmuring, and she held on tightly, her tears making wet splotches on his brown skin. "I knew that I had a chance to stay and *show* you the truth. But I couldn't betray your father. He loves you very much, and he did what he thought was best for you at the time. He said things would happen when they were supposed to happen, and he was right.

"Well, things have changed. Your father knows he can trust me. He can trust that my folks will keep an eye on your sister. And he can trust that I'll love you."

Alexandra's crying turned to hiccoughs as she purged herself. Parker felt the calming in her and leaned back to cup her tearstained face and tilted it up to his. "I couldn't even tell you how much I loved you, Alex," his voice was husky with emotions, "because I knew if I did, it wouldn't have mattered what your father wanted for you. When I suddenly found you again, I knew I was going to do everything in my power to make it up to you. To us. I cared, and I always have. My reason for being here, right now, is because I love you." He kissed her forehead and tried to wipe the tears from her face.

Alexandra shook her head slowly in continuing amazement. "I can't believe what he did," she sniffled.

Parker smiled kindly. "You were nineteen years old. How could he not? Think of how hard it must have been for him, trying to do the right thing."

"But to let me think it was all your fault. I thought I hated you."

Parker pulled her close again, soothing her and inadvertently loosening the terrycloth towel wrapped around her slender body. "I've already gotten a confession that you don't hate me, Alex. But you haven't mentioned love."

Alexandra's crying had stopped, and she gazed at Parker through wet, spiky lashes, and from eyes that were shimmering and bright.

"Of course I love you. That was the one thing I never doubted." Alexandra's chin quivered as she tried a weak smile and lifted her shoulders in a shrug. "There goes my pride."

He hadn't realized how anxiously he'd awaited that response until Alex had actually said the words. Parker just stared at her. "I'd rather have your love," he said, letting his fingers trace along her jaw and touch her still trembling lips. "Pride never kept anyone warm at night, and I think we're much better together than we are apart."

Very slowly Parker lowered his head, his mouth lightly touching Alexandra's. It was a tender new discovery of love. It was much more than the past or the present because their feelings, now spoken and shared, laid the groundwork for a future.

Alexandra let out a deep sigh of relief, love, joy, and wonder as she leaned into Parker, feeling safe and secure in his solid presence.

"Alex, I love you," he said earnestly against her mouth. "I've always loved you."

He pressed his lips against hers. She reacted by lifting her face, bringing her waiting mouth closer to accommodate him.

This time Parker took gentle possession, carefully brushing against her mouth, settling into a position that allowed his warm tongue to test and tease and seek entry. His hand released her face and glided down her arms. Parker's arms, closing around her back, tangled in the towel, pulling it loose. His right hand continued a journey to her hip, his fingers massaging her flesh through the towel, pressing her to the bold, hard outlines of his growing desire. He was slow, taking his time to earn Alexandra's trust again, taking his time to prove his love.

His mouth slowly became heated, more insistent and hungry, his tongue and lips making passionate demands that Alexandra was more than willing to meet. He finally released her mouth, taking in a deep breath of air. He moved his mouth along her skin, leaving kisses from the corner of her mouth to her ear and neck.

The towel was slipping away, leaving Alexandra's breasts exposed. Parker groaned deep in his chest, and he looked down. He could see the hard, brown nipples, the softness surrounding the centers as her breasts pressed against him.

Parker rested his forehead against hers, closing his eyes, controlling the potent surge of feelings that made his breathing ragged. His middle was hard and undulating against Alexandra's hips, his hands seeking her warm skin under the towel, until he grabbed it and simply pulled it away.

Alex gasped softly at the sudden exposure of her skin to the cool air and Parker's exploring hands. The touch of his hands was an erotic warmth on her skin, heating her all over. Her own desire lent boldness to her actions, and Alexandra began to press a series of kisses across Parker's chest. She kissed his nipple and turned her head to rest a cheek against his chest.

"I love you," Alexandra whispered. The absolute truth of it was heartfelt. Alexandra's admission was more for herself than it was a confession for Parker. It didn't matter if he heard her or not.

Parker stroked her shoulders. "When I finally met your

father face to face, the night you took me home to dinner, he and I both knew."

"Knew what?" Alexandra asked dreamily, following the sensual wanderings of Parker's hands, the alternate hesitancy and daring of his touch.

"That my feelings hadn't changed in all those years. I haven't lived the life of a monk, Alex, but I've never been in love with anyone else. Not even close. You are still the only woman I can just be myself with."

Parker slowly began kissing Alexandra's face, his breath whispering over her skin, his lips teasing at her mouth again, moistening the surface with his tongue. He was feeling a certain level of wonder and reverence toward her. He was feeling lucky that after so many years, he'd found his true love. That conviction lent power to Parker's next words.

"I don't know what I did to deserve seeing you again, but I'm not going anywhere unless you're with me. I don't care if you want to be another Leontyne Price or Shirley Bassey, as long as we can love each other." His hands smoothed down over the contours of her back and gently, gripped her buttocks, Parker pulled her to the heated need of his body and moaned deep in his throat. "I don't want to talk anymore about your father, your sister, the past, or music. I want to love you, *make* love to you."

Parker released her and Alexandra retrieved the yellow towel to hold in front of her as she watched Parker unsnap his jeans and push them and his shorts down over his narrow hips.

Seeing the blatant display of his masculinity sent a wave of pure longing rippling through her. All Alexandra wanted, too, in that moment was to have Parker make love to her. She wanted to *feel* his love within her.

Her eyes were bright with need and love when she met

his intense gaze. He stood naked and magnificent before her. Mesmerized by the message he sent her with his slumberous gaze, she dropped the towel and stepped toward him.

He reached for her hand and led her back to the bedroom. He pulled her into his arms and began to kiss her with deep erotic urgency, as if he was using this instant to ask for forgiveness, declare his love, give to her and take from her all the moments they'd both needed all the time they were apart.

His mouth manipulated and demanded, and Alexandra was too overwhelmed and helpless to do anything but comply. The muscles in her stomach twisted and tensed with a need that seemed out of control. She didn't have to ask him, for Parker, too, needed a gratification that would bind them together.

Parker lowered Alexandra to the cool fresh linens, their mouths and tongues still fused. He levered his long, trim body over hers, and settled easily and comfortably to fit her soft contours.

Alexandra felt protected and safe under the weight of Parker's body. It was very like the trusting feelings she'd granted Parker the very first time they'd ever made love. And now, having reestablished that connection and trust, Alexandra experienced the heightening of her senses, her desire growing and leaving her limp in Parker's embrace. He began to move against her, to rub his thighs and stomach against her so that his intentions were so clear that Alexandra drew in her breath sharply as she felt herself melting and wanting him almost with desperation.

"Oh, Parker . . ." Alexandra sighed, as his mouth once again robbed her of words. There was an eloquent demonstration of his love as he stroked her sides and thighs lightly with his hands, and his hips pressed against her.

Alexandra's legs separated, and she and Parker both moaned deeply at their coming together, which was quick and electrifying. For long moments they lay entangled, until Parker began a rhythm, a cadence that created more sounds, deeply felt utterings of satisfaction and delight. There was music that played perfectly between them, through movements fast and slow, until the ending was a crescendo, expertly pitched and timed. But there was no way such heights could be sustained. The ebbing and flow of their playing peaked. Alexandra's back arched from the bed, allowing Parker easy access to her pert, uplifted breasts with his warm, rough tongue. Her climax was enough to trigger his own, and Parker buried his mouth in her neck and groaned deeply his release and pleasure. Their movements were a gentle swaying together until their bodies finally came to rest. Heavy breathing and little mews of expression were the only sounds thereafter for a long time.

Alexandra kissed Parker's neck, her nose buried in the strong male essence of him. Parker began slowly with her shoulder, kissing his way along a collarbone to her throat, her chin, her slightly parted lips. His voice was raspy and thick when he finally spoke, coming up on his elbows and letting his gaze search over the shadowy glow of Alexandra's face.

"That was to settle any doubt in your mind that I've always loved you and wanted you. God, it's been such a long time," Parker said with feeling.

Alexandra sighed, tilting her head to let Parker's lips continue their journey. "I never knew," she whispered in a trembling voice, tears of happiness gathering in her eyes again.

Parker chuckled lightly. "That's my fault," he said,

moving his body, rubbing against her sensuously. "But I plan on taking the rest of the night to apologize."

"And after tonight?" Alexandra asked softly. She could see Parker beginning to smile rather lovingly at her.

"Then we talk about being a two-career family," he responded, kissing her and putting an end to further talk for the time being. "You sing, and I'll play."

Epilogue

When Alexandra stepped off the elevator, four pairs of alert eyes greeted her with varying degrees of expectation. The sight both surprised and amused her and, walking toward the support group of family and friends, she began to laugh merrily.

Debby looked maternally anxious as she gnawed on her bottom lip, her eyes rounded behind her glasses. Her expression seemed to convey sympathy without yet knowing if it was needed. Mr. Morrow, looking decidedly uncomfortable in a dark blue suit that hung on his spare frame, had his hands stuffed in his pockets and looked like an expectant father-to-be. Christine's tapping foot and impatient air hid her need to ask "Well, how did it go?"

And then there was Parker, lounging casually against a pillar in the main lobby of the empty recital hall.

Alexandra wore a white angora knit dress, its hem hiding the top of her brown high-heeled boots. Her hair, full and loosened in waves around her face, was topped by a black beret pulled saucily on an angle. Her outfit, at once bright and warm like her dark eyes and sunny smile, was like a harbinger of spring which had finally arrived. The four silent adults before her were as much stilled by her appearance as they were with their own anticipation of the outcome of Alexandra's audition.

"You all look like I've just been given a reprieve by the governor." Alexandra laughed. She squeezed her father's arm reassuringly as she passed him, but continued past her sister and Debby, right up to Parker.

"Well, are you going to end the suspense and put us out of our misery, or what?" Debby begged plaintively.

Alexandra gave her friend a brief smile over her shoulder but still said nothing. Christine made an impatient sound and flounced over to her father.

"Boy, is she going to play this for all it's worth. We already know she won," Christine said with conviction, but still she cast a speculative glance at her sister, who, for all intents and purposes, only had eyes for Parker.

For Alexandra, it was impossible to describe to the other three witnesses what passed between her and Parker. It was a secret communication between kindred spirits.

Parker's brows raised and he lifted a corner of his mouth in a half-smile. He was thoroughly enjoying the animation on Alexandra's teak-brown features, the dark, sparkling eyes that showed a joy that truly only the two of them could know. It was a sense of "being there," of having reached the very top of her form, of having executed something very well, and knowing that others realized it, too. But beyond the *others,* the judges and pianist and nervous competitors, Alexandra knew that this day she had at last truly achieved her dream. And wherever else today led her, *today,* this moment, was the epitome and culmination of all she'd worked for. If it all ended in the next hour, or the next year, she still would have accomplished what she'd set out to do so many years ago.

Cupping a hand at the back of Alex's head, Parker

gently pulled her forward to kiss her. The kiss said everything—I love you, congratulations, you look gorgeous.
"You look like the cat that was given a bowl of rich
cream," he drawled in amusement.

"And lapped up every ounce of it," Alexandra said
softly. She sighed. "I was good, Parker, *very* good. I did
everything right, and I'm happy with how I performed."

"But?" he asked easily.

Alexandra turned to encompass the rest of her entourage. "But I didn't place first," she said comfortably, with
neither rancor nor disappointment.

"What? Are they *crazy?*" Christine burst out in surprising defense.

Alexandra gave her sister a wry affectionate grin.

"Oh, Alexandra," Debby moaned her disappointment,
clicking her tongue against her teeth in a soothing manner, as though Alexandra was a child.

"Well, I know you did your best, Baby. That's all that's
important," George Morrow said awkwardly, not sure
how to ease his daughter's defeat.

Alexandra raised her brows and her eyes quickly
glanced at each person around her. "Come on, guys. This
isn't the end of the world. I was first choice for the chorus,
and I'll understudy the female lead in next fall's produc-
tion."

There was a long moment of stunned silence while this
information sank in before Debby let out an uncontrolled
squeal of delight, and everyone converged at once on
Alexandra, surrounding her with love and hugs. Everyone
started talking at once, and Alexandra laughed and shook
her head at all the confusion, appealing to Parker over the
top of everyone's head to be rescued.

Parker came to stand next to Alexandra, draping an
arm around her shoulder and pulling her against his side.

"Look, let's give her a change to catch her breath, and she'll tell us everything."

However, the talking began at once as Parker led them all to a bank of leather banquettes. They all sat, with Alexandra in the middle, and Parker next to her, holding her hand.

"So, talk," Debby urged excitedly.

Alexandra took a deep breath and gave them the details they wanted to hear. Only Parker knew that beneath the routine of waiting in a dim hall, and on an even dimmer backstage with a dozen or so other hopefuls, was the essence of the experience.

He acknowledged, as Alexandra had, that her talent, her God-given gift from which she might personally derive so much pleasure, was to be judged and censored by a group of strangers who knew nothing at all about why she did what she did. Still, within that spectrum was the need for their approval. He knew that there was validation Alex received for all the years of belief in her own talents and worth. There was the knowledge now that all the years of work and worry had paid off.

As she talked, Alexandra repeatedly sought Parker's attention, as if to say to him, *Now I know what it's like.*

When she was finished, she shrugged. "Well, that's all of it," she said, and looked around at the pleased faces. "I just want you all to know I couldn't have done it, couldn't be here today, without your love and support. You deserve congratulations, too."

Christine gave an exasperated sigh, her beautiful face grimacing with charm nonetheless. "I still think you should have won."

Alexandra smiled. "It's not a matter of winning, but of earning a place. I earned not one but *two* spots, Christine."

"That's even better," Debby exclaimed.

"Does this mean you're going to be famous, after all?"
Christine suddenly asked.

Alexandra laughed at her sister, easily seeing the drift
of her thoughts.

"I hope not," Alexandra said, and looked at Parker.
"One famous musician in the family is quite enough," she
conceded. It meant much more to her to be loved than to
be well known.

Parker basked in Alexandra's glow. Yes, he knew what
it was like, how it felt to have the recognition and ac-
colades. But he also knew what it was like to come home
to an empty place after the fans and your manager have
told you how hot you are. It doesn't last forever. Realisti-
cally, it shouldn't. What he always wanted to have instead
was something that required more of a commitment, real
compromises and work. A family. *That* he could have
forever.

"So, what happens now?" Parker aked her, squeezing
her hand.

"Well, I told them I was opening a concert in New
York, and I told them I am getting married in June."

"See? I told you you'd let your private life get in the
way of your music and career," Christine said.

"No, you don't understand, Christine. I won't let *music*
get in the way of my private life." She looked with glowing
eyes to Parker again. "After all, there *are* priorities. I love
to sing. But it's *not* the most important thing in my life."

"But what if you have to go on tour?" Debby asked.

Alexandra was shaking her head. "One of the reasons
the Light Opera Company of Washington is so perfect for
me is because the repertory never does tours." She looked
at Parker. "I never really expected to do concerts and
nightclub acts."

"If either of us goes on tour, the other will go along, if it's possible," Parker added. "But I'm going to begin to limit my tours to a few a year."

"What about your teaching?" George Morrow asked.

"Oh, I'll continue with that, too, but I'll probably limit it to advance preparation for recitals and tryouts. Like David Evans. Thanks to his impromptu meeting with Parker while I was sick, he's discovered a new interest in music and he's back to his piano lessons."

"And I suppose you'll start having babies?" Christine said, with a bored but still curious tone.

At that, however, Alexandra became tongue-tied. She glanced at Parker. They had not, as yet, talked about having children, although there was no question that they both wanted them.

Parker arched a disapproving brow at Christine's question. It was still too personal to be bandied about like cocktail conversation.

"Alex is going to take her shot at performing first. Our babies will come after a year or two. There's no rush."

"How many?" Christine asked impertinently.

"Okay, that's it. Enough questions," Parker said, standing up abruptly. "I've made reservations for dinner at a great restaurant in Georgetown. There's a whole lot of celebrating that has to be done."

"How nice," Debby chirped. "I sure wish Brian could have been here, instead of at a recording studio."

"I could use something to eat," George Morrow said, patting his flat stomach. "I'm getting too old for all this excitement."

"Are you trying to get rid of us?" Christine asked suspiciously.

"Yes," Parker didn't deny. "The reservation is for the three of you. I have something else in mind for Alex and myself." He stood and helped Alexandra into her coat, and turned to usher Debby, Christine, and George Morrow to the exit.

"But . . ." Christine started to protest.

"Good. Now that that's settled," Parker overrode her, and everyone laughed. Parker knew exactly how to keep Christine in line.

Alexandra was very curious about what Parker had in mind, but made no objection as they waved to the departing cab headed for Georgetown. She turned to him, however, trusting whatever decision he'd made. She was happy that it meant they could be alone and away from the curiosity of everyone. Alexandra didn't mind sharing her victory and her excitement, but she'd rather have Parker to herself. They still had a lot to catch up on.

"Now . . ." Parker said on a deep sigh, as he faced Alexandra and put his arms around her. "I had plans for a candlelight dinner, and soft, romantic music. *Not* mine." She giggled. "Champagne, and maybe even dancing."

Alexandra smiled up at him, and circled her arms around his waist. "Ummm. That sounds lovely. I hope I have enough time to change before we have to be there."

"No problem. The reservation will hold."

Alexandra was curious. "Really? You must know a maître d' in high places."

"Ummm," Parker said noncommittally. "And there's no need to change. As a matter of fact, this is an occasion to dress down, not up."

Alexandra's frown deepened. *"Really?"* she said again, more intrigued than ever. Parker began kissing her cheek, trying to distract her as he signaled for another cab. "Just where are we going?"

Parker kissed her nose. "My place," he said hoarsely, hugging her close. "I figure it's going to take at least five or six hours for me to congratulate you," he said wickedly.

Alexandra looked coyly at him. "Oh? And what happens after dinner?"

Parker's grin grew broader and broader. "Dessert, of course," he said softly, and bent to kiss her soundly as the cab pulled up before them.

FUN AND LOVE!

THE DUMBEST DUMB BLONDE JOKE BOOK (889, $4.50)
by Joey West

They say that blondes have more fun . . . but we can all have a hoot
with THE DUMBEST DUMB BLONDE JOKE BOOK. Here's a
hilarious collection of hundreds of dumb blonde jokes — including
dumb blonde GUY jokes — that are certain to send you over the
edge!

THE I HATE MADONNA JOKE BOOK (798, $4.50)
by Joey West

She's Hollywood's most controversial star. Her raunchy reputation's brought her fame and fortune. Now here is a sensational collection of hilarious material on America's most talked about
MATERIAL GIRL!

LOVE'S LITTLE INSTRUCTION BOOK (774, $4.99)
by Annie Pigeon

Filled from cover to cover with romantic hints — one for every day
of the year — this delightful book will liven up your life and make
you and your lover smile. Discover these amusing tips for making
your lover happy . . . tips like — ask her mother to dance — have his
car washed — take turns being irrational . . . and many, many
more!

MOM'S LITTLE INSTRUCTION BOOK (0009, $4.99)
by Annie Pigeon

Mom needs as much help as she can get, what with chaotic sched-
ules, wedding fiascos, Barneymania and all. Now, here comes the
best mother's helper yet. Filled with funny comforting advice for
moms of all ages. What better way to show mother how very much
you love her by giving her a gift guaranteed to make her smile
everyday of the year.

*Available wherever paperbacks are sold, or order direct from the
Publisher. Send cover price plus 50¢ per copy for mailing and han-
dling to Penguin USA, P.O. Box 999, c/o Dept. 17109, Bergen-
field, NJ 07621. Residents of New York and Tennessee must
include sales tax. DO NOT SEND CASH.*